T0149513

THE RECKONING
OF JACK THE RIPPER

Entity Unknown

Mark Barresi

authorHouse®

AuthorHouse™
1663 Liberty Drive
Bloomington, IN 47403
www.authorhouse.com
Phone: 1-800-839-8640

Published by AuthorHouse   10/02/2012

ISBN: 978-1-4772-7616-7 (sc)
ISBN: 978-1-4772-7615-0 (e)

When a series of murders and mutilations of female victims throws the city of San Diego into a panic-stricken frenzy, a citywide task force is put in place to catch the unknown killer, who the police have called "The Entity" because of his ability to conceal his identity from police, forensic experts, and witnesses. That is, until Detective Ed Brooks confronts the killer in a bloody last-ditch effort to stop him—an encounter that almost costs Brooks his life. Now, four years later, the Entity murders have started again. Brooks and his team are once again charged to stop the killer and unearth his motives for committing the most brutal serial slayings since the original Jack the Ripper murders more than a century before in Whitechapel, England. With the help of FBI profiler Stephanie Morgan, they will uncover a connection between the recent murders and the original Ripper suspect so many years ago—a link that will connect modern forensics and the history of the world's most infamous first serial killer. *The Reckoning of Jack the Ripper* will culminate in action and fury and a shocking ending.

Combining both fiction and historical facts from the Jack the Ripper murders of 1888 England, author Mark Barresi has set out on his own personal quest to name the most likely suspect of the first and most elusive serial killer the world has ever known.

Preface

History of Researchers of Jack the Ripper

I want to first say that I never intended to write a book about Jack the Ripper. My first thoughts were to write a novel about a serial killer in San Diego that was possessed by a demon. But I stopped and thought about this idea, and it didn't sound very appealing to me. I knew at that point that a story of that kind would not be very interesting to my readers. So I began to investigate the history of Jack the Ripper.

As we all know, his identity has never discovered, despite being investigated by all the lead detectives on Scotland Yard—most notable of all, Inspector Frederick Abberline—and a whole list of other prominent police detectives and officials who worked the case even beyond 1888, the year the murders began and ended in Whitechapel, England. I read many books about the Ripper and watched many documentaries and have a whole list of known suspects, and many potential suspects were repeatedly mentioned every year all the way to present day. Some suspects and theories sound believable, but most are very ridiculous, leading investigators and researchers to just laugh and not even bother to follow the leads.

The best-known researches to whom I give my utmost admiration and respect and whose work I believe and follow are Martin Fido, Paul

Begg, Stewart Evans, Richard Jones, and Donald Rumbelow. I have read their works and watched them give their personal thoughts in interviews on who the Ripper could have been. On the journey from 1888 to present day, our advanced criminology system has taken us to DNA evidence. We can now list up to six plausible suspects we believe may have committed the slayings. Some of these suspects were even named in secret archived notes locked away in Scotland Yard until more recent years. But years have passed, and we have no DNA evidence to link any suspect or any confession made by arrested suspects or any valuable witnesses to the crimes. Until the day comes that we can find something that truly links one outstanding suspect to the crimes, we can only offer opinions and suggestions for who Jack the Ripper really was. This book is only my opinion of who I feel committed the most brutal serial slayings of all time, a conclusion I came to after two years of research and investigation. I agree with some of the best researchers and authors that we might have found our killer. In all, I dedicate this book to all Jack the Ripper authors and researchers around today.

—*Mark Barresi*

Acknowledgments

I want to thank my family and close friends who helped me and supported me in writing this book as I faced some personal hardships along the way. I will always be indebted to you all. Most of all, I want to thank my mother for her love and support.

Prologue

Discovery of the Journal

I t was a very dark night, and strong winds carried a continuous downpour of heavy rain throughout the massive city of San Diego. It was just past 11:00 p.m. as he sat at his desk, reading the latest news on his laptop. The top story read, *A prominent physician for the pharmaceutical company, Quasar Pharmaceuticals, was terminated yesterday for his ongoing illegal attempts to bring in GHB and other drugs that are not legal for most American and other companies who sell and distribute a wide variety of brands of drugs and pharmaceuticals around the world. The doctor's name is being withheld at this time by the board of directors of Quasar.*

He laughed to himself as he took a long drag of his Dunhill Fine Cut cigarette. He placed it in the glass ashtray on the left side of the desk and then picked up a shot glass of Wild Turkey bourbon. He took a fast gulp of it and squeezed his eyes tightly shut from the effects of the strong alcohol. He stopped reading the online news article about him; he already knew what was to follow. He would be brought up on federal charges for distributing illegal prescription drugs, both steroids and other GHB performance-enhancing drugs, to sports athletes and other well-known physicians to give to their patients.

The illegal distribution had made him wealthy and attracted many powerful and influential friends. Now he was about to lose all his money, his luxurious home and cars, not to mention all the personal things he had gathered over the years. He thought of being alone in a federal prison, unable to access any of the enjoyable comforts that even the everyday person had. He knew he would be found guilty and sentenced to many years in prison.

Losing his freedom and his will to live, he clenched his fists and banged them down hard on the wooden desk. He then smiled as he thought to himself, *If I'm about to lose everything I have built around me to those who feel they are the champions of the good and just of the people, I will not give in to them without exacting my bold taste of vengeance against these fools.*

I have long held my hatred for men and women who have achieved happiness in life that I was never able to cherish and enjoy. Money and power did not bring it to me, and true love I never found, just a brief failed marriage to that bitch who never loved me but gave all her love and devotion to our only child. I have longed for her to suffer in hell since the day she passed away from Alzheimer's. He had been overjoyed to watch her suffer as she lost all memory of her loved ones and happy life.

To him, her suffering was well deserved. He blamed her for their divorce and his many years of unhappiness when they were together. She had taken him for a lot of money in the divorce, which she had received in the settlement along with custody of their only child—the only thing he had truly loved in his bitter and twisted life. His disdain for women had started with her, and he now knew the true bloodline of hatred and vengeance. It had all begun within his family tree many years ago, which he had discovered while sorting through an old trunk from the early 1900s. The truck of old family items had belonged to his father and had been stowed away for many years, unopened until just the other day when he found an old box in it.

He spun in his leather chair to reach the old nineteenth-century box made of dark Calamander wood. He opened it and took out a very old journal and two brass rings that had at one time belonged to a female.

The journal was from the 1800s, leather bound with a brass latch in the center. As he opened the latch to read the very worn and frail pages of the journal, he saw the name of its owner and author on the inside cover. The journal had belonged to a distant relative. The name had been signed with a fine fountain pen matching the era of the book. The water-based liquid ink was still legible, and the fine blue script read, *Francis J. Tumblety*—the author of the journal. It held a total of two hundred pages, but only one hundred and thirty seven pages were completed with detailed written passages by Tumblety, who in fact had been a physician himself dealing in ancient Indian herbs and other forms of medicines found during that era.

But it was the last twenty pages or so that really caught his attention. As Francis Tumblety recounted his visits to Europe in the mid—to late 1800s, he described traveling to a poverty-stricken area known as Whitechapel, England, in late 1888. He had spent time there as one of the most infamous crimes in world history took place. He admitted that Whitechapel was home to a large immigrant population of Polish Jews who had found refuge in the abundance of very cheap lodging houses known as doss-houses. The result was very tight quarters for the occupants and a shared toilet on each floor or outhouses.

He went on to write that these people where beneath him and said that he found them repulsive. He hated them because they drank heavily and became violent toward one another in an area that was already very tight to live in, with overcrowded streets and very small alleys. He noted that their drink of choice was gin, and the women had very puffed-out cheeks from heavy drinking. The ones who took to prostitution in order to make a living walked the streets of Whitechapel to find a few pennies to cover the cost of lodging for the nights. He wrote of his hatred for these women. *I have become sick to my insides of these grotesque and foul women who need to sell themselves to earn refuge for a night's stay. For my first wife was a woman of the street, which she did not admit to me until after we were already husband and wife. I shall fix these women while I am here in Whitechapel.*

Tumblety went on to say how he committed the most unspeakable act one can do to another person—the act of bloody murder—and how he got away with it after he had savagely taken five women's lives. He had escaped England and went to France. Then he had made his way by boat across the Atlantic Ocean to return to New York and be in America again.

He smiled as he read who his great uncle really was: I escaped the fools in England right after I slaughtered the last whore. I managed to slip by the great detectives of Scotland Yard just as they gave me my true name, Jack the Ripper.

He looked up from the journal and spoke to himself, "My dear uncle, how true I hold what you did so many years ago to my heart. I will carry on your legacy of vengeance to rid the world of these foul women and all others who get in my way. The Ripper shall be born again!" He put down the journal and picked up a very sharp stainless steel postmortem knife. Then he smiled and said, "A century ago you were immortalized, and now I will join you in the present time!"

Chapter 1

Veronica Wood was walking the unsafe streets of National City, just south of downtown San Diego. The area was a mixture of commercial and residential areas. Veronica earned her living meeting men at truck stops and rest areas and taking her charges back to one of the many cheap motels or better-class hotels nearby. Veronica was a very attractive twenty-six-year-old brunette. She was about five foot four with long black hair and dark brown eyes. She wore very short Daisy Duke denim shorts, a black button-down blouse under a short leather jacket, and black heels. She wanted to bare as much of her body as she could in an effort draw the attention of men walking or driving by to her very slim and athletic body.

She was walking around the corner of the diner, a spot most frequented by truck drivers stopping and parking to get coffee or a bite to eat as they got ready to embark upon their long journeys on the interstate north out of San Diego. It was just past 1:00 a.m. Veronica looked up and noticed a four-door sedan driving slowly past her from behind. She smiled in case the driver was male, trying to get his attention. As she smiled, she hoped she didn't have to walk the streets for long to find a man on this particular cool night of May 17. She would charge him the usual amount for a three-hour meeting: four hundred dollars cash. *Not an expensive amount for an escort to ask these days*, she thought. She stood in place as the car made a U-turn over the double yellow line to come back in her direction.

His heart started to beat faster. This was his first meeting with a prostitute and would be his first cleansing of the low-class women he had come to hate. He did not think of the act he was about to commit as murder but rather as a cleansing of the scum and pure trash he wanted to think of them as, just like his great uncle had. So many years before, he would have been taken in by Veronica's exquisite body and nice shapely long legs. He slowed to a stop and lowered the passenger side window to greet the woman.

"Hello, sugar," she said with a wide smile, showing off nice white teeth. She asked him if he was interested in a good time tonight.

"Hello, my dear. How are you this fine evening?" the doctor asked her. "I'm sorry, but I am nervous being that this is my first time meeting a young lady in this manner."

Veronica, amused by his innocent demeanor. thought he was too well mannered and too soft spoken to be an undercover cop out to bust her tonight.

"Well, why don't you open the door and let me in, and we can talk about it, sugar?" she replied with a laugh.

He unlocked the passenger side door. She gently opened it and slid into the leather seat. It was a nice car, and he was very pleasant and mature, she thought. This was a good catch for her tonight.

"I'm Veronica. Thank you for stopping by and meeting me," she told him.

He smiled and said it was a pleasure to meet a very beautiful woman on this pleasant early morning.

"So what's your name?" she asked him.

He told her his name was Nathan.

"Is that your first name or last name, Nathan?"

"Does that really matter? I don't mean to sound rude, but I don't like being very open to you right now, since this is the first time I have ever met with someone like you," he replied with a nervous look in his eyes.

"It's all right, Nathan. No need to be nervous with me. I just want you to relax and let me give you a first time you will never forget."

With that reaction from her, Nathan became more confident as he got to know her more each moment. He asked her if she met her men at her place or at motels only. She remarked that she only met her contacts at motels and hotels, especially since this was their first meeting. She felt safer being in a public place. He smiled and asked if they could meet at the Twin Palms Motel. That was less than a mile away. She smiled at him and said that motel was fine with her.

Nathan told her, "Great," and drove off toward the motel.

"What made you pick that motel?" she asked him.

"It is small and kind of cozy, I thought. Being that this is my first time, I just wanted to be in a very comfortable setting for myself," he replied.

Veronica asked him to tell her about himself—what he did for work and how old he was. He told her he was fifty-six years old and divorced with no children. As for work, he told her he was in medicine but did not go into any details about what he actually did.

After they entered the parking lot of the small motel of twenty-four rooms on two floors, Nathan parked his car in the middle row. He explained that he would go into the office and secure a room for them. The hotel seemed to be very empty except for two other vehicles parked in the motel's lot. As he exited the car, Veronica thought to herself that Nathan kept himself in very good shape for his age. His fit appearance gave the impression that he exercised and ate well. He had a full head of dark gray hair, which was brushed straight back. His height was just under six foot tall.

She watched as he entered the office, and then she opened her small purse and took out her compact powder and lipstick. She lowered her passenger side visor, opened the mirror, and added more makeup to her beautiful face. As she noticed him returning to the car with a key in his right hand, she quickly placed the items back into her small purse. He went to the back of the car, opened the trunk, and took out a vinyl carry bag about eighteen inches long. As Veronica exited the car to meet him, he told her their room was room 12, straight ahead from where he parked. She informed him of the amount of her donation and told him that she would only meet with him for three hours for that amount. He agreed that it was all right with him. She looked at the bag in his left hand, puzzled.

"I hope you're not into anything kinky. Because I'm not into that sort of thing," she said with a look of seriousness in her eyes.

"Neither am I," he replied, and they both smiled.

He motioned for them to enter the room, which he opened with his key. Veronica went over to the king-sized bed, removed her jacket, and placed her purse on the side table next to the lamp, which she turned on. Nathan left only the light to the foyer of the room on. He watched her remove her blouse and shorts. She kicked off her pumps and now stood in her matching black lace bra and panties. Nathan opened his wallet and took out four crisp hundred dollar bills. He handed them to her, and Veronica pleasantly took the money from him and placed it in her purse. Then she returned the purse to the side table.

"Come on, handsome. Don't you want to have the time of your life now?" she said as she slid back the comforter and bedsheets, climbed in, and relaxed her sexy body to entice him to join her.

He took off his button-down denim shirt, kicked off his black leather shoes, and removed his jeans. Veronica was stunned; she had expected to see him in his underwear, but he was now wearing what seemed to be black hospital scrubs. She asked in surprise what he was wearing. He replied that they were cotton pajamas that helped make him feel very comfortable before they got started. As he joined her on the bed, he glided his hand up her very smooth left thigh to her left hand. She pulled him toward her face, and they kissed one another deeply. As she pushed him down onto the bed, he removed her bra while they continued kissing. He gently removed her panties.

Veronica tried to remove his top, but he stopped her hands and held them down as he kept kissing her. She then tried to remove his bottoms, but he again stopped her hands and spread them against her sides.

Uneasy about how this was going, she asked, "Hey now, what's with you? Are we going to get on with it or what, sugar"?

He looked into her eyes and smiled. "Can we first play a nice game?" he asked her.

She made a face and asked if he wanted to role-play. She wasn't into that sort of thing.

"No, not role-play. Just a very romantic game of blindfolded sex."

She asked what he had in mind, and Nathan explained that he would blindfold her with a black scarf while they had sex.

Amused by this, she smiled at him. "You really are nervous about this being your first time, aren't you, handsome?" she said. Fond of the idea, she agreed to have him blindfold her.

He reached into his bag and took out the scarf. He then placed it around her eyes and double knotted it at the back of her head and made sure it was secure. As he pushed her back down to the bed gently, he began to kiss her deeply once again. Then he reached back down to his carry bag, which he had left on the floor near the bed, and took out a sharp stainless steel knife with his right hand. He very quickly covered her mouth tightly with his left hand and muttered softly into her ear, "Whore!"

He cut her throat deeply from left to right with the sharp blade and then again from right to left. He squeezed his hand tightly over

Veronica's mouth. She flailed her hands about, and all he could hear was her gasping for air and choking on her own blood. Then she stopped gasping, and her hands fell to her sides.

He watched in peace now as she looked at him in shock and closed her eyelids. Blood gushed all over her neck from the two open straight cuts to her throat. As he removed his hand from her mouth, he quickly got up from the bed and pulled open his bag. He produced a few white gauze pads and a bottle of sterile water. He put on long latex gloves to cover his hands and then produced two sterile shoe covers. He quickly covered his feet and all was now secure; he would not leave any of his DNA behind.

After wetting the gauze pads with water, he quickly washed her body, legs, face, lips, and hands. Then he wiped down the inside of the room, the room key, the inside doorknob, and the light switch. He knew he would clean his hands when he was done. But now it was time for the real cleansing to commence.

With anger in his eyes, he took out a sterile black cap and full plastic visor mask. He picked up the knife again, took her right hand, inserted the blade under her index fingernail, and violently pulled away from her skin. He dropped the fingernail into a clear plastic bag and then did the same thing to the next finger. As he repeated the process on the other hand, he laughed to himself. "No DNA evidence, people." He placed the plastic bag in the side pouch of his carry bag. Then he looked at the time on the digital clock on the table. It read 2:25 a.m. Still enough time for him to finish what he had set out to do.

He took hold of her left breast, remembering what his great uncle had done to his last victim in England, Mary Jane Kelly. Nathan would also brutally separate this whore's body from all her flesh and organs and leave her faceless—a death no one deserved. But this was the start of no remorse for him; this was his way of continuing Francis's hatred toward women. He thrust the blade into the edge of her breast and sliced all around the tissue and ligaments. Her blood stained her whole chest red. He removed her breast and placed it at the foot of the bed and then did the same to the other. He stopped and thought to himself again.

"The Ripper took trophies from his victims, a uterus and a kidney from each. They deserved to have their bodies cleansed from the whores they became in life!" he shouted the idea to himself as he spread her legs open wide and inserted the blade deep into her vagina. He wanted her womb out. He used both hands to open her vaginal cavity. Well schooled as a medical doctor, he knew human anatomy. He took hold of her fallopian tubes and then cut and tore them from the womb. He ripped her insides out of her as he extracted her uterus. He held it in his hand and smiled as he looked at her lifeless body.

"This is what makes a woman a whore!"

He wanted to take the bloody organ with him, just like Francis had written in his journal; he'd had a large collection of female wombs in glass jars. But Nathan couldn't take it with him, for it was too bloody and messy. He placed it at the foot of the bed, next to the extracted breasts.

Next he turned her over on her side and tore into her lower back. He wanted both her kidneys out of her. He thrust the knife into her again, tearing through skin and muscle until he felt her left kidney, and then cut away all the organs that held it. He took it out of her body and then stopped, paused again, and thought of the "From Hell" letter that had been mailed along with a bloody kidney to George Lusk, the head of the Whitechapel vigilance committee at the time.

Nathan placed the kidney next to the other organs and knew he needed to stop. This was modern-day San Diego. People would be up early for work, and he needed to hurry and clean up now. He tore into the body again hurriedly and extracted her right kidney, wet with blood. He placed it in the neat row formed by both breasts, the uterus, and the other kidney. He then turned her over onto her back once again.

Next, Nathan quickly took out a large black plastic garbage bag. He took off all his sterile garments and placed them, along with the bloody surgical knife, in the bag. He took out a small bottle of clear hand sanitizer and rubbed his hands very well with it. Then he took out one last sterile gauze pad and stopped to look at his amazing and bloody work. To him it was an art of true wonder. This act proved him to be a true man and personal hero to his own cause, just like Jack the Ripper. He laughed as he left her eyes blindfolded and walked to the door. He used a gauze pad to turn the brass doorknob and close it behind him. He then dropped the pad into the black garbage bag.

Once in the parking lot, he opened his car door, climbed inside, and started the vehicle. After putting the car into reverse and then into drive, he drove out of the parking lot very slowly. There was not a soul around at 2:50 a.m.

Nathan smiled to himself. "I have done it, my first murder of a whore! But it will not be my last. I will go home and burn my scrubs and knife. I will always follow the same pattern and strike a new whore each time. The fools will not catch me!"

He made his way onto the on-ramp of the interstate, which would take him home to hide.

It was just after 8:00 a.m. when homicide detective Edward Brooks got a call from the Central Division of the San Diego Police Department. A body had been discovered at the Twin Palms Motel, just south of downtown San Diego but still within the jurisdiction of the Central Division. Ed's partner, Robert Cullen, picked him up in their unmarked sedan. When they pulled into the motel parking lot, they saw it was swarming with Central Division squad cruisers and the county coroner's forensic van. Brooks and Cullen exited their vehicle to be briefed on what had happened inside room 12.

Ed Brooks was six-foot-one and very muscular. He had a vigorous exercise routine, which included lifting weights every night at his house and running up to five miles on the weekends. Ed was a navy veteran who had served just fewer than six years, which had earned him the rank of petty officer second class, E-5 pay grade. Ed had been with Central Division PD for eighteen years. He had been a patrol officer and sergeant for the first ten years and lead homicide detective for the last eight years. He was now forty-one years old, and his partner, Rob, was only thirty-six, having joined the force straight out of college at the age of twenty-four. The two had been partners for four years; Rob had replaced Ed's last partner, who retired.

The first squad officer on the scene walked up to them to brief them on what was known so far. "Hey, guys. We got ourselves a bad scene here. According to the victim's driver's license, which was found inside her purse, she is a twenty-six-year-old female named Veronica Wood. She is a known prostitute from the area; we've picked her up a few times for solicitation."

Rob asked had been in the room so far and who had discovered the body.

"The body was first discovered by a housekeeper, Betty Flores. She screamed, ran into the office, and notified the night manager, who was still on duty and in turn called us. The first call came into dispatch at 7:23 a.m. The forensic team just entered the room to gather evidence only, per the instructions of your boss, Lieutenant Stanford."

"Was the night manager on duty when the guests came to rent this room during the night?" Ed asked him.

"He was on duty, and he assigned room 12 to a gentleman by the name of Mason Albert. Probably a fake name, but we are checking on that. The manager stated that the man came into the office alone, paid cash for the room, a total of sixty-five dollars. And he was alone. He signed for the room at 1:50 a.m.," the officer read from his notes.

Ed and Rob said they would interview the night manager once they were done looking at the body. With that, they entered the room and closed the door behind them. As the three-man forensic team dusted for prints in the bathroom and around the entryway, both detectives put on latex gloves and sterile foot coverings before moving anywhere near the body, which was lying on the bed, with a black scarf tied around her head and eyes. Ed and Rob looked at one another when they saw the amount of blood that had seeped all over the bed and into the carpeting of the room. Rob clenched his teeth in surprise when he saw the organs spread out at the foot of the bed.

Ed whispered to him, "The killer positioned them in his own symbolic way to show us that he has no fear of law enforcement. I can tell right away."

Rob nodded in agreement. Ed approached the lead forensic specialist and asked him how long ago the victim died judging by the body temperature.

"I estimate the murder happened between 1:00 and 2:30 a.m. So just about five hours ago, not a long time at all," he told Ed.

"Any signs of a struggle or skin tissue under her fingernails?" Rob asked him.

"We will never be able to tell. The killer removed all ten of her fingernails. The cause of death was two deep straight cuts to the throat and larynx from ear to ear, left to right first and then right to left. That makes our killer right-handed," stated the forensic specialist.

Ed continued to gather all the information known so far as he looked around the room for clues. He walked over to the body and lifted the blindfold on Veronica's head.

"So no signs of a struggle and no fingerprints so far. If you had to guess, were all these organs removed with the same weapon?" Ed asked him.

"Well, I didn't turn her body over to look at the wounds on her back, as it appeared the killer turned her onto her back again once he removed her kidneys. But from what I can see of the throat lacerations and the deep cuts to her vagina to remove her womb, I can tell you that this guy knows what he is doing. He's smart, and he had it planned out very well."

Ed took a breath and let it out slowly. "I agree with you on that. Look, bag the blindfold and send it with all the DNA swabs of the body and blood. If we are lucky, they had sexual intercourse, and maybe his semen is on her vaginal walls. Also, get lots of pictures of the body and room. Let's hope this is the first and last victim, but my guess is it's just the start of a serial pattern to come," Ed told them.

The lead forensic specialist acknowledged his requests. Rob told Ed to look at her eyes. They were closed peacefully, and there was no fear on her face. Ed looked and thought, *What a very pretty girl. What a waste of a young life.*

"She has no fear in her eyes because of the blindfold, and she was very comfortable with him. This means our man is well groomed, well mannered, and well-spoken enough to persuade any young lady to be with him. Another thing for us to worry about is if he is indeed a serial killer," Ed explained to Rob, who agreed with him.

Ed's cell phone rang. He took it out of his inside pocket and answered it. It was their boss, the lieutenant in charge of the homicide division, Rick Stanford. He informed Ed that he was on-site and coming to the room now.

Rick entered and put on latex gloves and sterile shoe covers. He approached his two detectives, and Ed and Rob briefed him on the findings up to that point. Rick was a very skilled detective himself and had been on the force for more than twenty years. He enjoyed his job and the nice weather of San Diego, and he liked every one of the men in his division. Rick had no intention of retiring any time soon.

As Rick looked around the room and body, he agreed with Ed and the forensic team that the killer might have made a mistake by not taking the blindfold with him. He hoped the killer had touched it before he put on gloves. The three men then exited the room to go talk to the night manager.

Rob interviewed the night manager and asked for him to describe the suspect to him and their forensic sketch artist so the artist could make a detailed composite drawing of the suspect. Rob asked about all the man's features: his weight, hairstyle, facial hair, and race.

The night manager replied to his list of questions, "Look, as I already stated before to the other policemen, the guy walked in here at ten minutes to 2:00 a.m. He paid cash for the room and signed the ledger as Mason Albert. The guy was white. He was about five foot nine to five foot eleven. He had a full head of straight gray hair that was slicked back and kind of high. He had a dark gray mustache and long sideburns, I believe. As far as what he was wearing, I think it was a dark shirt and a jacket. Look, I only dealt with him for about three minutes. He paid me. I gave him the room key. I didn't see whether he was with her or if he was with another guy. We have no surveillance camera system here, which I know is a state violation by the owner of the motel," he admitted to Rob and Ed.

Rob said, "Yes, it is a very big violation."

As the forensic artist finished his sketch of the suspect, Rob thanked the manger. Rick asked to talk to them outside. The artist handed his sketch to Ed, who thanked him and showed it to both Rick and Rob. They then walked outside the office and stood in the parking lot right outside the room. They watched as the body being was removed in a body bag and placed into the county coroner's white van.

"So what do you guys think so far?" Rick asked them.

"Well, he scouted out this location beforehand and knew they didn't have a surveillance system. He parked his vehicle right in the parking spot by room 12 for an easy in-and-out getaway. And just by looking at the sketch, my guess is he was wearing a fake mustache, wig, and sideburns," Ed explained his thoughts about the killer to them.

"And by the looks of the patterns of the wounds and the knowledge it would have taken to find and extract the victim's organs, I say we are dealing with a doctor or some person with anatomical knowledge of the human body," Rob suggested to them, and both Rick and Ed agreed.

"Okay, we will wait and see if Dr. Cate Adams finds anything with the gathered swabs and the blindfold. Till then, run this guy's face against our database of known convicts. Plus check around with surrounding counties and states to see if there have been any similar killings like this one, guys," Rick instructed them.

Ed told Rob to go back to the precinct and begin work there, as they would also need to contact Veronica Wood's next of kin and break the sad news to them.

That night he sat at home in his living room, watching the evening news and smoking another Dunhill Fine Cut cigarette. As he exhaled a long puff of smoke slowly from his mouth, he listened as the female newscaster told of the horrific discovery of a young female's body at the Twin Palms Motel. She said the police were holding back the victim's name at that time, as well as the grizzly details of the murder. He was just about finished with the cigarette and smashed it into the glass ashtray on his marble coffee table. He then picked up his great uncle's old journal and read more of its chilling passages.

> *I was able to get by the fools by using other men's names to hide my own. I even went as far as to grow my mustache very long and wear clothing the fools would not have known I would wear. I am a true hider of my identity and a traveler who escapes all those who seek me out. For I am the one who did not end with the five the fools believe me to have murdered. I continued until number ten.*

Nathan read the passage in the journal, and it made him feel as if he was now equal to Francis Tumblety in more ways than one. He had achieved his goal of concealing his identity so far, and he'd been able to disguise himself and commit murder. He looked up from the journal and laughed out loud.

"Dear Uncle, I wish to surpass your number ten until I kill a number of whores so great that will shock not only this large city but shake the world at the core of its foundation." He laughed again as he thought and planned his next murder. He would allow time to pass between them, as the Ripper had done with his victims.

Chapter 2

It had been two days since the murder. Ed Brooks and his partner, Rob Cullen, were going over the crime scene DNA results from county medical forensic scientist Dr. Cate Adams. Rob read her findings to Ed. "No fingerprints were on the blindfold because Dr. Adams found that the blindfold had been dampened with sterile water, maybe before or after the killer placed it over her eyes."

Ed looked up at Rob from his desk, which faced Rob's, and said, "This guy is very clever." Then he continued, "So if he follows this same pattern again, avoids surveillance cameras, and disguises himself well, we are going to need an eye witness to his next killing to identify him. That will be the only way we will have anything to go on about him. But I am sorry to say this: there will be another murder to happen soon," Ed told Rob just as Lieutenant Stanford came by. He already knew of all the DNA findings because he had been in a relationship with Dr. Adams for quite some time.

"Hey, boss, how about the idea of using female undercovers as prostitutes to flush him out? We have done it before on raids of male solicitors in the downtown area. Why not for this case?" Ed threw out an idea for him to think about regarding how they could catch the killer in the act.

"I already talked to the captain about that idea, and for now he said no. He doesn't want to place anyone's life on the line in undercover work on this just yet. But being as we have little to nothing to go on,

I agree with you that another murder is bound to happen. So for now we are heating up patrols by our uniformed cops through late evenings till early mornings to see if we spot any suspicious men driving around the downtown areas," Stanford informed them. He told them to stay sharp and that they would get a break eventually.

On Monday, June 22, Nathan picked up the very lovely Sharon Kessler just after 6:00 p.m. More than a month had passed since he had picked up Veronica Wood. This time he planned his routine differently. He met Sharon as she was walking through a strip mall and the thought crossed his mind that she was a street walker. She was wearing skin-tight leather pants and high black suede boots that reached almost to her knees. She also had on a dark blue sweater, which had a deep neckline that showed off her bare shoulders.

Sharon was a beautiful African American woman who had nice wavy hair that hung to her shoulders and a body that was almost identical to Veronica Wood's. As he slowed his sedan next to her in the parking lot, he was not nervous like he had been before. He used his same mellow voice and charm to ask her if she wanted to show him a good time tonight. As Sharon entered his car, he agreed upon her donation of six hundred dollars for five hours. But he made one different request than the first time; he asked if they could meet at her residence instead of a motel.

Sharon gave some consideration to the request. She felt that Nathan seemed harmless because of his older age, so she agreed and told him where she lived. They drove off to her residence in the northern district of San Diego. Soon they came upon the nice apartment she shared with her roommate just off Carlton Hills Boulevard. As they entered her nice, spacious two-bedroom apartment, Sharon informed Nathan that her roommate would not be home until later that evening and that if he was still there when she arrived, he shouldn't worry because her roommate was also an escort and they kept the names of the men with whom they met confidential. Nathan told her that made him very comfortable indeed. Sharon closed and locked the door behind them and then asked Nathan what was with the nylon bag he had strapped over his shoulder.

"Oh, this is just a change of clothes and clean underwear I have for myself so my wife will not be suspicious of me when I return home," he answered her as they entered her bedroom.

She closed the door behind them. "Your wife? But I thought you said you were divorced now," she replied. Her back was to him as she dimmed the room's lights. All of a sudden a gloved hand came over her mouth very quickly and held it shut with a powerful grip.

"Yes, I made a mistake, whore!" he spoke very softly into her left ear as his right hand held a steel postmortem knife to her neck.

The sharp blade came across her neck, cutting deep into her flesh. It cut very easily, and her blood flowed down from the open wound and colored his left arm red. Sharon didn't even have time to react or make a sound. She couldn't gasp for air. As she lost all life in her muscles, she collapsed in Nathan's arms. He quickly picked her up, carried her still body to her bed, and laid her down. He then undressed himself, put on black sterile scrubs, and fixed the head cap, clear face mask, and shoe coverings to be certain that none of his DNA would be exposed to the body or left in the room.

"Just like the first bitch I cleansed, I have plenty of time to destroy this whore's body and cleanse all the shameful acts she has reaped and sowed in her wretched life!" he snarled as he took hold of the sharp knife and stabbed hard into her chest.

Blood flew up onto his face mask and all over the nice cotton sheets. He stabbed again. The blood flew upward even higher now, and dark blood began to seep from the open wound in her chest. He wanted to extract the most valuable organ in the human body. He wanted her heart first. He soon found it. He began to cut away the arteries and muscles that held it in the thoracic cavity. When he was done, he pulled it out of her chest cavity, leaving the enormous open wound he had cut and torn into her chest in order to extract the bloody heart he now held in his left hand.

"My prize gift to myself. I have taken it from this foul bitch, for I remember what he did to those women one at a time. I will do the same now," he whispered to himself in a dark and evil voice. He turned his attention to her ears and used the sharp blade to slit just behind her earlobe. The blade sheared away her muscle, and blood oozed down his blade and gloved hand as he severed her ear from her head. He held it in his hand, bloody and still with its gold hoop earring dangling down. He smiled to himself again as he placed it right beneath the heart. He repeated the extraction of her right ear and also displayed it at the foot of the bed with her other organs. He was still smiling as he looked at her body over, still not satisfied with his work.

"What else does she still have that I would need to take from her to prove to these street walkers that the life they lead is true filth?" he spoke softly to himself as he looked at her eyes. Then he knew what he wanted to take next. He also knew he had to work fast so he could remove her fingernails, just like he had with the first whore.

It was 9:37 p.m. when Linda Rivera opened the door with her key. As she entered her apartment, she only saw a few lights on in the living room and no lights coming from her roommate's bedroom as she passed by the closed door. She didn't know what time Sharon would be home, so she decided to give her a call on her cell phone. She dialed the saved number. Only three seconds passed before the sound of a musical ring came from within Sharon's bedroom. Stunned by the sound of the phone, Linda went back over to Sharon's room and knocked lightly on the door.

"Sharon?" she called, but there was no answer.

Concerned now, Linda turned the doorknob slowly to the right. The door was unlocked. She pushed the door inward halfway, reached out to find the light switch on the wall, and turned on the lights. Her eyes fixed upon the purse on the floor, which contained the still-ringing cell phone. Linda then looked at the bed. Her eyes shot open wide in horror, and she let out a loud, piercing scream at the top of her lungs. She could not bring herself to look any longer at the bloody corpse on the bed. She ran out of the apartment and into the hallway. The neighbor from the apartment above looked down the stairs to see what had caused the loud scream.

As Linda looked up and saw her, she calmed herself enough to scream up to her, "Call the police!"

At eleven o'clock, Ed Brooks was relaxing on his leather sofa, drinking a cup of coffee, and listening to "Hey Joe," one of his favorite Jimi Hendrix songs, on the sound system of his deluxe Bose stereo system. His wife, Kayla, came into the living room, wearing a short silver silk robe over some nice lingerie that she had just put on. Ed's eyes fixated on his beautiful wife, her long red hair, and her sparkling hazel eyes. Kayla was barely shorter than five foot nine, and she was a middle school teacher. As she came over and sat in Ed's lap, he placed the hot mug of coffee on the end table next to him.

"So, is there something you would rather do than listen to Jimi Hendrix CDs all night? Or would you rather join me for some fun?" Kayla asked him with a gleaming smile.

Ed grasped her tightly around her waist and pulled her face close to his. They kissed deeply. Ed asked her what kind of lingerie she had on under her robe.

Kayla smiled at him and answered, "Well, I will give you a hint. You got it for me as a gift this past Valentine's Day."

Ed raised his eyebrows and knew what it was. "Wow. So I think we better make sure it was a special gift I got you." Ed used his remote control to turn off the CD player and then picked Kayla up in his strong arms. They kissed deeply again. As Ed carried her toward their bedroom, he heard his home phone start to ring. Kayla broke their kiss and softly told him not to answer it. Ed told her he didn't want to answer it, but he had to. After he sat Kayla down on the couch, he picked up the phone just after the fourth ring. "Hello?"

"Ed, it's Rick. Look, come meet me and Rob at 475 Carlton Hills Boulevard. We have similar style case on our hands," Rick informed him.

Ed looked at Kayla, who gave him a sad look as he told Rick he would be there as soon as he could. He hung up the phone, bent down to her, and held her hands with his. "Hey, I got to go out for a while, but I will be back as soon as I can. I'm sorry, sweetheart," he told her.

A tear ran down her right cheek. "Go, Ed. I will be up waiting for you. Just be careful please," she told him.

Ed kissed his wife again gently and went and retrieved his 9mm sidearm and his jacket. Then he headed out the door. Ed arrived at the crime scene nearly a half an hour later. He saw that the whole block had been blocked by Northern Division squad cars. He glimpsed another county coroner van parked in front of the apartment building. Rick and Rob walked over to him as he got out of his GMC Envoy. Ed knew this wasn't their jurisdiction; this murder scene was located in the northern part of San Diego. He knew then that the crime must be very similar to the Veronica Wood murder.

"The forensic crew is already inside doing the whole ten yards on the scene and the victim," Rick told Ed. He also said that the two detectives from this division were already interviewing the victim's roommate and neighbors about any suspects seen with her that evening.

Rob asked Rick for the victim's name.

"The latest casualty is twenty-nine-year-old Sharon Kessler. She lived here with her roommate, thirty-two-year-old Linda Rivera. Both women are escorts who advertised their services privately on the Internet. So it looks like either our suspect sought her out through an online search, or he happened to approach her on the street. Linda told one of the other investigating detectives that Sharon had told her she had no clients set for this evening." Rick then told him the rest of the information he had been told up to that point.

"So how is this case similar to ours?" Ed asked them.

Rick told them to glove up and cover their shoes. He said this scene was far worse than the other one. When the three detectives were ready, they entered through the door of the apartment and walked through the living room, where they saw Linda Rivera crying as she spoke to the detectives. The door to the bedroom was closed, so Rick knocked on it. When a crime scene technician opened the door, they saw three other technicians in the room; one was taking photographs of the body and the room, and the others were dusting for prints and gathering swab traces for DNA evidence. Ed and Rob just stood in place in absolute shock and horror. They were speechless as they looked at the poor girl's remains.

"Oh my God," Rob muttered softly as they walked closer to the bed.

The head technician, who had also worked the first crime scene, removed his mask to talk to Rick and his men. He explained that just like the first victim, her fingernails had been removed and taken by the killer. The killer had placed the organs he removed from the body at the foot of the bed, just like he had with the last girl. Ed looked at the organs—her eyes, heart, and both ears. They were placed in such a way that the eyes and the two ears made what looked like a happy face. Ed thought of a famous crime committed years before. Rick called his name, but Ed didn't respond. Rick called his name a second time, this time louder. Ed turned to his boss. He was standing next to the two lead detectives assigned to this case. The men all huddled around to talk and share notes and knowledge of both cases.

"Guys, these are Detectives Jack Kerns and Ken Rogers. I filled them in with what we know so far on Veronica Wood, and we are already in agreement that this is the same suspect."

All five men confirmed their agreement.

"So, so far he preys on escorts. He travels all around the city, not worried about sticking to one sector or pattern of where to commit the murder. He takes the victim's fingernails with him as both a trophy of the crime and mostly to prevent his DNA from being scraped from under the fingernails," Ed told them as he looked at Ken Roger's shirt, which seemed to be stained with water.

Ken's partner looked at Ed and said, "Ken and I were so shocked by the nature of the crime that Ken threw up on himself."

Ken admitted he was still in shock at the brutality of this killer's work.

"So do you think the chief would want to set up a task force now? Or do we need more murders on our hands? I'm sure he's smart enough to know we have a serial killer on the loose now in the city of San Diego," Rob told them.

"Okay, guys, just relax for a minute. Lieutenant, I need to talk with these guys about this. Since the first crime happened in our division, we would take point on the investigation. As far as a task force goes, that is up to Chief John Chase, so I will be briefing him and his staff tonight. Let Kerns and Rogers here take care of the crime scene and witnesses' contact information. I will make a brief statement to the media about what we know so far," Rick instructed them.

Ed smiled and said to himself, *What is he going to tell them? We don't know anything about this guy just yet ourselves.*

Detective Kerns told Rick that the crime scene crew would forward everything to Dr. Adams for complete DNA analysis like with the first murder, and she would brief them when she got her results back. The men agreed to stay in touch, exchanged their cell and office numbers, and said good-bye for the time being.

It was just 2:00 a.m. when Ed got home. He parked his Envoy in his garage, right next to Kayla's car. As the garage door closed, Ed glanced over and smiled at his prized Fat Boy motorcycle, which was custom painted black and had chrome trim. Ed exited through the garage and went up the stairs. He knew Kayla would be sleeping, so he was quiet as he took off his jacket and removed his gun from his right-side holster. Then he went into his office and turned on his computer. He closed the door so he would not wake his wife and sat down at his desk, where he did an Internet search of Jack the Ripper.

Ed started to read the history of the Ripper's victims, their names, and the state of their murders. There were five known victims of the Ripper, but there may have been as many as eight altogether. But the police officials who investigated the crimes in the Whitechapel section of England in the autumn of 1888 were never sure. Ed was reading about the lead investigators assigned to the case from Scotland Yard when the door was slowly pushed inward and Kayla entered his office. Ed quickly closed the screen to his laptop, not wanting to show her what he was looking at. As she pulled a chair from the corner of the room to sit next to him, she knew from the look on his face that he was disturbed by something.

"Ed, are you all right? I know you can't discuss anything with me about the cases, but I watched the eleven o'clock news, and they said another young woman was found brutally murdered. I'm scared now living here; I'm scared for you being involved in this case," Kayla whispered to him.

"Look, nothing is going to happen to me or you. You know I will never let anyone harm you, Kayla. But this is part of my job, and after all my time on the force here in this city, we are now faced with the worst serial killer in decades. But don't worry, because we have so many cops and forensic specialists working the case, we will get a top lead, and then we will get him. I promise you." Ed tried to sound positive for Kayla. They both got up and embraced one another, and Ed told her, "Let's finish what we didn't start before I left." Kissing Kayla gently, he picked her up in his strong arms and carried her to the master bedroom.

He read from the old journal again about his great uncle Francis Tumblety. He had been born in Ireland and grew up in the small town or Rochester in upstate New York. He had traveled across the states, selling Indian herd remedies and calling himself a doctor of herbal medicines. He wrote about how he treated patients for minor ailments, but the fools were so taken by his persuasive act as a physician that they bought his remedies in hopes they would be cured. From Detroit to Washington D.C. and parts of Maryland and across Europe, he traveled, gaining knowledge of how to perfect his con scheme and meeting very important figures in history such as Charles Dickens, and he even was awarded for treating Louis Napoleon, the second president of the republic of France at the time.

He also mentioned being a suspect in the assassination of President Abraham Lincoln. In St. Louis in May of 1865, he was sought by the federal police and Union soldiers; the false name he was going by at the time had somehow been involved with the assignation plot orchestrated by John Wilkes Booth and others. But he wrote that he was released when it became known that he was using a false name and there was no evidence to charge him with conspiracy.

As Nathan read more of a passage, he was greatly intrigued.

> *The fools thought they had me days after I dissected the body of Mary. But when they could not hold me, I escaped to France. There I boarded the ship back to America and used the secret name Frank Townset. I then fled to Brooklyn. When the fools came looking for me, I evaded them once again. The great police of Scotland Yard were too late and powerless to capture me a second time.*

Francis wrote this passage with arrogance and novice, praising himself for his choice of false names and disguises to elude capture by Scotland Yard, who had sent detectives to New York to apprehend Francis Tumblety in December 1888. But they were too late, as he had already moved out of his apartment in Brooklyn and fled to another state. Very impressed by Francis's cleverness and cunning and the fact that he was never caught and was a master of disguise, Nathan smiled as he looked up from the journal and stared out the window. He wondered, *So now that I have taken two whores, to sicken them even more and shock the great police of this city, I will move on the next one soon, for I can't wait to start to cleanse again.*

Nathan laughed out loud as he closed the journal and locked its latch into place.

At 11:30 a.m. two days after the shocking murder of Sharon Kessler, Ed and Rob had just been briefed along with the other two investigating officers, Rogers and Kerns, who had come over to Central Division to listen to the latest crime scene findings from Dr. Cate Adams. She had found that, like the first victim, Sharon's body had been cleaned with sterile water, and the killer had to have worn complete scrubs or a sterile suit. He was very smart, but it was stomach turning that he had taken all ten of her fingernails, just like he had with Veronica Wood.

Rogers and Kerns said they were returning to the strip mall where Sharon Kessler was last seen and may have encountered the killer. They were going to see if there were any surveillance cameras in the parking lot or businesses and interview people around there to see if anyone had seen anything that night.

An hour later, around noontime, Rob looked up from his computer and asked Ed what he felt like for lunch. He noticed that Ed was engrossed in a book he had open on his desk. Rob then saw another book faceup on Ed's desk and was surprised as he read the title: *History of Jack the Ripper*. Rob looked back at Ed, who was still deep into his read.

"Ed, come on now. Don't tell me you think this guy is a copycat of the original Ripper from way back when," Rob said to his partner.

Ed looked up at him with a serious look in his eyes. "Well, look. He mutilated his victims just like our suspect now, and if you read about Jack the Ripper's last victim, Mary Kelly, you'll discover that he hacked up the poor women's body, including her face. So there is no doubt in my mind that our man has been reading up on the original Ripper crimes," Ed told him.

Rob asked if he could look at the book Ed was reading. He looked at the photograph of the crime scene of Mary Kelly. She lay on her bed in her one-room flat. Her body and face were completely destroyed, and the flesh had been taken off her face and placed with her intestines on the night table beside the bed. Rob read the caption under the picture, which stated that the crime scene had shocked even the most veteran detectives of Scotland Yard. Rob now agreed with Ed that their suspect had knowledge of the Ripper and his style of body mutilation. When they saw Lieutenant Stanford walking toward their desks, they quickly put the books away.

Rick had come over to inform them of another victim. "Guys, we just got a call from Western Division. It looks like another body was discovered in Shoreline Park. It's a female with similarities to our cases."

Ed and Rob logged off their computers and put the books and files away. The trio went on their way to see the latest victim's body.

A short time later, they entered the park's main road. Many squad cars and the county medical examiner team were already there. The detectives were allowed in by four patrol officers who were keeping everyone except the police investigators away from the crime scene. Ed noticed two Northern Division officers being briefed by two other plain-clothes detectives, and he knew those two had to be with the Western Division.

"Let's see what they are talking about," Rick told his men as they approached.

They all greeted one another. Detective Jack Kerns introduced the two detectives assigned to this latest murder. "Ed and Rob, this is Skip Jones and Julie O'Keefe from homicide. They will be working on this case now."

As they all shook hands and introduced themselves, Rick was called away by a uniformed officer to go meet with higher-ups in the departments.

"What are the known details about this victim?" Ed asked the two new cops.

Julie O'Keefe read off the details to them. "The body was discovered around 8:00 a.m. by an elderly female walking her dog. The victim is thirty-two-year-old Lauren Morton. Her neck has multiple deep stab wounds, and she was decapitated," she read to them very softly, her voice full of shock and remorse.

The macho men just looked at one another and knew that to leave the body in as public of place as a park, their suspect had no fear of the police or anyone else.

Skip Jones led them under the police caution tape, which had been set up many yards away from the crime scene. They walked into the grassy wooded park; the grass was still wet with dew. The victim lay on her back in a spread-eagle position. The crime scene unit took pictures of the body. Already there to take DNA samples and examine the body was county medical examiner Dr. Cate Adams. She greeted all the detectives as Rick Stanford approached the crime scene to join them. He smiled at his girlfriend.

Cate began to tell them the similarities between this body and the other two. "This young woman's fingernails were also removed. It looks like the same kind of knife has inflicted the deep wounds. But the decapitation weapon has to be a small axe. I can tell that by the clean sharp-edged wound to her neck. But what makes this murder different from the others is that it seems she tried to fight him off. I can tell that because of the bruising on her arms and hands and the deep bruise to her right cheek. That tells me he killed her somewhere else and placed her body here," Dr. Adams told the group.

Rick also had something important to tell them. "Okay, everyone, this is coming straight from Chief Chase and his office. He is going to have a press conference within the hour at Central Division, and after the press conference, which we will all attend, he will brief us, as he has charged us to be the task force to investigate and apprehend our suspect. He will be giving us more details in our confidential briefing."

Ed nodded in agreement with his lieutenant as he looked at the body of Lauren Morton, quickly becoming enraged that another young woman's life had been cut short for no reason by a mad psychopath on the loose in his city.

Just a half hour after the major press conference conducted by the police chief of San Diego and the mayor at San Diego Police Department headquarters, the briefing of the organized task force of detectives was about to take place in the large conference room. The two lead detectives of each division where the three murders happened were present, and because of his overwhelming experience on the force and status as a longtime resident of San Diego, Lieutenant Rick Stanford was made lead lieutenant of the squad.

They were all seated around the large oval wooden table as they viewed a large LCD-projected map of San Diego. The points where the three bodies had been found were marked. Each detective had a folder sitting in front of him or her containing crime scene photos and the names of the victims. There was also a sketch of the only known suspect and some other details about the forensic findings. Dr. Cate Adams was also present for the briefing.

Chief John Chase walked into the room with Rick and closed and locked the door behind them. He took his seat at the head of the table, and Rick sat beside him. All the partners were seated next to one another as Chase began to go over what he had told the media a short time ago. He had shared with the public the names and ages of all three women and revealed that they had been escorts. He had explained that they were dealing with a male serial killer and released the composite sketch of his face. He was a white male about five foot nine to six foot tall. Chase had warned that the suspect might use fake mustaches and beards to disguise himself and conceal his true identity. Then he had stated that the police were doing everything in their power to make sure every citizen of San Diego was safe and advised people not to venture out alone late at night, though all divisions would have more patrol units on the streets around the clock.

He now looked up at all the detectives and introduced them to one another: Ed Brooks and Robert Cullen from Central Division, Ken Rogers and Jack Kerns from Northern Division, and Julie

O'Keeffe and Skip Jones from Western Division. Next, he laid out who the point team for the task force was.

"Okay, people, since the first murder happened right here in Central Division's jurisdiction, Ed and Rob are the lead detectives for the task force. We have now dubbed our suspect, "the Entity," for his use of disguises and his ability to conceal his identity and every move from us up to this point," Chief Chase told them. "Rick Stanford is your lead lieutenant, and he will forward everything over to me and my staff. I want only a small number of people in on this task force. The fewer people, the better and less confusing it will be for you to work together. Dr. Adams will now go over what she has found so far in the forensics for each victim," he concluded.

Dr. Adams took out her folders, which contained many pages of DNA analysis, and began to speak to the group. "Well, so far he has the same pattern of removing the fingernails of each victim, which gives me decreases my chances of finding any of his skin cells under the women's nails. He washed the first two bodies clean with sterile pads or gauze and sterile water, so he knows how to not leave any of his DNA around. I also believe he wears latex or vinyl gloves and some sort of sterile suit when he disembowels their bodies. From the patterns of the knife wounds, we can tell he is right-handed. We found very strong bruising on the third female's skin. I believe she got into the car with him and tried to fight him off once she knew she was in trouble or didn't want to go to the location he suggested. So he killed her in his own car and placed her body in Shoreline Park, where I believe he then decapitated her with a sharp-edged ax. However, he also stabbed her in the chest eleven times with a knife. Judging by the bruising on her arms and face, I believe he forcefully held her down in his vehicle as he stabbed her," Dr. Adams finished reading off her results.

As the group looked at the crime scene photos, Julie O'Keefe asked Dr. Adams what kind of knife she thought was used. Dr. Adams stated that she thought he was using a very sharp postmortem knife made of stainless steel. She also said he must be disposing of them; he was smart to use a new one for each victim.

Just like Jack the Ripper," Ed whispered to Rob under his breath.

Rick asked Ed if he had a comment, but Ed said no and that he had just been agreeing with Dr. Adams.

"So by looking at the map of where he supposedly meets and then kills his victims, we can tell that he knows the city well, and he doesn't seem to follow any symbolic ritual or pattern on where to leave the bodies. Neither does he care if we find them. It seems he wants us to see how he mutilates the bodies and the way he can cover his tracks. It's as if he is daring us to try to stop him," Ed offered his opinion, and then Detective Rogers asked the chief if he had any plans to bring the FBI in on this.

"As long as the murders don't go beyond our city limits, we can keep this all right here in our jurisdiction. But if he happens to kill someone outside our limits, then I'm certain the FBI will get involved. But this is why I decided to bring us all together, to stop this now and keep this whole thing from getting into national headlines and making the San Diego police look incapable of finding a serial killer. That's another reason why I don't want the FBI involved in this one," Chief Chase added, sounding upset at the idea of the FBI and excessive media exposure taking hold of his city. He didn't want any more negative press.

"So if he is very cunning and knows we are out looking for him now, I say we don't just sit around and hope our uniforms can seek him out and stop him in the dead of night. We need a way to draw him out into the open and conceal ourselves if we are to get the drop on him," Rob openly told them.

The task force couldn't play a wait-and-see game with the Entity. They needed to do something to stop him now. Chief Chase and Rick looked at one another, and then they stared at the very attractive Detective Julie O'Keefe. She smiled back at them, and then all the men looked at her and smiled. They knew what the chief and Rick had in mind to draw their suspect out into the open.

Chapter 3

He was frustrated that he hadn't been able to have his way with the last female; he had wanted to get her alone in a place where he could have time to perfect his fun, to open her up and gut her insides like the first two women. But no, this young woman had been smart. She had known something was wrong when Nathan suggested they go to a secluded location rather than the hotel she had suggested when she got into the car with him.

If he hadn't locked the doors to his car, she would have gotten away and told the police about him. She had fought back hard, scratching his face as he tried to hold her hands down, but she had been strong and in good shape. He'd had no choice but to stab her hard many times with his knife, and her blood had shot out all over him and onto the dashboard and upholstery of his car. He had taken her to the park after he killed her and had quickly beheaded her, taken her fingernails, and washed her body clean. She was the most disappointing victim of the three, he thought as he sat at his desk, reading more of the journal.

He read how Francis hadn't been able to enjoy one of his victims either: the Ripper's third victim, Elizabeth Stride, who Francis had approached in the early morning hours on September 30, 1888. Nathan read the passage describing how Francis had been interrupted and unable to enjoy the whore.

I first met this tall and slender street walker at Berner Street. I talked with her a few minutes, wearing my long wool coat and deerstalker hat. I had proposed we go to a cheap lodging house, but she refused when she saw I had my satchel of knives and instruments for my work. She grew loud, and I was forced to push her into Dutfield's Yard, where I slit her throat with one sharp stroke of my blade.

As her body fell to the cold pavement, I took out my other knives and bulls-eye lantern to give me light to see in the pitch of darkness and fog of this night. As I was about to gut her up, I heard the steps of a beast and carriage coming close. I quickly shoved my tools in my bag and hid behind the wooden fence in the dark. I saw the driver and pony come into view, and the driver's beast reared and bellowed loudly in fright. He was unable to move forward, as the body of the whore had startled him. His driver got off the carriage and lit a match to see what had startled his pony. He saw what I had done, and he called for a constable to come and help him. I quietly slid out from the alleyway and walked quickly till I was far away from them, and I found a new whore to deal with. This time, I had my way with her.

Nathan continued to read what had led to the night of what was historically known as the "double event," when Francis Tumblety was interrupted with his first victim by the passing of Louis Diemschutz on his cart and pony. He hadn't been able to mutilate the body of his third victim, Elizabeth Stride, but he had walked a mile away, where he found his fourth victim, Catherine Eddowes. This time he had been able to not only slit her throat deep but mutilate her in Mitre Square, where her remains were found just a short time after the body of Stride was discovered. Francis wrote that he was satisfied with this cleansing, as he had also taken two brass rings he'd found among Catherine Eddowes's possessions. Francis wrote,

This night was not a total loss. I was able to find another streetwalker and cleanse her good. I even took a small

memento of my two kills. Two cheap brass rings, one for each whore.

Nathan held the old brass rings in his hand. He smiled to himself, as he now knew he had to make plans to move on from San Diego because he felt like the police might close in on him at any moment. Or maybe they already knew who he really was. Perhaps his moments of freedom were counting down, and he would be caught soon. But he would not be taken alive. No, he would go down to death before he would be dragged to a police cell and mocked in the media.

"Oh, Francis, how I tried to be like you in disguise and good with your skills of cleaning their foul bodies, but I am against more modern times and better-skilled policeman than you dealt with. Oh, I will make certain they do not capture me alive, but I will have at least one more thrill to enjoy, unlike the last one. I will truly enjoy opening this next whore's insides. I will take my time and commit a last kill even more shocking than your last victim, Mary Kelly."

Nathan closed his hand tightly upon the two rings as he closed the journal for what could be the last time. He placed it and the rings back in the Calamander wood box and locked it closed. He knew he had to prepare to either move on or get ready to meet his uncle in hell.

"I will plan one more kill, but I hope it will not be my last. This Friday night will be the perfect time for it to happen, and I will plan a direct avenue of escape for these fools who think they can stop me. I will have my name go down in infamy!" he swore to himself as he got up from his desk to prepare for what he felt could be his last murder and coming death.

Kayla had just made dinner for herself and Ed, and they were seated together in the dining room. It was Friday evening on June 29. Kayla looked up at Ed, who seemed distant and was barely touching his food. He just kept drinking his ice water. Kayla was getting upset with him because he had been acting this way ever since the last murder. She also wanted to confront him about something that was bothering her.

"Ed, can you please talk to me? For almost four days now we have just talked about things around the house and what's for dinner. Please talk to me. I want to support you through all of this," she pleaded.

Ed put down his fork, pushed his chair away from the table, and got up. "What do you want me to say? I have a murdering psychopath on the loose, I am the lead detective of this new unit we hope will bring him in, plus we are about to do a sting operation I'm not in favor of. Of course I'm mad and upset, but not with you, Kayla. You know I love you," Ed told her. He now stood in the living room.

Kayla got up and walked over to him. Ed could see her frustration in her face.

"Ed, besides all this, I am tired of you avoiding the issue of when we are going to have a baby. I'm not getting any younger, and we have been married for a while now. All my friends and sisters are mothers now and very happy. I want us to have at least one child together," she told him.

Ed rolled his eyes and sat down on his leather couch. Kayla sat down with him.

"Look, this isn't the time to be talking about this now. I know how you feel. You want a baby, but we lost the first one when you miscarried, remember? So let me get through this and we will talk about it then, okay?" Ed told her.

Kayla started to cry as she remembered losing their baby in the early stages of pregnancy two years ago. "So let's talk about something else," she said. "The thing you have been devoting all your time to ever since these murders happened. I know you have been reading about and researching the Jack the Ripper murders. What the hell is this all about? I'm not comfortable with these books and you reading up on this stuff in my own house!" she shouted at him.

Ed rubbed his forehead. "I don't know yet, but these crimes are very similar to the Ripper murders from years ago. I haven't told anyone else in the unit except for Rob and now you. I feel there is a pattern between both cases, then and now," Ed told her.

Kayla just shook her head in disbelief. "Ed, I'm sorry, but I can't be here with you while all this is going on. I am going to stay with my parents until this is over. I don't feel safe being here alone while you're out looking for this person," she told him. She got up and quickly walked to their bedroom.

Ed called out after her, but she continued to walk away. "Fuck. Damn it!" he cursed to himself.

His cell phone started to ring. Ed went over to where it sat on the coffee table, right next to his black Smith & Wesson 9mm. He answered the phone; it was Rick telling him to come down to Central Division and that the chief had given their sting operation the go-ahead for that evening. Ed told him he understood. He got his gun and a few other things together and heard Kayla taking her suitcases out of the closet to pack with clothes for herself. He knew she was getting ready to move out of the house, but Ed just picked up his Envoy keys and shook his head as he slammed the door behind him. Kayla stopped packing when she heard the door close.

She softly prayed, "God, please look over Ed for me," and started to cry again.

A little while later, Ed and Rob walked toward the conference room. As they passed the other cops in the hall, they saw the serious looks they had on their faces; they all knew something was going down tonight. Upon entering the conference room, they saw Rick Stanford and Chief John Chase, along with one of his deputy chiefs. All the detectives in the task force were seated except for Julie O'Keefe, who wasn't present. Ed and Rob took their seats. Chief Chase began to talk about the operation, which was going to take place that night. The lights dimmed, and the LCD screen showed a huge image of the city of San Diego.

"Thanks for coming so quickly. I'm sorry we couldn't call you guys sooner, but the mayor just gave us to go-ahead on this a short time ago. Rick and my staff have been busy pulling the top patrol teams from each division who we feel will be best suited to work this operation with you people. So, as we know, he doesn't seem to stay in a particular pattern when he meets a woman and then kills her. But since the last murder took place in the western area of La Playa, where we believe he met Lauren Morton before leaving her body in Shoreline Park, we feel this is the area we want to concentrate our focus on tonight and see if he will take the bait," the chief informed them. He told Rick to go over the plan of action that they had both devised.

"We will have our female operative work this area of Liberty Station. We feel it's a great industrial sector of the city, where truck drivers and cabbies meet people and stop on their way to the nearby San Diego International Airport. We feel if we have our patrol men cordon off this seven-mile radius of Liberty Station and have cruisers set on all on-ramps and exits off Lanning Drive and North Harbor Road, we can contain him in these seven square miles. The chief, you men, and I will be the only units close to our operative, all in plain-colored cars. We will be on one-channel radios so that we will be the only ones able to communicate with the cruisers if we have to box him in; this way we'll avoid too much radio confusion. We have the best body armor for all you guys to wear, and we want you to carry only a sidearm, extra clips, and the small earpiece radios just in case we have to give a foot chase. We will be able to move swiftly with less to carry. Do we all agree with this assignment? Are there any questions?" Rick asked them.

All the detectives looked at one another, and everyone seemed very comfortable with this plan.

Then Ken Rogers raised his hand and asked, "Rick, who is the decoy?"

Rick and the chief smiled, and Rick asked for Skip Jones to bring her in. Skip left the conference room and came back with Julie O'Keefe, who wore a long black raincoat. As Skip closed the door behind them, Julie smiled and took off the coat, revealing to them her undercover uniform. She wore a short black skirt that ended just above her knees, black stockings, short black leather boots, a black sweater, and a short dark blue denim jacket. Her medium-length brown hair was done very nicely, and her face was made up with cosmetics. Her brown eyes shined in the light of the room. Rob and Jack Kerns whistled loudly to let everyone know they thought Julie looked very attractive.

She placed her hands on her hips and smiled at them. "So you men didn't think I was good enough to be the undercover target for this creep, did you, guys?" she asked them, being very coy. She laughed as all the men agreed that she was the right choice for the decoy.

Next, Rick instructed Julie and the team how they were going to set this up. "Julie, this is where you're going to walk, on the main stretch of Central Avenue. It has two lanes of traffic, and we want you to walk on the northbound side so it will be easy for us to pick up any vehicle that comes into contact with you. We will be in three unmarked vehicles—myself and Skip, Ed and Rob, followed by Ken and Jack. All three units will be no less than two blocks apart. We will have you under night vision surveillance from all vehicles, and we will have our helicopter airborne once you're picked up by any vehicle, so they can detect you by FLARE night vision from above. You will have the small earpiece radio and the microphone disguised as the gold butterfly broach on your jacket, but you will only be able to carry mace in your small hand purse. So you will be vulnerable if we lose track of you and he has you cornered alone somewhere. Are you certain you want to carry on with this plan?" Rick asked, concerned for her safety.

"Look, Rick, I know all you guys will be there looking after me. But I also know this might be the only way to stop this person. I am afraid to put myself in this position, but I'm also mad that he took three young lives for no reason. I want to do this. I will be fine, I promise you all." Julie told them, sounding confident that she would be able to pull this sting operation off.

Chief Chase looked at the time on the wall and then at his watch. He knew they had to move into position now, and he gave some last directions on what to do. "All right, Rick. I will be in mobile command unit one, situated right off of North Harbor Drive. My team and I will be listening to all your radio transmissions and watching you all on our monitors. I will not break into radio transmission until Julie is picked up by a vehicle, and we can have our units start blocking off the main intersections to box the suspect's vehicle in. Any questions, people?"

No one answered the chief.

"Good. Let's move then," he said.

All the men rose from their seats, gathered their things, and walked out to the parking lot. Rick instructed Julie that she would ride with him and Skip, and they would drop her off on Central Avenue.

As she put on her raincoat, Ed came over to her and whispered to her softly, "Hey, don't worry. We have your back covered, and I will not let you get hurt tonight. You got that?"

Julie smiled at him and placed her hand on Ed's chest. "I know, Ed. Just you be careful yourself and no big hero stuff for either of us if it does happen that way. Promise me?" she asked.

Ed smiled at her and said, "I promise. Come on. Let's go," he told her, and they walked out the back exit and into the parking lot, got into their vehicles, and drove toward the target location.

Rick was able to watch Julie with his single night vision scope as she walked up and down the street, smiling at passing cars. He was staying in communication with the other two vehicles. They had been on the scene for over an hour now, and so far four vehicles had approached Julie, but the male drivers had just complimented her on her sexy figure; they did not offer to pick her up. Ed told Rob that their killer might not show up that night. Rob told him to be patient; it was only 11:45 p.m. The chief had instructed that the operation be called off at 1:00 a.m. if they had made no contact with any suspect by then.

"I see she is using her cell phone. Was she instructed to have it visible?" Rob asked Ed, who nodded in response.

"The chief and Rick thought that her talking and texting on her cell phone would really make it look like she was an escort in contact with a client to set up a date for tonight. Besides, they told her to text Rick a quick description if she was in a vehicle with a suspicious person, if she could," Ed informed Rob.

Rob told Ed that the chief and Rick had thought of a good plan for this. He just hoped their suspect would show up.

Nathan drove slowly along Lanning Road, scanning for his next target. He passed a few females on the way but none who really piqued his interest. If this was to be his last offering, he wanted her to be very special. He had the ultimate cleansing planned for her. He had driven one of his other vehicles, a metallic gray Jaguar X-Type. He hadn't had time to clean and wash all the blood out of his other car, which still had the smell of death in it from the last meeting.

He was looking for the perfect female tonight and was wearing a dark blue suit over his black scrubs. As he turned and looked at his bag in the backseat, he knew he would not make the same mistake as last time. He would earn her trust and then get away from the populated roads. Once alone, he would slit her throat right away, not even give her a chance to breathe. Then he would take her to the place he had already picked out, where he would be able to pick away at her body without worry or interruptions.

He made a right turn onto Central Avenue. He saw one female and then another, but he was not satisfied until his right eye caught a glimpse of a female walking up ahead with her back to him. Even from behind he knew this one was different from the rest. He started to reduce his speed and got into the right lane.

He was parallel with her left shoulder when Julie noticed the gray jaguar to her left. She put her cell phone in her bag, looked directly into the vehicle's passenger side window, and gave the driver a smile. As she was smiling, she whispered into her microphone, "Rick, gray Jaguar to my left."

Rick responded to her that he saw the vehicle. "Approach him, Julie. Guys, get ready to move," he instructed the team.

Julie walked over to the gray vehicle, and the driver lowered the window to greet her.

"Hello, nice man with the fine looking car," Julie said to him as she took a good look at him, ready to send back a detailed description to her fellow detectives. She noticed his short gray curly hair and long sideburns, but he was clean shaven and wearing a dark blue suit.

"Good evening, my dear. Would you care to have a nice getaway for the two of us in this great cosmopolitan city of ours tonight?" he asked her.

Julie knew right away this man was educated and suave with his words—something the team thought their suspect must use to earn the victims' trust.

"My goodness. You're an educated man and very handsome. I will be honored to spend the evening with you," Julie answered him.

He opened the passenger door for her. Julie got into the Jaguar, very slowly brought her legs together, rested her purse on her lap, and closed the door. He smiled at her and then looked for oncoming traffic as he slowly merged onto the northbound lane of Central Avenue. As Nathan and Julie introduced themselves to each other, Rick and the others saw them drive off. Rick softly told his men to follow them. All three vehicles moved onto Central Avenue. Rick told Skip to stay two vehicle lengths behind the jaguar and Rob and Ken to stay three vehicle lengths behind them so they did not raise the man's suspicions.

Chief John Chase, hearing everything that was taking place, ordered the helicopter to take off and follow the gray Jaguar. He also ordered his patrol vehicles to start to close off the intersections at Barnett Avenue and Rosecrans Street. He wanted to get Julie out of that vehicle as quickly as possible. Rick focused on the vehicle's license plate number, which read CBQ-7298. Rick told mobile command the plate number. Once the officer in contact with him confirmed the number, he started a computer search to find out to whom it was registered. The vehicle's speed was only forty miles per hour; they confirmed that he was being cautious.

"So where do you want to go tonight? Any hotel you have in mind?" Julie asked him.

He looked over and smiled at her. Julie knew just by looking that he was wearing a wig and fake gray sideburns. The color of gray in his hair did not match the color of his sideburns very well. She took out her iPhone and sent Skip a quick text: *He's in a disguise, dark blue suit.* Skip held up his cell phone and read the text to Rick. Rick then told everyone on the radio what the suspect was wearing.

Taken in by her stunning beauty, Nathan knew she was the perfect catch tonight. He already has it planned out. "Julie, my dear, on this perfect night, how would you like to see the nice rays of the full moon shine off the crystal blue waters of the Pacific Ocean at Ocean Beach?" he asked her.

Julie quickly thought that the Ocean Beach area had many remote, deserted locations this time of night. Knowing he had plans for her, she went along with him. "That sounds romantic for us. May I ask what you do for a living? You being a fine-tailored, educated man?" she asked.

He turned and smiled at her, feeling uncomfortable that she had asked him this inconsequential question, and so far she hadn't mentioned what her donation would be. Nathan was already suspicious of her when Julie again texted in her lap. He was about to answer her when he noticed her sending a message on her phone again.

"I'm a real estate agent, my dear. And who are you texting again this late at night?" he asked as Julie quickly sent the last text to Skip.

Skip read it to Rick. "Ocean Beach. That's where he's taking her!" Skip yelled.

Rick radioed it over to the other two cars and the mobile command. Chief Chase ordered patrol vehicles to Ocean Beach at once. Hearing all this, Ed noticed the Jaguar begin to pick up speed. He ordered Rob to drive faster, and their car started to pass Rick's vehicle in the left-hand lane. Rick became angry and tried to motion to Ed and Rob to stay back.

"Come on, Ed. We can't get too close to his car. He might get tipped off that we are tailing him," Rob explained.

Ed, convinced this had to be the suspect, yelled back at Rob, "Rob, it's him! I know it! Just stay close to him now and cut him off before he makes the left turn onto Barnett Avenue!" Ed ordered.

Rob told him they couldn't; the man hadn't done anything wrong yet. Ed screamed at him again to just do it. Rob shook his head and completely passed Rick's vehicle. Now they were next to the Jaguar, and Ed stared at Nathan, who was looking straight ahead at the road, waiting to make the left turn up ahead. Julie looked past Nathan at Ed in confusion, knowing this wasn't going the way Rick and the chief had planned it.

Rick, furious with Ed and Rob, yelled over the radio, "Units, close off Barnett Avenue! Don't let him turn onto it! Ed, what the fuck are you doing?" he shouted across the radio as the mobile command acknowledged his orders.

Two squad cars quickly closed in from the shoulders of the road. As Nathan turned to his left, he saw the vehicle keeping pace with his and locked gazes with Ed. Ed stared at him with deep hatred; he knew this man was the Entity.

"You son of a bitch!" Ed screamed in anger.

Nathan sent him an evil smile and responded to Ed, "She's mine!" He locked the doors to the car and quickly slammed on the brakes.

Rob passed his vehicle, and Skip stopped short along with Ken's vehicle in the right-hand lane. Nathan turned into the opposite lane and now headed southbound. Ed screamed at Rob to turn around and follow them. The tires screeched hard as they spun around. Two patrol cars barely missed their vehicle. Skip and Ken also turned around. The four vehicles collided head-on violently.

Rob floored the gas to keep up with the Jaguar as Ed yelled at him to hurry and stay with them. Julie's life was in peril.

Nathan looked behind at the black sedan gaining on them. He turned to Julie, who was trying to open her side door even though it was locked. Nathan screamed at her, "You bitch cop!"

He grabbed her arm, pulled her away from the door, and slapped her across the face. The force of the slap cut her bottom lip, and blood started to flow down the right side of her chin. As Nathan came to the intersection, he thought fast about what to do. He made a hard right turn onto North Harbor Drive. He tried to think of an escape route for himself, but he wanted to kill Julie first. If this was to be his last day on Earth, he swore to himself that he would take her life with him.

Rob came to the intersection and floored it hard to make the right turn. After they barely missed colliding with another vehicle, the chase continued eastbound toward San Diego International Airport, and where the mobile command was based. Ed yelled their position into the radio. The helicopter circled above and shined its blue searchlight down on the Jaguar. Nathan cursed to himself as he looked up at it. He was without a firearm to match the police's firepower. He hadn't thought he would need to carry one, being that he thought he would always get away with his crimes.

Julie desperately tried to grab hold of the steering wheel and force him to crash. Nathan punched her hard in the face, and Julie flew back into her seat. He reached into his inside pocket, and produced a steel scalpel to slit her throat. Julie quickly took out her small mace bottle and sprayed it right into his left eye. Nathan screamed in pain. Julie again tried the door; this time she was able to unlock it and pushed herself out onto the road. She hit the pavement hard but kept her hands over her face. As she spun and rolled across the hard surface, it burned her skin and scraped and cut her knees and arms. Through his pain, Nathan was able to glimpse the airport up ahead. He made a hard left turn into the entrance, smashing through the arms of the checkpoint gate. Rob came to a stop when he saw Julie on the right shoulder of the road. He and Ed exited the vehicle and ran over to her.

"Julie, are you all right?" Ed shouted to her, holding her in his arms.

When she came to, she started to cry and held him tight. Rob took out a clean handkerchief and covered her right knee, which was bleeding heavily. Ed thanked God she was alive. He then became enraged.

"Rob, stay with her!" Ed screamed as he ran to the Ford.

He slammed both doors shut and took off after Nathan. Two squad cars came and stopped to aid Rob and Julie; Rick and Skip were inside one of them. Rob told Rick that Ed was now in pursuit of the Jaguar, and the helicopter's copilot confirmed the suspect's vehicle had entered the airport. But the helicopter couldn't follow overhead because of air regulations forbidding even police aircraft from flying over free airspace for safety reasons. As Ed followed the path made by the Jaguar, he slowed down some because he was in a very populated area and had to be careful not to endanger innocent civilians. Ed drove slowly down a service area of the airport, knowing this was where the suspect would have likely driven because it was less populated.

When Rick and Rob arrived at mobile command with Julie, an ambulance was waiting to rush her to the nearest medical center for treatment. She was in shock and had multiple cuts to her hands and face, along with a deep gash to her right knee. But as they loaded her into the ambulance, she cried and thanked the team and Ed most of all for saving her life. As Rick stayed on the radio with Ed, twelve squad cars entered the airport and began to canvas the area. The security personnel at all the checkpoints were given a description of the suspect in case he tried to board a flight out of San Diego. As Ken and Jack were inside working with the security, Ed remained outside with the patrol cars. Rick turned to Chief Chase and told him this guy was very smart. He had known they would lose him once he went into the airport. Just then they received all call that the suspect's vehicle had been found at the west end of the airport.

Ed raced over there and was met by two squad cars. He quickly got out and glanced over the inside of the vehicle. He saw marks of fresh blood that had to be Julie's. The bag that Nathan had had in the backseat was gone, and Ed cursed to himself as he looked around the area for returned rental vehicles. He noticed two uniformed officers talking with a rental agent, asking him if he had seen anything. Ed joined the conversation as the man said he hadn't seen anything because he'd been behind the counter with his back to the window. But he had heard a car engine start and a car drive away toward the west end gate.

Ed shouted at him, "What kind of vehicle was here?"

The man replied that it was a new blue Nissan Altima. Ed raced to his Ford and drove out the west gate. He cut through the Midway District and headed onto the San Diego freeway, which was going to take him back westbound. He radioed, asking for help from the helicopter to find a blue Altima from above. They radioed back that the suspect must be keeping the speed limit to not to draw attention to himself. Ed cursed and yelled back to Rick to see if there had been any luck checking the vehicle's license plate number.

Back at the airport, Rick was handed a printout by another officer. "We got something, Ed! The vehicle is registered to a Dr. Nathan Malcolm, 8540 Hill Street, Sunset Cliff Estates!" Rick yelled to Ed over the radio. Then Rick and Rob headed to a vehicle as Ken and Jack raced out of the airport with the patrol vehicles.

Chief Chase announced the suspect's name and address over the radio. "Every unit is to converge on this location. The order is to shoot the suspect if you deem him hostile!" the chief ordered as he raced out of mobile command and got into a squad car that would meet all the other units at the suspect's home.

Ed, who already had a head start, placed his flashers on and gunned his car up to eighty miles per hour. He knew this area of San Diego; only well-off people lived here. *Dr. Nathan Malcolm*, he thought, *the man who is embroiled in that pharmaceutical drug case. His trial is set to start at the end of the month. He was released on his own recognizance since he posted bail, and he wasn't charged with a crime that involved hurting another individual.* Ed took the exit for Chatsworth Boulevard; it would take him right to Sunset Cliff Estates.

Nathan had parked the car down the street in order to buy himself some time. As he entered his large home, he began to gather the two small carry bags he had packed for himself. He knew he couldn't carry anything larger to get away, since he had to hurry. He quickly went over to his desktop computer and smashed it with a baseball bat, wanting to destroy all evidence of searches on the hard drive. But he knew that wasn't good enough. He had to get his plan ready if he was going to deceive them. He had to destroy his home. He went behind the bar in his living room and poured bottles of alcohol all over the walls and curtains. Then he ran to the kitchen and blew out stove pilot flames to let the gas seep and collect in the house.

Next he lit a match and dropped it to the carpeting of the living room, igniting a line of flames that quickly climbed the curtains and walls. As fire engulfed the inside of his house, Nathan tried to focus his left eye, which still burned from the mace. He then threw a bottle of vodka onto the wood stairs and lit another match to light the stairs on fire. He dowsed one last object on the floor with alcohol. He was about to pick up his bags when Ed came crashing through the front door. Ed's gun flew out of his right hand from the sheer force it has taken to break the wood framed door. Nathan stood there in shock. The men locked eyes as Ed got to his feet.

"You bastard!" Ed yelled and charged Nathan.

The men collided and fell to the floor. Scorching flames grew all around them as they rolled on the floor. Ed pulled back his hand and drove his tightly clenched fist hard into Nathan's face once and then again. As he hit him a third time, Ed raised Nathan's head off the floor and smashed it back down. He pummeled the man without mercy because of all the brutalities he had committed. Ed cursed and swore as blood poured from Nathan's nose, mouth, and the back of his head.

Nathan reached down and was able to grasp the sharp doubled-edged knife he kept strapped to his left ankle. He took hold of the handle, thrust the blade deep into Ed's left side, and then pushed it in deeper.

"Die, you foul cop! You're too late to stop me!" Nathan screamed at Ed as Ed fell off him, screaming in pain.

Wet blood rushing out of the deep open wound in his side, Ed looked around for his gun but couldn't see clearly because of the smoke from the raging fire, which was beginning to blaze out of control.

Nathan approached Ed, the knife still clutched in his right hand. He reached down, grabbed Ed's shirt with his left hand, and prepared to strike him in the neck with the steel knife. Ed blocked the swing with a roundhouse right hook, and the knife flew from Nathan's hand. Ed then hit him hard in the face twice. Then he grabbed Nathan by his jacket and flung him into the raging fire. Nathan screamed in mortal pain, and Ed saw him burning from the waist up.

Ed struggled to his feet and leapt through a nearby large window. He crashed through the glass panes and onto the front lawn of the home. Rob and Rick had just pulled into the driveway with the other units. They got Ed to his feet and pulled him behind the safety of the cars just as the home exploded outward, glass shards and debris flying past them. They took cover just in time. After the explosion, Rick looked up and saw that the fire was out of control. He reached into the car for his radio and called for the fire department and an ambulance.

Rob looked down at Ed and saw he was shaking in pain. He asked what was wrong as other vehicles arrived with Ken and Jack. Ed didn't answer Rob but kept shaking in pain. Rob then felt wet blood all over his hands and knew Ed had a major stab wound to his left abdomen.

"Shit!" Rob yelled as he took off his jacket and pressed it against the wound.

Rick and the other detectives raced over to Ed.

"The ambulance is coming!" Rick yelled, but Rob knew by the amount of blood Ed was losing that they couldn't wait.

"We have to take him to the hospital ourselves!" he said.

As the three men helped Ed into the backseat, Rick got into the driver's seat of the Ford. Once everyone was secure, he floored the gas pedal, and they took Ed to the emergency room. Rick made Ken call the ER on his cell phone so they would be prepared for an incoming male patient with a major stab wound to his left side and would be ready to take him into surgery upon arrival.

Ed lay on his back in the backseat, and Rob kept pressure on the wound. Ed started to close his eyes; he was losing consciousness and going into shock.

"Ed, stay with me! Don't you dare die!" Rob yelled at him.

Rick wove in and out of vehicles on the freeway and told Rob they were less than a mile from the hospital. Rob told Ed he had gotten the bastard and that the fire department had arrived and was fighting the fire Nathan set at his home. Rick told Rob not to worry about that right now. He pulled into the entrance of the ER, where four nurses and a trauma surgeon were already waiting with a gurney to take Ed to the OR. Rick screeched to a stop, and the men pulled Ed from the car and onto the gurney. As they rolled him into the ER and toward the elevators, Rick answered the doctor's questions about the injury. Once in the elevator, they headed up to the fourth floor and hurried the stretcher inside the open double doors to the operating room. Rick and Rob were told they couldn't go any farther, and they watched the doors close.

Rob looked at all the blood on his hands and then up at Rick, who told him, "He's going to make it, Rob. Don't worry."

As the trauma team prepared Ed for surgery, the two head surgeons looked at the wound. Their team prepared Ed with intravenous lines and anesthesia. The head nurse, who was monitoring his vital signs, told the doctors he was stable now. They prepared to take a closer look at the deep wound to his upper abdomen. One surgeon announced his spleen had been punctured and an artery had been severed. He asked for clamps to stop the blood gushing from the deep wounds. As the nurses changed bloody dressings around the wound, the other doctor asked Ed's blood type; they needed to start a flow of blood into the IV line because he was losing too much. As the team raced around one another, the surgeon began to suture the artery closed, but the spleen continued to bleed. The two doctors looked at one another, and the head surgeon shook his head at his colleague. The nurse told them Ed's vitals were dropping.

"Look, we are going to have to close both wounds at the same time. If we don't, we are going to lose him!" the head surgeon shouted. The other surgeon agreed and asked what he should do.

"Here. Clamp the spleen in four places and begin to close the wound from the smaller gap up to the major gap. I will work on the severed artery. It's the only way to save him!"

The staff agreed with the lead surgeon, and he then asked the head nurse to help keep the suction of the blood going as he worked on the artery.

Rick was in the waiting room of the OR, along with all the detectives. Skip Jones had just joined them; he had been with Julie, who was admitted for observation after receiving stitches to her right knee and having other various cuts cleaned and bandaged. She was now sedated and resting, unaware of what had happened to Ed. Skip and the others didn't want her to worry for now.

Rob's wife, Antonella, met Kayla in the lobby, and they walked into the waiting room together. Rob had called them not long ago and told them to get to the hospital as soon as possible. Rob and his wife embraced. Kayla, confused, asked Rick where Ed was. He took her hands, sat with her on the couch, and told her what happened. He told her they hadn't yet received word from the doctors about his status. Kayla became hysterical and started to scream. Rob and his wife tried to comfort her. Rick and his men were full of remorse. They looked at the wall clock and noted that Ed had been in surgery for over an hour now. Rick felt it didn't look good for his friend, but he said to himself, "Come on, Ed. You can make it, buddy."

More than two hours later, the two surgeons entered the waiting room and came over to Kayla, who was seated next to Antonella. The lead surgeon, Dr. Stewart Foster, took her hands and spoke softly to her.

"Mrs. Brooks, we were able to close the wounds to Ed's spleen and one of its major arteries, which was heavily torn open. He lost a tremendous amount of blood, and we had to administer blood to keep his heart and other major organs functional while we operated. I'm happy to say that he will make it, but he will have a long recovery."

Kayla smiled and began to cry. She hugged and thanked Dr. Foster for saving Ed's life, and all his friends shook each other's hand and thanked God that he would be all right. Chief Chase, who was now at the hospital, was briefed on the status of both detectives. He was now prepared to give his press conference about what had transpired that night.

Chief John Chase took the podium as Rick and other top officials lined behind him. This late breaking news conference was going on at four o'clock in the morning. He was instructed that he could begin to talk now, so he said, "At exactly 11:00 p.m. last night, we set into motion a sting operation to flush out the suspect in the brutal slayings of three prostitutes in our city. Myself and others in my staff formed an elite task force of veteran detectives to work this complex case. We were forced to take unorthodox measures to flush out our suspect, who we had named the Entity because of his methods of concealing his identity from us and his medical knowledge. We had to use a female operative to go undercover as an escort to lure the suspect into the open. She was wired and under constant surveillance and in contact with our team when she was picked up by our suspect in the Liberty Station section of the city, which we had cordoned off for the operation.

"Our female operative made contact with the suspect at around 12:10 a.m. She was picked up in his vehicle, and he had plans to take her to a secluded location to carry out another mutilation similar to the three previous victims. But our team moved in to save our detective and apprehend the suspect, at which time our female detective was assaulted in the vehicle but was able to throw herself out of the moving car. A car chased ensued in the area of the San Diego International Airport. We were able to safely secure our operative and get her medical attention right away. She is currently here at Mercy Hospital for several non-life-threatening injuries.

"During the car chase, we were able to trace the suspect's license plate number back to its registered owner, a Dr. Nathan Malcolm, who was set to stand trial in the Quasar Pharmaceutical scandal case. Our lead detective followed Dr. Malcolm back to his residence in the Sunset Cliff Estates area. Dr. Malcolm attempted to escape, but first, in an effort conceal evidence of the crimes, he set fire to his home and destroyed vital evidence of his involvement. Our lead detective was able to confront the suspect in his home, and a violent struggle took place. Our operative was severely injured, and the suspect ended up perishing in the fire, which caused a gas explosion that destroyed the house.

"The fire department discovered the remains of the suspect's very charred body at 2:00 a.m. this morning, and we used the suspect's medical and dental records to make a positive identification. The badly burned body was that of Dr. Nathan Malcolm. Lead Detective

Edward Brooks received a deep stab wound to his left abdomen that took surgeons hours to close. He and our female operative, whose name we are withholding at this time for her safety, are both resting and are expected to make full recoveries."

After the chief finished giving all the facts, he then announced that Brooks and the entire task force would receive Stella awards from the mayor and the city of San Diego for their work on this case.

Chapter 4

Four Years Later

Ed lifted the barbell and two hundred and fifty pound in weights over his chest and exhaled deeply through his mouth. He brought it back down and then raised it up high once again before placing onto the rests of his free weight bench press unit in his spare bedroom.

He sat up and drank some bottled water to cool him down. Loud heavy metal songs played on his stereo system to motivate him as he worked out this early Tuesday morning. As Ed got up and went to shut off the CD player, he used a towel to wipe the sweat off his forehead and arms. He went into the master bathroom to shower and shave and get ready for work. He took off his white tank top. As he stared at himself in the full mirror, Ed turned to his left to look at the remains of the scar he had from his only encounter with serial slayer Dr. Nathan Malcolm. Ed gently glided his hand over the long scar. It didn't hurt anymore; it was just a reminder of how the case still affected his life. He then took off his gray sweat bottoms and entered his glass-enclosed shower. The warm water relaxed him as he thought of what this day would bring at work.

At 9:00 a.m., Ed met Rob in the employee lounge at the station. They sat down and talked over breakfast and coffee. They made small talk, knowing they had been slow lately with no major cases on their agendas. Neither man minded not being busy. Rob told Ed that he and his wife were busy enough these days with their four-year-old daughter, Megan. His wife, Antonella, wanted her enrolled in modeling for toddler clothing ads and commercials because she believed their daughter had the look and early talent to be a future model and actress. Ed wished them good luck with Megan. Rob thanked him and noticed Ed was still wearing his wedding band on his left ring finger. He knew it was the time to bring it up to him.

"Hey, Ed, you know I don't like to pry into your personal life, but it's been three years now since you and Kayla got divorced. It's time for you to ditch that ring and move on. Antonella and I were talking about you last night. We want you to move on and be happy again. So get rid of that cheap gold ring and come out with us this Friday night for dinner," Rob told him.

Ed just looked at his partner and knew he was concerned about him. "I know you guys really care for me, and I know I should take off my ring. But Kayla and I still talk, and she asked me to come over this weekend to paint the bedroom for her. Her husband is out of town on a business trip, so I agreed to do it for her. I don't mind. It gives me something to do besides always lifting weights and playing my guitar," Ed told him, laughing.

"Well, just think about coming over to the house for dinner with us. Antonella is going to make another one of her top Italian pasta and veal dishes, so I know you don't want to miss a free meal like that," Rob told him.

Ed thanked him and said he would be at Rob's house at 6:00 p.m. sharp for dinner on Friday night. Then they got up from the lounge table and headed to their desks in the homicide division.

They sat down and started going over the cases they had been assigned this week. No homicides, just two gang-related assaults and one domestic violence case. They could go interview the witnesses and the gang members who were involved and maybe have it all done by 3:00 p.m. and call it an early day. Just then Rick came by to talk to them.

"Hey, guys. How's it going?" he asked them.

"Not much, boss. Anything new with you or around here today?" Rob asked him.

"Here it's been slow, so that's good. Marrying Cate has been a blessing in my life because now I have her to make the bed in the morning and cook me dinner when I get home," he said, and they all laughed. Rick suggested they go out for drinks after work at the usual cop hangout bar just three blocks down the street. Ed and Rob agreed to meet Rick there around 8:00 p.m. that evening.

Later that evening, just after eight o'clock, the three cops were seated in the back of Four Clover's Pub, sharing drinks and talking about how they all had to get together with their wives and go out to eat at a restaurant sometime soon. Rob knew he shouldn't have mentioned *wives*, being that Ed wasn't married any more. But he looked at Ed's ring finger and noticed he had taken off his wedding band. Rob was pleased that Ed had listened to him.

He was going to let Rick be the one to ask Ed the next question; it was the real reason they wanted to get him alone tonight at the pub. Rob glanced at Rick, and Rick knew it was time to talk to Ed.

"Hey, Ed, Rob and I have been talking lately. We know you been through a lot, not only being alone again but we know what happened four years ago is still haunting you. Maybe it's time you considered retiring and moving on with your life. Find a new woman and settle down again while you're still young and able to have kids like us," Rick suggested to him.

Ed looked up from his beer and smiled at them. "I know I can retire any time now and get my full pension, but I need to still be active with the job. It keeps me busy, and I just want to be able to help our city by being out there and preventing more murders and bad crimes," Ed responded to their suggestion that he retire.

Rob was getting frustrated over this. He had to come out and tell his partner how he really felt about what had been going on in his life the last four years. "Ed, it's over! You got him four years ago. Now let it go! It almost cost you your life, and it wound up costing you your marriage. You need to let this go. There is no connection between Malcolm and Jack the Ripper more than a hundred years ago! Now move on for your own peace of mind," Rob told him boldly.

When he mentioned Jack the Ripper, a few people in the bar looked over at them. Ed shot Rob a cold stare, a look that told him to back off, and Rick told Rob to relax.

"Look, I have been looking into the Ripper case for more than four years now, and I'm convinced that Nathan Malcolm was related to one of the top suspects of the Ripper murders back then. He must have found out shortly before he started his own crazed rampage, and it gave him his motivation to kill those women," Ed explained.

Rick shook his head in disbelief. "Ed, even if you're right about this, it doesn't matter anymore. Malcolm is dead. Jack the Ripper, even though we may never know who he really was, is long dead, unless Malcolm came back to life as him in reincarnation. Let it go! There is nothing left for you to prove. You should be very happy that you saved Julie's life that night. And God knows how many more innocent young women at the same time," Rick told him as Rob nodded in agreement.

Ed looked down at his cold glass of beer, feeling that they might be right. Four years of investigating the Ripper murders on his own had consumed him and stressed him out. He was about to answer them when Rick's cell phone rang. Rick got up and excused himself to answer it. Ed and Rob felt it might be Cate asking him where he was at this time of night. Ed thanked Rob for his and Rick's concern about his well-being. Rob told him not to mention it. He, Rick, and their wives wanted nothing but the best for Ed.

They looked over at Rick, who was standing in the corner, still talking on his cell phone, and they knew by the serious look on his face as he finished his phone call that he wasn't talking to his wife.

He walked back over to their table, and Rob asked Ed what that had all been about.

"Hey, guys, we have a body that was just discovered a short time ago, a young female, and it looks like a homicide," Rick told them, and Ed studied the upset look in his eyes.

"Why do you look so upset? Is there something more to it? Ed asked.

Rick hesitated to answer. "The body was discovered in Shoreline Park, and the victim has been badly mutilated," he told them.

Ed's and Rob's jaws dropped. Shoreline Park had been the location of the last Dr. Nathan Malcolm murder four years ago. The three detectives got up and shot out the door to the parking lot in order to get to the crime scene as soon as possible.

At 9:15 p.m., the three detectives from Central Division were being briefed by uniformed police officers from Western Division when two familiar detectives joined them to talk about the victim. Detectives Skip Jones and Julie O'Keefe said their hellos to their former colleagues from original serial killings task force. Julie smiled at Ed, who just smiled back and winked at her. Julie was still very grateful to Ed for saving her life four years ago. Skip began to give them the details on the latest victim.

"We were able to identify the victim by the driver's license in her purse, which was found near the body. Twenty-four-year-old Caucasian female Ashley Cook is not a known prostitute, but she is a waitress at Perlisis Steakhouse in Old Town. We think she was picked up by the killer, whom she might have known because there were no defensive wounds to indicate a struggle," Jones told them.

Rob asked what the cause of death was and how the body was mutilated.

"Cause of death was a deep cut to the throat of the victim, and her fingernails removed, all ten of them," Skip said.

All the men and Julie looked surprised. This recent murder had a pattern of inflicted wounds they had seen before.

"Any other wounds or body parts taken by the killer?" Rick asked.

Julie told him the victim's breasts had also been removed, and she had a deep straight knife wound down the center of her chest. But besides that wound and the cut to her neck, the only body parts removed were her fingernails and breasts. The breasts had been placed at victim's feet, and the fingernails were presumed to have been taken by the killer. Ed looked at Rob and then in the direction of the area where the body was located; it had been taped off with yellow caution tape.

Rick and the others went to look at the body, which was very easy to see because the forensic team had set up large mobile floodlights that illuminated the area of the park, even in the dark of night. Ed already knew it had to be a copycat killer. But how were they going to approach this new case, he wondered as he saw Rick talking with one of the police chief's staff members off to the side of the crime scene. Rick seemed to be agreeing with his orders. He then returned to brief the detectives, calling for everyone to gather around him.

"Look, people, I was just instructed by the deputy chief that there will be a press conference in the morning to announce the discovery of this victim. But the chief is not going to reveal that there was any type of mutilation to the victim. We don't want to stir up panic in the city. He wants a complete autopsy done on the body, and then he will go from there on how he wants us to react on this new series or possible copycat series of murders," Rick informed them.

They watched the forensic team place the body of Ashley Cook in a body bag. Detective Jones informed them that he would contact the victim's family. *Another young life taken away by a vicious unknown killer*, Ed thought.

The next day, just after 2:00 p.m. at Central Division, Ed and Rob were contacted to come meet Rick and others in the conference room for a briefing. As they walked down the hallway together, they noticed two other familiar faces: Northern Division homicide detectives Jack Kerns and Ken Rogers. The men greeted each other and entered the conference room, where they saw Julie O'Keefe and Skip Jones already seated along with County Medical Examiner Dr. Cate Adams. The original task force from four years ago was now back together for what seemed to be an obvious copycat of the Dr. Malcolm slayings.

As everyone took their seats, Rick told them to listen to Dr. Adams's brief before asking any questions. Rick then took his seat. Dr. Adams thanked her husband and turned on the projector so the team could view the massive wounds that had been inflicted upon the body of Ashley Cook.

"I want to first say that just by looking at the wounds and type of sharp-edged knife used, I can tell that whoever committed this murder has some deep insight into the murders four years ago. I also want to point out that we haven't gotten any DNA evidence back yet. I don't expect we are going to find any DNA from the killer, as I don't believe any oral or vaginal sex occurred before she was killed. I do think this killer has followed the same MO as the previous killer, Dr. Nathan Malcolm. It's obvious enough to leave the body in the same park where the last victim was left four years ago."

All the detectives in the room just looked at one another, stunned that whoever this new killer was must have known Nathan Malcolm and his ways of mutilating his victims. Ed raised his hand to ask Dr. Adams a question.

"Doc, the type of knife wounds on this victim, how similar are they to the victims' wounds four years ago?" he questioned her.

"Just by looking at the wounds, I see that the knife was very similar, but the angles and the penetration depth are not the same as the previous murders. So we definitely have a similar killer, but we all know Nathan Malcolm perished in the fire at his home. His body was given a full autopsy by me and criminologist forensic scientist Dr. Diana Farrell. We confirmed that Malcolm perished in the blaze, and his remains were cremated by order of the state," Dr. Adams said.

Rick stood to advise them why Chief Chase had called the task force together again. "Okay, as ordered by Chief Chase, we are reforming the task force under top-secret circumstances until we find out more about this new killer. We can all expect another murder to happen again soon, but when and where is the big question. We have taken precautions and contacted the FBI, and they are sending us their best West Coast profiler to help us on this case. The profiler will be working mostly with Ed and Rob, who will again be taking point on the task force," Rick instructed them.

Ed frowned to himself, thinking, *What is an FBI profiler going to find out that I don't already know about these murders?* As everyone stood to leave the conference room and look into leads of the new killer, Rick asked Ed and Rob to stay behind. Rick and his wife, Dr. Adams, wanted to warn Ed about this new suspect.

"Look, Ed, Cate and I were talking about this, just between us. If this new killer has any ties to Nathan Malcolm, he is probably going to target you for being the one who killed him," Rick advised him. Cate also stated that criminal physique was not her specialty but that the mind of a psychopath would always follow the pattern of murder and revenge.

"Thanks for the warning, but I'm in this one to the end, just like four years ago. I don't have any worries about whoever this new killer is or if he is indeed related to Dr. Malcolm. I just want to catch this person without any more bloodshed," Ed told his lieutenant and then asked when the profiler would be coming to work with him and Rob.

"I was told by the chief that the profiler is leaving LA tonight on a flight and will be here early tomorrow morning to start work with you and Rob," Rick told them, and they understood that they were going to be working directly with the profiler.

They walked out into the hallway to catch up to the other detectives and begin sharing notes on this new case.

Rob turn to Ed to ask his opinion on the profiler. "What do you think this profiler dude is going to look like? I bet he will be in his fifties, all gray, and overweight. These guys are always out of shape, being that they are office bookworms," Rob told Ed, laughing.

Ed agreed with him, hoping this new case ended soon. He did not want the profiler to make it a three's-a-crowd atmosphere.

That night, Ed was home working on his computer, comparing the latest crime file to the past victims. He was also checking the original Ripper victims for any patterns that matched the most recent victim.

Five victims were known Ripper victims, but there might have been seven or eight because there were two murders prior to the first known Ripper victim, Mary Ann Nichols. But some say the Martha Tabram murder was not related; even though she was stabbed thirty-nine times, she was not slashed or mutilated like the five noted Ripper victims, Ed thought. He continued reading until he looked at the time in the lower right-hand corner of his computer; it was 2:10 in the morning. Ed logged off his computer, knowing he would not mutter another word about his belief that these crimes were in some way related to Jack the Ripper. He got up, stretched his muscles, and headed to his bedroom for some sleep.

Wednesday morning, just after 9:00 a.m., Rick left Ed a voice mail saying he was going to pick the profiler up at the hotel and then head to the office. Ed and Rob patiently awaited their arrival.

"So, what do you think we should do for this guy when he gets here? Take him out to Starbucks or Dunkin' Doughnuts so he can stuff his face while we fill him in on the case?" Ed asked.

Rob laughed. He looked up and noticed an embarrassed Rick standing behind Ed with a very attractive female. The pretty brunette smiled and responded to Ed's remark.

"Well, Detective Brooks, I would like it if you and your partner would please take me out to a nice diner and fill me in on the case. But I have no intentions of stuffing my face. I'm into a very healthy diet and exercise routine, just as you are."

Ed turned around and stared into the black eyes of the lead profiler in the FBI's LA division.

Rick introduced them to her, "Ed and Rob, this is FBI Profiler Stephanie Morgan. I apologize for Detective Brooks's remarks," Rick told her as Ed and Rob got up from their seats to greet her.

Stephanie told Rick it was all right as she shook Rob's hand and then Ed's hand. Ed was very upset with himself, and she smiled gingerly at him.

"I'm very sorry. I didn't mean that. I didn't know you were a—" Ed wanted to finish his sentence but couldn't.

"You didn't expect me to be a female?" Stephanie finished for him. "Is that it, Ed?"

Ed now felt very embarrassed in front of Rick and Rob. He just smiled at Stephanie, and she grinned.

"I know a diner where we can all go and have some good coffee and talk," he stated.

Rob got his jacket and car keys and said he would drive. Ed showed Stephanie to the back door leading to the parking lot. Rick grabbed Ed's arm and told him to keep cool and behave himself with her. Ed smiled back and said he would treat her like a true lady.

An hour into sharing coffees and going over the victims and forensic findings from all four murders, Stephanie asked Ed and Rob if they had done any checking to see if Dr. Malcolm had any know relatives or a wife. She knew of his illegal doings in the Quasar Pharmaceutical scandal he was involved in at the same time of the murders. Rob filled her in on what they knew about his private life.

"Nathan Malcolm was the top international sales buyer and distributor for Quasar. He made a big fortune for himself and others. They were able to distribute many illegals drugs into the country and Mexico primarily, drugs like illegal steroids and GHB tablets and the drug Soma, which is a heavy painkiller he gave to many pro athletes without a prescription. They relied on it heavily to fight injuries and keep them quiet from teams physicians," Rob explained.

Stephanie asked Ed if Nathan Malcolm had been married or if there was any known next of kin.

"We looked into this very heavily. We found out he was divorced, and his wife received a lot of money from him in their settlement. She passed away a few years later from Alzheimer's disease. They did have one child together, but it seems his ex-wife must have changed their last name, because we have not found any records on their child or whether or not their son or daughter is deceased," Ed told her.

Stephanie nodded and then looked back down to read the case file. Ed studied her face and appearance. *She has to be around thirty-eight or thirty-nine years old. What a beautiful face and long black hair. She has to work out often to maintain that athletic physique,* he thought. Rob noticed Ed staring at Stephanie and kicked him under the table, not wanting him to embarrass himself with her again.

"So what are your personal thoughts about this new killer? Do you have a theory on whether or not he has a connection to Dr. Malcolm?" Stephanie asked him.

Ed looked up and thought to himself before he answered her, stuttering, "I guess, being that Malcolm had medical knowledge when it came to removing victims' organs and the way he was very cautious not to leave any DNA evidence behind, I feel this new killer has to possess medical skill. He also has to have insight into the killings four years ago to know to leave his victim in Shoreline Park. But I believe we are dealing with a copycat killer," Ed gave her his opinion, and Rob said he agreed with his partner.

Ed looked at Stephanie's ring fingers on both hands, trying to see if she wore an engagement ring or wedding band. He didn't spot one, but that didn't mean she was single. From the corner of her eye, Stephanie noticed him looking at her. She calmly ignored it, thinking she was just working with two macho detectives. She said that in order for her to get a feel for this killer, the best thing would be to see the crime scene at Shoreline Park, along with the other crime scenes from four years ago. They got up, gathered their things, and headed out to start working together.

The trio made their way from the first murder at the Palms Motel to the apartment of the second victim, Sharon Kessler. Then they rounded back up to Shoreline Park. The area where the body had been found was still cordoned off by police tape. Stephanie looked around the area, trying to get a feel for the victims and killer. What could have drawn him to this park to kill his victims, besides the fact that it was secluded and deserted late at night? And why would the second killer want to come back to the same area as the first killer?

Ed and Rob looked around for themselves, and Rob asked Ed what he thought of Stephanie's work so far.

"Well, being a profiler, she is very educated and sharp. But unless she has some psychic abilities that we don't know about, she can't figure this killer's motives or if he is someone tied to Malcolm until we just catch him ourselves," Ed responded.

They saw Stephanie coming toward them, her dark sunglasses covering her black eyes in the bright light of the afternoon. Ed smiled at her as she joined them. "So, we have been going at this now for five hours. It's now 2:30. We just had coffee for lunch. What do you want to do now, Mrs. Morgan?" he questioned her.

Rob couldn't believe Ed had thrown out that remark to see if she was indeed married or single.

"For starters, it's Miss Morgan, Mr. Brooks. And yes, I know we have been all over the crimes scenes now, but I want you to take me to the county morgue so I can view the body of Ashley Cook. I have some questions for Dr. Adams, who conducted the autopsies."

Ed agreed to take her to view the body at the county coroner's facility. As they were driving on the interstate, Stephanie asked Rob if it was true that Rick was married to Dr. Adams.

Rob answered, "It's true. They got married right after the Entity murders ended, a little less than four years ago now. Funny. It's Rick's first marriage at his ripe young age of forty-five."

She absorbed the thought and decided to make a comeback response to Ed's straight-forward question to her earlier.

"Oh and, Ed, hasn't it been three years now since you divorced from Kayla, if I may ask?"

Ed slowly turned around in the passenger seat to face her, and Rob made a face under his sunglasses as he looked straight ahead at the road. Ed glared at Stephanie and then smiled at her.

"You seem to know a lot about us, including my private life, Miss Morgan. I will be honest with you. Yes, I have been divorced from my ex-wife going on three years now, if you really need to know."

Stephanie smiled back at him. "Well, I really like to know who I'm working with when I'm in an unfamiliar city and working a very important case with men I just met today," she told him. Ed faced forward again as they pulled into the parking lot of the facility.

Dr. Adams led them into the cold chamber, where she opened the door to pull out the remains of Ashley Cook. Stephanie looked at the wounds to the body and then at photographs of the other victims to see if she could extrapolate a pattern from the killer's style of inflicting the wounds. She asked Cate about the differences between the knife wounds and gouges on the latest victim and the others before.

"From what I could tell, both killers are right-handed. I can surmise that Nathan Malcolm was more powerful than the new killer because the wounds he inflicted on his three victims were deeper lacerations, and he seemed to take his time, wanting to remove the organs and not hide his hatred for these women," Dr. Adams gave Stephanie her opinion.

"I can add that this killer wants us to think he is like Nathan Malcolm, not only in the sense of his similar style murder but in the way Malcolm thought and used disguises," Stephanie said. "I have no doubt that this killer wants to taunt the police and make us play a game of cat and mouse with him. Judging by the fact that he did not choose a prostitute for his first victim, I think we can expect more murders to happen because he will be taking young women at random now."

Ed and Rob shook their heads, hoping her hunch was wrong. Ed thanked Dr. Adams for her time, and they left the county coroner's building and headed back to Central Division to brief Rick on what they had gone over. Ed asked Stephanie what hotel she was staying at. She told him that for now she was staying at the Capri Hotel on Mission Boulevard and that Chief Chase and Rick would find a condo for her while she was there helping them on the case. Rob pulled into the parking lot of Central Division, and they all went into Rick's office and briefed him on how Stephanie was helping them and asked what Rick had planned for tomorrow's task force meeting.

"So you guys saw the body of Ashley Cook and spoke to my wife, Dr. Adams. I know, Stephanie, that you might have more insight into what this new killer has going on in his mind and methods compared to Malcolm. I know it's late in the afternoon and you must be tired from your flight late last night, so I'm going to let you go back to your hotel now. We will have the task force here early in the morning so you can meet them and begin working with them all," Rick told her.

He also told her that he and the chief had found a condo for her to stay in; it was located in the area of Bird Rock. Rick asked Ed if he would mind taking her back to Capri Hotel, since it was on his way home. Ed agreed, and Stephanie thanked Rick and told him to thank Chief Chase for his kindness. She left with Ed. They got into his Envoy and headed off to the interstate.

While they drove, Stephanie looked out her window, gazing around at the beautiful sights of San Diego. Ed asked her if this was her first time in the city. Stephanie told him yes and that she had grown up in Encino, California, which was a suburb outside Los Angeles. Ed proposed to her that if she would like, he would help her move her things into her condo, being that he lived only a few miles away in Lower Hermosa. Stephanie told him that would be great. She hadn't unpacked yet, and she didn't care for hotels much anyway.

Ed pulled into the Capri Hotel and went up to help her bring her bags down to his SUV. He was shocked to find that Stephanie had five large bags, along with her briefcase and a small carry bag for her laptop. Ed saw the smile on her face and knew she had gotten back at him again for his behavior when they first met. After Ed secured the luggage in the trunk, they took off for Bird Rock.

"Look, Stephanie, I'm sorry for the way I acted when I thought we would be working with a male profiler. I'm not like that at all. I just wanted to let you know that," Ed told her, hoping she would accept his apology.

Stephanie faced him and removed her sunglasses. "Let me see, Detective Ed Brooks. You had a stellar naval record when you were enlisted in the navy. You have received many awards and commendations on the force, and you have worked four very difficult homicide cases and were able to solve them all. You were made the lead detective for the task force, not only because the first murder happened in your division's precinct but because your dedication and hard-nosed attitude helps you catch your suspects. How's that for a summed-up profile of you by me?" she asked.

Ed just stared at her, shocked that she knew so much about him.

"So how is it that you know so much about me and I know nothing about you?" Ed asked, and Stephanie told him her boss had filled her in on all the people she would be working with on the task force.

She knew how Ed had almost been killed by Nathan Malcolm in the bloody sting operation the night Ed killed him. Stephanie told him she was sorry for what he went through and that it had cost him his marriage. Ed smiled and thanked her and asked if they could be friends now.

Stephanie smiled and said, "We can be friendly and work together, but as for friends, we'll have to wait and see."

Ed pulled into the nice condo complex and made a face that he would have to unload all the bags and carry them to her apartment. Stephanie read the key number and told him the good news. Her condo number was number 1-D; it was on the first floor.

Ed whispered to himself, "Thank you, Lord," and helped her inside her spacious apartment. He placed her bags down in her bedroom. She thanked him as she walked him to the door. Ed looked at his watch. It was just after 6:00 p.m.

"May I ask if you have plans for dinner? Unless you packed yourself microwavable dinners in one of your bags?" Ed asked.

She smiled at him. "No, Ed, I don't have plans for dinner, and I don't have any food with me. I was going to look online for the best place to order food," she told him.

Ed asked if she would like to go out to dinner with him. He knew a very nice Spanish restaurant close by in La Jolla Mesa. Stephanie just studied the handsome look on Ed's face. She knew she was safe with him and felt this would be a good way to earn his trust. She smiled and said she would love some Spanish food for dinner, but she wanted to shower and change first. Ed told her that was great and that he would be back to pick her up around 8:00 p.m. sharp. They exchange cell phone numbers.

Ed walked to his truck and smiled to himself. "Thanks again, God," he said to the good Lord as he headed home to shower and change.

Just a little before 8:00 p.m., Ed arrived at Stephanie's door dressed in a casual black shirt and dark gray slacks and shoes. He popped a Tic Tac into his mouth for fresh breath. As he was about to knock, Stephanie opened the door slowly. Ed was stunned to see her dressed in a pure white dress that was low-cut, sleeveless, and knee-length. She also wore nice black sandal type shoes. Her hair flowed softly down the back of her neck. Ed was blown away by her beauty, and Stephanie was also taken by his tall, clean-shaven, and handsome appearance. Ed couldn't talk, and Stephanie laughed.

She had her purse in her hands and said, "How about we go to dinner?

Ed said, "Yes, of course." When they were down in the parking lot, he opened the door for her, and she got into his truck. As Ed pulled out of the parking lot, he said, "The name of the restaurant is *El Sabio.*"

Stephanie repeated the name, and Ed thought she said it perfectly in Spanish, so he asked if she spoke Spanish.

"Just a little," she said.

A short time later, Stephanie admired El Sabio's old Spanish decor as she and Ed were seated in a small booth in the middle of the restaurant. Ed thanked the male host for seating them. She knew Ed must have come here often before. As they read their menus, Ed asked her what she felt like. She said she didn't know yet and asked him what he felt like having. Ed showed her his menu and pointed at the dish. He said he couldn't pronounce the word. Stephanie told him not to worry and that she would tell the waiter the name of the dish for him. When their waiter came over to them, Stephanie told him in Spanish that she would have the *arroz negro paella negra* seafood dish and that Ed would have the Andalusia meat dish. Then she told the waiter that they would both have just water to drink. She thanked him again in Spanish. Ed felt like the words coming out of her mouth were so sweet and polite that they should be put to music for her to sing.

"Wow, did you take Spanish in school?" he asked.

Stephanie smiled and said yes. She had also traveled to Mexico and Spain on vacations, so she was quiet fluent in the language. She then changed the subject. "So, Ed, tell me. You have obviously been here before with other women. I can tell."

He told her it had been one of his ex-wife's favorite places to go to for a nice dinner on the weekends. Stephanie's expression saddened when he mentioned his ex-wife. Then Ed asked her why she was still Miss Morgan and not Mrs. Morgan. She frowned; she had known he would ask this question.

"Because, Ed, I just haven't found the right man yet. I was in a long relationship for a while. He was a nice guy. It just didn't work out for us because we are still dedicated to our careers, so we decided to just move on. We ended our relationship a few months ago. I know you're going to ask me if he was an FBI person too, and the answer is no. He is a dentist, and his name is none of your business," she said, laughing as the waiter brought their food.

As they began to eat, Ed raised his glass of water and said, "To new friends and good luck on this case."

She touched her glass to his. After they told one another how good their food was, Stephanie asked him what his thoughts were on the case. Ed just talked about it being another similar style killer but said they would catch him with her help. He didn't want to talk about the case; he just wanted to enjoy her company. Stephanie felt that he was holding something back from her or even hiding something. But she didn't want to press him on it. She was enjoying her dinner and his company. After dinner, they relaxed with coffee, and Ed asked her about her family.

"My parents live in Santa Monica. My father is retired LAPD, and my mother is still working as a behavioral therapist in her own practice. So you can see where I got the inspiration to become a profiler for the FBI. I have one brother, who is a captain in the marine corps and stationed overseas right now."

Ed smiled and said, "Semper Fi!"

Stephanie asked Ed about his family, and he said, "My parents are retired and living quietly in northern California, where I was raised in Redding. I have one brother, who is married with a family in San Francisco. He and his wife are both lawyers and have two daughters. I moved to San Diego when I left the navy a long time ago, and I have been with the PD ever since." He briefly mentioned his marriage to Kayla and said they still talked once in a while and that she was now remarried, and still living in San Diego with her husband.

Stephanie didn't want to ask him any more questions about Kayla because she didn't want to upset Ed. When Ed received the check, he paid the waiter and left him a generous tip. He knew it was getting late, so he suggested he take her back to her place. When they walked outside, Stephanie wrapped her arms across her body, and Ed knew she was cold. He covered her shoulders with his leather jacket, and she thanked him. Moments later, they got into his truck.

"So here you are," Ed said a little while later as he pulled into her complex and got out to open her door.

They walked to the door of the building and into the foyer together. She thanked him for dinner and said she'd had a nice time. She also had something on her mind.

"Ed, I know we just met, and I also know that besides working together, we have to trust one another no matter what happens, right?" she asked him.

Confused, Ed said, "Right."

"So then tell me what's on your mind about this case, because I know you're not afraid of anything, but you are holding something back from me. I sense it, Ed."

Ed took a breath and let it out slowly. He told her he would open up to her in time about it.

Stephanie smiled and nodded. "Okay. You better get going, Detective Brooks," she told him.

Ed smiled at her, and they shook hands. Ed then put his hand on her waist, pulled Stephanie to his chest, and kissed her gently on the lips. Stephanie returned the kiss and then pushed him slowly away with a hand on his chest.

"Ed, let's take this slow, please? We just met, but I am attracted to you."

Ed smiled into her dark eyes and said, "I will pick you up at 8:30 in the morning, and I really like you, Miss Profiler."

They kissed softly again, and Stephanie gently pushed him out the door and closed it behind him. As Ed slowly walked back to his truck, he whispered, "Thanks again, God," knowing the man upstairs had answered Ed's prayer to bring another elegant woman into his life.

Chapter 5

Early Thursday morning, August 10, the task force again assembled in Central Division's conference room. Chief John Chase and some of his staff were there to brief his elite detectives and introduce them to Stephanie Morgan. As she entered the conference room with Ed Brooks, Rick and Rob smiled at one another, feeling Ed that had started more than a friendship with the profiler. Ed took his seat next to Rob, and Stephanie went to the podium to talk to the detectives. The pictures of the three previous victims and the most recent victim were projected onto the large screen, along with their names and the dates of their deaths and discoveries by police. Rick turned the podium over to Stephanie.

"Good morning, all. I had the privilege of meeting a few of you yesterday and have spoken with Chief Chase quite a bit on the phone about these cases before I was brought in to assist you. My name is Stephanie Morgan. I have been with the FBI for more than twelve years now as a profiler working in the LA office. I helped our agents there and LAPD detectives apprehend Louis Stolla, the serial strangler who killed six young women, and the serial rapist Stan Wilson, who raped more than eight women but did not kill them.

"After looking over the three murders committed four years ago and the most recent victim, I have no doubt that this killer wants to follow the same methods and style of killings as Nathan Malcolm," Stephanie told the task force and then explained that the new killer had done a lot of research into Malcolm's patterns and now wanted to taunt the police into thinking he and Nathan Malcolm were one in the same.

The detectives began to question Stephanie on who this new killer was. Skip Jones was the first speak up: "Stephanie, you said this new killer wants to match the patterns of Malcolm's killings. Is there a chance he may be related to Nathan Malcolm somehow? Or could Malcolm have revealed his ways of killing to a close friend?"

Ed spoke up and said he would answer part of that question for her. "Once we knew Nathan Malcolm was the serial killer, we did a complete and thorough check on him. He was divorced, and his wife passed away. They had one child together. We tried to trace records to see who their child was, but we believe Mrs. Malcolm had the child's named officially changed. We can't find any records or DMV listings of a surviving heir to Nathan Malcolm," he explained.

In addition, no next of kin had come forward to take possession of his badly charred remains. He had been cremated by order of the county judge after his autopsy was finished.

Stephanie spoke up to answer the second part of Jones's question, "You're asking me if I feel this killer has knowledge of Malcolm's patterns of murders. Yes, I believe he does, and he is going to continue killing young women like this until one of two things happen: either we track him down and stop him, or he is going to end up killing the same amount of victims as Malcolm did, stopping at three. But Malcolm did try to take one last victim, who was Detective Julie O'Keefe. So if this new killer is going to try for three more victims, and if he is not preying on prostitutes, which we can now assume because Ashley Cook was not a known escort, trying to anticipate this killer's next move is going to be more difficult," she told them.

"So if we can't set up another sting operation with an operative as an escort, how are we going to have a chance to be a step ahead of the killer?" Julie asked her.

"Well, we know the areas where Malcolm met and took his victims. I suggest for now that we have double patrols in all the areas the murders took place and any secluded parks and recreation areas that would be an inviting place for a killer to stalk a young woman. We can have an operative set up as a jogger or walking a small dog all alone in one of these places. It's really the best shot we have right now if I had to make a judgment call on this," Stephanie replied.

All the detectives looked at one another, and Chief Chase and Rick whispered back and forth. Chief Chase got up.

"Thank you, Stephanie, for giving us your detailed insight into this case. I want to let you know that Rick and I will be considering having an undercover officer pose as a possible target for our suspect. But we can't forget what happened to Julie and Ed four years ago. We almost lost two cops in one night. So this will be a last resort to draw this person out. I'm going to follow Stephanie's advice in patrolling those specific areas. We are going to look more deeply into Malcolm's personal past and see if he had close friends with whom he worked or a neighbor to whom he was close, as well as all recently released convicts who are known killers. We have to find something soon, people, because I don't want to get a call and be told that we have another victim on our hands. So let's get a move on quick!" the chief told them and then left with his staff members.

Ed and Rob went over to Stephanie, who was gathering her folders, and Rick came over to them and asked what they were going to do now.

"Boss, I think we are going to pay a visit to Quasar Pharmaceuticals and speak to their CEO or the people who knew Malcolm the best while he worked there. Stephanie thinks he could have said something to a fellow co-worker who may know something or may even be our killer," Ed told him, and Rick told them go for it.

The two detectives and Stephanie headed to Spring Valley, San Diego. Ed led the way into the big commercial facility of Quasar, and they checked in at the central security desk. The security guard made a call to the CEO's office and spoke to the secretary. She informed him that she would come down and escort them up to the office to meet with Mr. Aaron Byrne, the CEO of the company.

They waited a few moments, and soon a middle-aged woman wearing a business style dress welcomed the detectives to Quasar and told them to follow her to the elevators and up to the top floor to Mr. Byrne's office. As they walked through the large first floor of the facility, they saw many people working at work stations with lab tables and cold storage units and freezers for their work with pharmaceuticals. The secretary told them that the work floors went as high as the fourth floor. From the fourth floor up to the ninth floor were all the regular offices. The elevator stopped on the ninth floor, and she walked them across the very luxurious blue carpeted floors to the big double wooden doors of the CEO's office. She told them to have a seat and that Mr. Byrne would be right with them.

Only a few minutes had passed when a slender man of medium height walked through the double doors and into the lobby of his office. Mr. Byrne had gray hair and wore glasses. He shook all the detectives' hands, and introductions were made. After showing them into his office, he had them sit at an oval table. He already had an employee file sitting on the tabletop, the file of Dr. Nathan Malcolm. He then asked the three detectives how he could assist them.

Ed spoke first for his team, and they went over the history of Malcolm's work with the company and how he had begun to make large profits from his illegal steroid and other drug dealings. Then they went over who might have had any insights to his doings or if he had told someone he had indeed gone off the deep end and wanted to turn to murder. Mr. Byrne looked through some of the pages in the file, took out one sheet from the others, and handed it to Ed. As Ed looked it over, Byrne began to explain the person listed on the page.

"Nathan Malcolm worked closely with this man and former employee of ours, Fred Young. He was Malcolm's chief assistant in the pharmaceutical department. It was Fred Young who noticed shipping labels to countries outside the registered countries we are approved to ship legal pharmaceuticals to by the Food and Drug Administration. He found out what Nathan was doing and then reported it to our internal security, who followed up by gathering all the known evidence of who and where he was distributing these drugs to. Then we brought in the DEA to take over the case, and they arrested Malcolm and seized all his materials to get ready to start the trial against him. Fred Young never mentioned to me or anyone in our personnel department if Malcolm had made threats against anyone or if he had homicidal tendencies. He did give the appearance of not taking care of himself during his final weeks here. He looked very drained in the face, and it was obvious that he had been smoking and drinking heavily. But that is all I am aware of until he was terminated by myself and the board of directors. Then of course he did the unthinkable, which lead to his death four years ago," Byrne covered everything he knew about Malcolm's involvement with his company.

Stephanie asked him where Fred Young was now and said they needed to talk to him. Byrne told them that Young's address and home number were at the very bottom of the sheet. Ed and his partners rose from their seats and thanked Mr. Byrne for his time and cooperation in this case. They stated that if they needed any more help from him in the future, they would contact him. Ed handed him his business card, and the trio left the office and walked to the elevators to return to the ground floor. In the elevator, Ed asked Stephanie what she thought about Fred Young.

"Well look, we have the statements Fred Young gave to the police four years ago still in our files. You said he didn't mention ever hearing that Malcolm was going to hurt anyone. But that doesn't mean he didn't know something and just didn't tell you. So I say let's go pay him a visit, today if we can," Stephanie suggested.

As they got into Rob's four-door sedan, Stephanie called Young's home number. Ed and Rob listened to her talk to someone; it seemed she was having a pleasant conversation as she told the person who she was and what the call was all about. Stephanie thanked the voice on the other end of her cell phone. Then she looked at Ed and Rob from the backseat and smiled.

"So what did the person say?" Rob asked her.

"I spoke with Fred Young and told him what this was all about. He asked me if the recent murder was somehow connected with the past murders, and I told him maybe. He agreed to meet with us this evening at his home in Sorrento Valley," she told them.

Ed smiled and said he and Stephanie would meet with him. They agreed to head back to Central Division to make log entries about what they had found out and brief Rick and the others. As Rob pulled out of the parking lot and passed a string of parked vehicles on the service road, a pair of eyes that were concealed behind a dark pair of sunglasses watched the vehicle. The watcher sat in a nearby vehicle and pondered what do to next. *I will follow them for now, as I can imagine what their next move might be, but I will have something in store for them that they will not expect!* the watcher though coldly and eased the dark Ford SUV out of its space and accelerated to follow the trio to their next destination.

After Ed and Stephanie briefed Rick and the team on what they had found out earlier that day, they headed to one of the elegant neighborhoods in the Sorrento Valley to meet with Fred Young. Ed had picked Stephanie up at her condo and was now driving north on the 805 Freeway.

Ed remarked to her that she looked very attractive in her dark jeans and sweater but said he would like to see her in that elegant dress again soon. Stephanie winked at him and said maybe if they got done with interviewing Mr. Young early she would consider spending some quiet time alone with Ed at her place.

Ed smiled and said, "Let's get there fast." Then he asked if Young was married and had a family.

Stephanie said he had told her that his wife would be home to meet them. She didn't know if they had any children. As they searched for the home's address, they came up upon some very nice large homes of the valley.

"This is the house," Stephanie told him. "The one with the very long driveway and stucco sandstone design on the outside."

Ed pulled into the long driveway and parked his Envoy. He and Stephanie walked to the front door and rang the doorbell. They waited a few seconds, but there was no response from within the house. They looked at one another, and Ed told her there were lights on inside the home. He said he would go around back to see if there was another door. As he walked down the path on the side of the home, Stephanie again rang the bell. She then took out her cell phone and called the home's phone to see if she would get a response that way. Just then, Ed called to her in a low voice from the side entrance. Stephanie quickly went to him and saw Ed with his gun drawn and pointing to the door, which had been forced open. He motioned for her to stay outside as he went into the home to investigate.

Ed moved slowly down the tiled hallway and peered into the first room. It was the laundry room. He saw that the home was kept nice and neat. He moved again slowly toward a light that had been left on, but suddenly his rubber-soled shoes slipped on the ceramic tile. Luckily, Ed was able to catch himself. Looking down, he saw he had slipped on a trail of blood that started where he was standing and led all the way to the large living room. Ed called to Stephanie to call 911 right away.

Holding his gun ahead of him, he moved forward and came up the opening to the living room. He quickly turned his body to face whoever might be there. As he scanned the room, he saw two bodies lying in a pool of blood. A struggle had taken place; items had been knocked from walls, and tables were broken. As Ed turned and called for Stephanie to come inside, he was hit violently from behind by a blunt object and then hit once again as he fell to the floor.

The intruder dropped the object and ran down the hallway to exit the house, pushing Stephanie to the floor with a hard elbow to her chest. As she fell on her back, she looked behind her to see a person dressed in black running out the door. She took a breath and was able to get to her feet, only to see Ed on the floor, holding the back of his neck, which was bleeding. She quickly took some tissues and covered his wound as she helped him to his feet. She yelled to him, "Ed! Are you all right?"

Ed looked at her and nodded to indicate he was fine. They then looked at the bodies on the floor, a male and female who were covered in blood and what looked like tremendous stab wounds. Stephanie helped Ed to sit back on the sofa, and they waited for the police to arrive.

Some time passed before the police arrived on the scene. The whole task force was called to the residence. The forensic team removed the bodies and then began combing the home for evidence. Ed and Stephanie were taken outside to be treated by paramedics. Stephanie was fine; she just had a slight bruise to her left elbow from her impact with the floor. Ed had a gash behind his left ear caused by a blow from a wooden log the assailant used from the fireplace. Ed was told he was lucky and didn't need stiches. The wound was dressed and bandaged.

Rick and the team spoke to the detectives and uniformed police of the area's division. Stephanie came over and sat with Ed on the back step of the ambulance and asked him if he was all right. Ed told her he was okay, just shaken up, and she told him she felt the same way. Rick and the team came over to them.

"So this is what we can tell from the forensic team so far: It seems the suspect forced his or her way into the side door by shoving a screwdriver or long steel device into the doorjamb and forcing it open. Upon hearing the noise, Fred Young encountered the intruder in the hallway. As he tried to fight him off, his hands suffered knife wounds. He was stabbed multiple times in the chest and neck and forced into the living room. His wife, Clare Young, tried to call for help from the landline phone. The killer then turned his attention to her and slit her throat from behind, left to right. Then he stabbed her once deep in the chest and turned his attention back to Fred Young, who was on the floor, covered in blood. The intruder then slit Fred's throat from left to right and stabbed him again in the chest multiple times until he was suddenly stopped, presumably when you two rang the doorbell. Ed then entered and was hit with the wood log, and

Stephanie was pushed to the floor as the suspect fled," Rick recounted all the details he had been given by the detectives and forensic team.

Stephanie asked if any witnesses outside had seen the suspect flee.

"The detectives asked the neighbors within a two-block radius if they saw anything or anyone in the last two hours, but they all said no. We feel he parked his vehicle on the street behind the home and cut through the neighbor's backyard to make his way to the side entrance and then followed the same route to make his escape. There are signs of footprints in the blood, but it seems he had his feet covered with sterile shoe coverings, so he left no foot impressions in the house or outside on the dirt or pavement," Rick told them. He asked Ed and Stephanie if they had been able to make out anything about the killer.

Ed stated that all he had seen was the blood on the floor and the bodies. Then he had felt like someone broke a bat on his neck, and he saw stars. Rick then asked Stephanie what she had seen.

"I came inside once Ed yelled to me. I rushed into the hallway as a figure in black threw an elbow into me, and I fell to the floor. As I looked up, I only saw the dark outline of what look like a man in a hooded black jacket running out the door," Stephanie recounted.

Rick just shook his head.

"So the killer knew you two were coming here to meet with Young, and he planned this out very well to keep Young silenced forever. Seems like the same patterns used by Nathan Malcolm," Jack Kerns stated to them.

Some of the group agreed with him, and Julie said that it had to be a new killer because Malcolm was dead.

Rob looked at her and suggested, "What if Nathan Malcolm is still alive?"

"Then who was it that died in the fire that night at his home?" Skip replied.

Rick told everyone to calm down. He didn't want his team to start jumping to conclusions. He then gave the order on how to handle this now. "Julie and Skip, because this happened in your division's jurisdiction, you two follow this up with forensics and witnesses. Rob, you get back to Aaron Byrne at Quasar and find out if he mentioned to anyone that Ed and Stephanie planned on meeting with Young tonight. Ken and Jack, I want you two to go talk to Dr. Diana Farrell. She assisted Dr. Adams on the autopsy on Nathan Malcolm the day after his death, along with my wife. I want everything from her, including details about what she did to that body to confirm it was him before they cremated it. Let's get a move on this, people!" Rick told them.

As they moved out with their assignments, Rick turned his attention to Ed and Stephanie. "You two take it easy for the rest of the night and tomorrow morning too. I will call you both once we know something about this. Stephanie, will you drive Ed home for me, please?" Rick asked her, and Stephanie said she would.

Ed thanked Rick. Stephanie told Ed that she would drive his Envoy and then make him some hot cocoa to cheer him up. As they drove to his apartment in Lower Hermosa, Ed informed her that he didn't have any hot cocoa at home, just good old instant coffee.

When they arrived, Stephanie helped Ed up the stairs after parking his SUV in his garage, next to his motorcycle. They entered Ed's condo, which was right on the edge of the beach. Stephanie looked around the apartment and got a feel for what Ed liked. He had many pictures of Jimi Hendrix hanging on his walls and many weights in the center of his living room, which seemed out of place to her. She asked Ed why he didn't have them set up in the spare bedroom. Ed told her he had made the other room his office, and that was where his computer and other files were.

After Stephanie made two cups of coffee for them, she handed him his mug, and Ed suggested they walk out onto his deck. He wanted to show her the nice view of the Pacific Ocean at night. As they walked outside, the wind from the ocean's current picked up and blew Stephanie's long hair back. She told Ed what a breathtaking view he had from his deck. Ed smiled at her and held her hand.

Stephanie smiled back as Ed spoke softly to her. "I'm sorry I couldn't protect you in time. I lost my focus for that once split second, and we both could have been killed," Ed told her, sorry she had gotten hurt.

"Ed, I'm just thankful we didn't get killed. You did everything you could. We were taken by surprise by this new killer. Don't blame yourself for this; it would have happened even if we hadn't gone to meet with the Youngs tonight. We are faced with a killer who has knowledge and insight that might put him ahead of even me. It will be hard to get a step ahead of him," Stephanie told him softly as she took a sip of her hot coffee.

"You know I'm not going to let anyone hurt you. I care about you, Stephanie," Ed told her as he lowered his mouth to hers, and they shared a soft kiss.

When Ed pulled away, Stephanie asked him what was wrong. He told her she had coffee breath. They laughed, and she told him she had to go. It was getting late. After they walked back inside his living room, Ed secured the glass door to the deck. He watched her put on her short jacket. She came back over to him and asked if he was going to be all right. Ed told her he would take some Advil for the pain and then call her in the morning to pick her up.

He walked her to the door, opened it for her, and asked how she was going to get home. Stephanie smiled and said he was right. She would have to borrow his truck to drive home and then pick him up in the morning. Ed softly touched her face, and they kissed again passionately. He closed and locked the door and pulled Stephanie against his chest. He broke their kiss and whispered to her that he wanted her to stay with him tonight.

Stephanie tilted her head back so she could look into his eyes and whispered, "Yes, I want to stay with you, Ed."

They kissed again softly. Ed then picked Stephanie up in his arms and carried her to his bedroom. He closed the door with his foot and laid Stephanie down in his bed gently.

The Entity watched from inside his dark vehicle, which was concealed in the shadows of the adjoining alley next to Ed's apartment. The Entity knew his main adversary had a new love in his life. He smiled to himself, as he knew he could use Stephanie's love for Ed to trap him. He knew this would be his plan to get back at Ed Brooks for what happened four years ago. But Ed would fail to stop the Entity and his vengeance now. He started his vehicle and drove slowly away into the night.

As Stephanie awoke slowly in bed, she saw the very bright sunlight shining through the window, and she knew it was early morning. She sat up in bed and noticed Ed wasn't next to her. She then heard heavy breathing coming from the living room. She knew Ed was lifting heavy weights. She found his dress shirt, put it on, and went out to see him. She stood in the doorway and saw Ed bench-pressing heavy weights and sweating—a sign that he had been working out for a while. As Ed finished his last repetition, he placed the barbell back in place on the bench and sat up, taking heavy breaths. Stephanie came over and handed him a glass of water. Ed thanked her, and they kissed gently. Stephanie thanked him for last night and making her feel safe. They got up and sat on the sofa together. Ed prepared to suggest something to her.

"I want to ask you this not only because of the way we feel about each other but because I know you will be a lot safer too. Do you want to move in with me so I can make sure you're safe?" Ed asked her.

Stephanie held his face gently and whispered, "Yes, Ed. I would like that."

He smiled and told her, "Great," and they both admitted they had fallen in love with one another.

Suddenly Ed's home phone rang. He answered it. Rick had called to inform him that they had made some headway into the murders last night. They also had the detailed autopsy report from Dr. Farrell. Rick told him the task force would be ready for a noon briefing. Ed told him that he and Stephanie would be there. After hanging up, Ed informed her of the briefing and said they had four hours until they needed to be at Central Division. Stephanie suggested they take a shower together and then stop by her apartment so she could change into fresh clothes.

Ed agreed, and they kissed again. Ed removed his tank top, and Stephanie noticed the deep scar on his left abdomen from the deadly encounter he'd had with Malcolm. She hadn't noticed last night in the dark, but as they headed into the shower, she touched his side softly and told him she was very sorry. Ed smiled and told him he was all right now. He said this case had brought some comfort to him; it had brought her into his life. Stephanie smiled and said he was right. Ed turned the tap, and very cold water rained down onto their naked bodies in the marble-enclosed shower. Stephanie screamed that it was too cold. Ed laughed and told her it was only water. He turned the handle to the left to make it warmer, and they kissed gently as the water splashed down on their faces.

As they left Stephanie's apartment a few hours later, she looked at Ed, who was silent as he drove. His eyes were hidden behind his sunglasses. She knew something was on his mind again. He was thinking about the case and would not open up to her about what it was. She wanted to know what it was or else, now. She knew she would have to be outright blunt with him about it.

"Ed, I want to know what you have been hiding from me about this case. I want you to tell me because maybe I can help you piece it all together. Haven't I earned your trust yet and proven my love for you? Please talk to me. I'm frustrated that you will not open up to me about this," Stephanie said, pleading with Ed to trust her.

He turned his head to face her and saw the look of hurt and concern on her face. Then he turned back to look at the road. "Please, Stephanie. I'm not trying to hold anything back from you or Rick and the others. I have been looking at a theory of mine for some time now. And before I know for certain what it all is and who may be involved, I can't tell you just yet. So please, don't ask me this again. Okay?" he told her.

Disappointed, Stephanie just put on her sunglasses, looked out the side window, and whispered, "Fine, Ed."

Soon they pulled into the Central Division parking lot. As they entered the conference room together, Stephanie was very abruptly walking ahead of Ed as thought she was upset with him. She took her seat at the head of the table next to Rick, and Ed took his seat next to Rob. Everyone could tell she was upset with him.

Rob whispered to Ed, "There isn't trouble with you and your new profiler friend, is there, Ed?"

Ed shook his head and said, "She has a woman's insight beyond a profiler's intuition."

Rob smiled as Rick began to talk.

"Okay, we made some progress with the head of Quasar. He gave Ed and Stephanie the information that lead them to Fred Young. But someone killed Young and his wife last night to conceal the information he was going to give them on Nathan Malcolm. Rob visited with Aaron Byrne late last night, and he told Rob that except for his secretary knowing he talked to us about Mr. Young, no one knew the police were going to visit with him at his residence last night. So my guess is that the new Entity killer is tracking our movements in this investigation, unless someone in this very room is feeding the killer our information or is the Entity!" Rick told them.

As they all looked at one another in shock, he continued, "I had Ken and Jack meet with Dr. Diana Farrell early this morning and retrieve the autopsy report she completed on Nathan Malcolm the day after his death. After reading her full report twice, we have concluded that unless Malcolm is now a ghost, we have a brand new killer on our hands who has knowledge of our investigations and is now killing his victims at a faster rate and at random, unlike Malcolm, who just preyed on prostitutes. So we are now at a standstill in this new case, I believe. Now I will ask Stephanie to give us her opinion on where we can begin to focus our investigation now."

Stephanie took the podium, opened her folder, and began to talk to the group. "The most important thing I can suggest is that this new killer is trying to mimic the Nathan Malcolm murders. Malcolm's methods are reflected in where the killer left Ashley Cook's body and the remorseless way he killed Fred Young and his wife. But the main thing we need in order to be ready for his next move is trust in one another! A certain lead detective with whom I have been assigned to work is holding back information from me, which may be very detrimental to us all. This person, who is now my boyfriend and with whom I had passionate sex with last night and this morning, is being a stubborn asshole! So my biggest advice now is that we need to trust one another if we are going to solve this case. Thank you!"

Stephanie closed her folder, gathered her things, and stormed out of the conference room, leaving the whole group with their mouths hanging open in shock. They stared at Ed Brooks, who was beyond embarrassed. Rick got up slowly from his seat and thanked Stephanie Morgan for her honest opinions and advice. Rick stared at Ed and told everyone to work with their partners and decide amongst themselves how they wanted to work this case now. Ed immediately got up and stormed out the door angrily.

"Rob, leave him alone for now. Stephanie is the only one he will open up to about what he believes. Hopefully her little mind-blowing scheme has worked to get him to trust her," Rick told Rob.

Rob agreed with his lieutenant and suggested he would go find Ed. As Rob headed out the door, he saw Stephanie walking back to the conference room. Rob told her that Ed had stormed out and that he was going to look for him.

"I just saw Ed pull out of the parking lot," Stephanie said. "Let him go cool off. I did what I did in order for him to not only trust me but the whole task force. Can we go talk alone, please? You're his partner, so maybe you can share with me what Ed knows."

Rob agreed to talk to her but suggested they go somewhere alone to talk. After they got into Rob's car, they headed to the diner for some lunch.

A little while later, Rob had finished his sandwich and fries, but Stephanie had barely touched her salad. They were talking about Ed. Stephanie came out and asked Rob what he was holding back from her.

"Look, you have to understand, Stephanie. You're the first woman he has really been with since his divorce. Even though he was able to stop Nathan Malcolm, that case has never left his soul. Ed was convinced that Malcolm had a deep connection to a past serial killer, and he was determined to find out what it was. He has studied and researched this for going on four years now, ever since the first murders ended. But now with these new killings, I think Ed is more convinced than ever that the Malcolm murders and these murders are connected to another certain string of murders that happened a very long time ago," Rob told her, and Stephanie pressed Rob to tell her which case he was referring to.

Rob looked around the diner, knowing he couldn't mention the name there. She would have to find out for herself. "You know behind Ed's computer desk in his office? He has that enclosed marker board on the wall?"

"Yes," Stephanie answered.

"Open the doors to the board, and you will not only find notes Ed has made himself but pictures and dates with names of suspects and victims of the person Ed believes is connected to these cases. I'm sorry, Stephanie, but I can't tell you any more than this," Rob told her.

Stephanie thanked him and asked if he could take her back to her condo and help her pack her things because she would be moving in with Ed that evening. Rob agreed to help her move.

Ed was lifting weights to the song "Burning Desire" by Jimi Hendrix, which was blaring on the stereo. He heard the door unlock and open slowly. He stopped what he was doing and sat up to see who it was. Stephanie and Rob entered the apartment. Rob was holding her large bags, which she told him to set down by the sofa and then her strong new boyfriend would kindly help her with them. Ed smiled, and Rob told them he needed to get home and to have a good night. As he left, Stephanie stared at Ed, her expression sad. She went over and shut off the CD player.

Ed sarcastically thanked her for doing that, as he'd been enjoying that song along with his workout. He took a towel, wiped the sweat from his face, and headed into the bathroom to shower. Stephanie frowned angrily because he was ignoring her again. She ran into the bathroom before Ed could lock the door. He was naked.

"I hope I really embarrassed you this afternoon, because you needed a wake-up call to make you understand that you can trust me fully!" Stephanie yelled at him.

Ed went over and turned the tap to start his shower. He calmly asked Stephanie to give him an hour to shower and suggested they could then talk like rational adults. As Ed stepped into the shower, Stephanie stepped out of her slacks and blouse and then followed him in. She screamed again that the water was ice cold. Ed smiled at her, and they kissed. Stephanie whispered to him that she was sorry for what she did but asked if he could please tell her what was going on with this case. Ed told her they would relax for a short time after the shower, and he would tell her. As Stephanie started to cry, they kissed again.

Stephanie awoke in Ed's bed very slowly. She glimpsed the moon's rays coming through the bedroom window. She was surprised. After she and Ed had finished their shower together, he had carried her to the bedroom, where they had made love and she had fallen asleep. She turned her head and looked at the digital clock on the side table; it was 2:36 a.m. Stephanie very slowly turned to her left side, where Ed lay next to her, sound asleep. She remembered what Rob had told her about the whiteboard in Ed's office.

Very slowly Stephanie slid out from under the sheets and comforter. She put on Ed's pajama top, quietly opened the bedroom door, and closed it behind her. She walked down the short hallway to Ed's office, opened the door, went inside, and partially closed the door. She turned on the light and walked behind the desk to the large whiteboard that was covered by two side-by-side wood doors. She looked behind her and then very slowly opened the left door.

Her eyes widened in shock at what she was looking at. With an appalled look on her face, she slowly opened the right door. She noticed more shocking pictures and notes and then looked back at the left side again, were many more brutal and even scary crime photos of victims hung. They looked very old. Stephanie looked at pictures of several men's faces; Ed had written above their pictures, *Jack the Ripper suspects.*

Stephanie took a step back and said to herself, "My God." She took another step back and felt someone was standing behind her. She turned around and screamed. Ed was there, facing her. He reached out and held her hands. Stephanie said his name softly and began to cry. Ed hugged her tightly to comfort her.

"I'm sorry I didn't tell you this before. I didn't want to scare you, and I needed to dig up more information about him before I could be sure there was a connection between our crimes and the Ripper murders," he whispered.

Stephanie shook in his arms, very upset over seeing the graphic crime scene photographs of the Ripper's victims. As she calmed herself, she looked into Ed's eyes. "You really think Nathan Malcolm is somehow connected to Jack the Ripper?" she asked softly.

"Yes, I do," Ed replied.

Stephanie asked him to explain it to her. She needed to understand why Ed thought there was a possible connection with these crimes. Ed hugged her warmly again and looked up at the many photographs and written notes he had made on the Ripper murders. He whispered in her ear that he would explain it all to her in the morning. Ed closed the doors to the whiteboard and led her back to his bedroom.

Chapter 6

At 7:00 a.m., Ed and Stephanie were having coffee in the kitchen, and Ed had brought out some books and notes on Jack the Ripper. He explained it all to Stephanie, how even before they had known Nathan Malcolm was the serial killer, Ed had felt there was a connection between the Entity and the Ripper murders.

Ed showed her the crime scene photos of the five known Ripper victims and their names, and he told her how they were like Malcolm's first three victims. The five women Jack the Ripper had killed were prostitutes. Stephanie read off their names, and Ed told her the dates of their murders and about how the last victim, Mary Jane Kelly, had been brutally mutilated from her face to her legs. He warned Stephanie that the crime scene photo was very graphic, but Stephanie prepared herself and looked at the horrific picture. Ed told her that he had read that the crime scene of this murder had shocked even the lead investigator from Scotland Yard, Frederick Abberline, and his investigators. Mary Kelly's remains had been scattered around on a bedside table, and her body had been laid out on her bed. Her face had been completely hacked off. Stephanie asked Ed which suspect he believed Nathan Malcolm was related to and who, besides Rob, he had told this theory of his. Had he told Rick?

Ed took out a book and a list of Ripper suspects to show her. "This book was written in the 1990s by two former British police officers who found an amazing letter written by Detective Chief Inspector

John George Littlechild of the Metropolitan Police Service, who at the time of the Ripper murders was the detective chief inspector of the case. He wrote a letter in 1913 to author and journalist George R. Sims detailing how an American-born doctor by the name of Francis Tumblety was one of their main suspects. The two authors wrote of how Tumblety traveled to Europe and England frequently to sell his self-made Indian herbal medicines and remedies that he made a fortune on."

Ed explained that Tumblety had been considered a quack doctor at the time and was never really identified to be a true doctor. He had married at a very young age and found out that his wife was a prostitute, which explained why he would have a lot of hatred toward them and women in general. Ed went on to explain that Tumblety was also considered a homosexual. He had been arrested during the time of the Ripper murders for gross indecency with young men and released in time to commit the final murder of Mary Jane Kelly on November 9, 1888. He then fled to France and then by ship to America. Scotland Yard had sent two agents to New York to detain him and bring him back to England for questioning for his possible connections to the murders in Whitechapel, but they were unable to find him.

Ed showed Stephanie only the two known photographs of Dr. Francis Tumblety. He was stocky in appearance and had a very long mustache. Stephanie looked at the pictures and thought about everything Ed was filling her in on. She took a very long, deep breath and looked up at him.

"Look, Ed, you have done a lot of research here, and maybe those two former British police officers and the lead inspector at the time did indeed find this man, Dr. Tumblety, to be Jack the Ripper himself. But there was no DNA evidence back then, and there was no real evidence or even witnesses to tie any suspect they thought to be the Ripper. I studied the case for a while back in college, and I know the FBI even did a profile of the Ripper back in the eighties or nineties. Let me check with the head office in Washington D.C. and see if they can fax me anything they have from the profile match they did on him. And let's keep this between us for now and head to your office before we are late."

Ed told her okay, and they gathered all the notes and books together and headed out to Ed's SUV to drive to Central Division. As Ed was driving, Stephanie took out the crime scene photos of the women the Ripper had killed. Then she looked at one of the photos of Francis Tumblety. She thought, *What kind of an evil man could have done this to a human being?* She knew that even if Tumblety hadn't committed those murders, there was still a sense of evil in his photograph. He had an aurora about him of a man who had done evil things in his lifetime. Ed looked over at Stephanie and saw the upset expression on her face, but he didn't want to say a word about this until they got to his office.

They entered the building and met with Rob at his desk. Ed told him that he had told Stephanie all about the possible Jack the Ripper connection to these cases and suggested they now tell Rick and ask if they could formally investigate.

As they entered Rick's office, Ed said, "Hey, boss. The three of us have something to tell you, and then we need your permission to follow up on it."

Rick sat behind his desk, listening to what they had to tell him.

"I told Stephanie about my belief that these murders and the Malcolm murders are somehow related to the Jack the Ripper case way back when in England."

Rick stared at Ed long and hard and then at Rob and Stephanie. He knew if he let them investigate this angle, it could do more harm than good, not only for the task force but for the entire San Diego Department.

Ed told him that he had explained it all to Stephanie, and she could use the FBI's contacts in Washington to help them profile and even analyze the evidence they had to tie all the cases together.

Rick looked down at his own files of the murders. He knew they had brought Stephanie into this case to make headway. He looked back up at them and said, "Okay."

Ed and his partners smiled, pleased that he had given them permission.

"But look, we need to keep this between the four of us for now. Use the research office that is secured away from all the other cops in the building. I don't want this to get out and start a panic among cops and civilians at this point. Let me brief the others and have them follow up on the murders of the Youngs. You three work inside on this today." After Rick told them his orders, the trio headed to the office, which had two desktop computers, a fax machine, and an LCD projector to help them get started.

Rob and Ed set up the projector and posted the crime scene pictures on the whiteboard. Stephanie called the FBI office in Washington D.C. to ask them fax over everything they had on the Jack the Ripper case, along with the profile they had made of him years before. It took some time to get this all together and to them in California, so Ed began to brief Rob and Stephanie on the names of the Ripper victims and the dates they were killed. In order, they were Martha Tabram, Tuesday, August 7; Mary Ann Nichols, Friday, August 31; Annie Chapman, Saturday, September 8; Elizabeth Stride and Catherine Eddowes (both killed the same night, which was known as the double event), Sunday, September 30; and Mary Jane Kelly, Friday, November 9.

As Rob stared at the ghastly crime scene photo of Mary Jane Kelly, he felt the same way Stephanie had when she first saw it: horrified and shocked. Ed told them the women were all known prostitutes, but the police and Ripper experts couldn't say for certain if the first victim, Martha Tabram, had been a victim of the Ripper or a gang killing. She had been stabbed thirty-nine times, but she hadn't been slashed or mutilated like the other victims.

As Stephanie looked at their faces, she saw that the first five women had all been in their forties and not very attractive, except the last victim, Mary Jane Kelly, who had been only twenty-five years old. Stephanie looked at an artist's drawing of what Kelly would have looked like before her murder. Stephanie felt very bad for this young woman, who had been very pretty and hadn't deserved to die like that.

They were now an hour into the investigation. The fax machine beeped, and they started to receive the incoming faxes on the case. Rob took the faxes from the machine and handed them to Stephanie. She looked through them as Ed explained why he thought Francis Tumblety was the killer.

"He was living at a lodging house in the center of Whitechapel, 22 Batty Street, just a ten-minute walking distance from where all the victims were found. The police had this lodging house under surveillance, as they knew an American doctor was living there and one of the city's nearby museums had stated an American doctor was interested in buying preserved female wombs; he collected them in glass jars as a collection for himself," Ed described in detail from a book he'd read.

Rob nodded, thinking the Ripper likely lived a close distance from where the murders took place so he could commit a murder and escape back to his loft unseen. Ed taped a map of the Whitechapel district to the whiteboard and pegged all the crime scenes to show the short distance Dr. Tumblety would have to travel to from each block back to 22 Batty Street. Stephanie continued to read the FBI's profile on the Ripper as Ed continued to explain details that would no doubt tie Tumblety to the murders.

"So he collected and wanted female wombs and uteruses, and two of the victims had their wombs removed. What average killer would have known how to extract a person's organs if he did not in fact have medical and anatomical knowledge? And don't forget, there was no electricity back then. The street lights were gas lamps, and rooms were kept lit with candles and fireplaces. I bet my money that the Ripper have a satchel bag with him when he committed each murder, not only to carry his sharp knives but also to carry a bulls-eye lantern just like police constables carried with them to illuminate the surroundings just enough for him to see what he was doing in the dark nights and early mornings in the crowded areas of Whitechapel," Ed briefed them.

Rob believed everything Ed was saying. Stephanie was still reading the Ripper's FBI profile.

Ed looked at her and said her name loud to get her attention. "Stephanie! Are you going to say anything here, or are you just going to sit there with your legs crossed and keep reading what your so-called experts in Washington D.C. think?"

Stephanie sent him a long stare. She put down the papers and looked at the map of Whitechapel, which was detailed to 1888, the period in which the crimes happened. She told them what the FBI profiler believed to be the characteristics of Jack the Ripper.

"Ed, look. Lead FBI profiler John Douglas made this profile of the Ripper. Let me read to you some of the qualities he believed the Ripper had. A male of average height and weight, never married or maybe a very short marriage, a profound hatred for women. He was a loner with very little social contact. He was very familiar to the area of Whitechapel. Douglas believed he'd always lived there. He had the skill and profession of a butcher or mortician's assistant," Stephanie read aloud.

Ed agreed and disagreed with some of the profile's findings. "Well, I don't agree that a plain butcher or mortician's assistant would have the medical know-how to remove these kinds of organs from a female in the dark of night and very quickly. He would have had to carry a bag or some kind of box to place the organs in and then preserve them in jars, as Tumblety is said to have done. Did you read and compare the two letters that were said to have been written by the Ripper to the police? The "Dear Boss" and the "From Hell" letters? Both were signed *Jack the Ripper.*"

Ed handed Stephanie copies of both letters, and she prepared to read them aloud. She first let them know that there were many spelling and punctuation errors. Then she began to read:

Dear Boss,

I keep on hearing the police have caught me but they wont fix me just yet. I have laughed when they look so clever and talk about being on the right track. That joke about Leather Apron gave me real fits. I am down on whores and I shant quit ripping them till I do get buckled. Grand work the last job was. I gave the lady no time to squeal. How can they catch me now. I love my work and want to start again. You will soon hear of me with my funny little games. I saved some of the proper red stuff in a ginger beer bottle over the last job to write with but it went thick like glue and I can't use it. Red ink is fit enough I hope ha. ha. The next job I do I shall clip the ladys ears off and send to the police officers just for jolly wouldn't you. Keep this letter back till I do a bit more work, then give it out straight. My knife's so nice and sharp I want to get to work right away if I get a chance. Good Luck. Yours truly

Jack the Ripper

Dont mind me giving the trade name

PS Wasnt good enough to post this before I got all the red ink off my hands curse it No luck yet. They say I'm a doctor now. ha ha

"So he is denying he's a doctor in the letter. But, Ed, I myself have read and believe this letter was a forgery made by one of the local journalists who worked at one of the papers in London at the time. He did it just to draw attention and controversy to the case and sell papers. Even back then bad news and controversial stories that involved the royal monarchy were an open field day for tabloid papers, and it got the whole world talking," Stephanie said.

Rob agreed with her that most experts then and now believed the "Dear Boss" letter to be a fake. Ed agreed and then asked her to read the "From Hell" letter. Stephanie cleared her throat and made a face as she began to read. It letter was addressed and sent to George Lusk, the head of the Whitechapel Vigilance Committee at the time because he owned a small business in the area.

From hell

Mr Lusk

Sor

I send you half the Kidne I took from one women prasarved it for you tother piece I fried and ate it was very nise. I may send you the bloody knif that took it out if you only wate a whil longer

signed

Catch me when you Can Mishter Lusk

Stephanie again pointed out the errors in spelling and punctuation. Ed told them that this letter had been sent to Lusk in a box that contained half of a human kidney, and just around the time he had received it, one of the victims, Catherine Eddowes, had one of her kidneys removed. The letter was also covered in blood and was thought by some researchers to have been written in blood. Ed told them the two authors of the book that stated that Francis Tumblety was the Ripper had a handwriting expert compare the letter and copies of letters Tumblety had written. The expert had come to the conclusion that Tumblety did in fact write the "From Hell" letter to George Lusk.

Stephanie shook her head in amazement at what Ed was implying. "Fuck the movie with Johnny Depp! And the stupid theory that the royal physician Sir William Gull was Jack the Ripper. You convinced me, Ed. Francis Tumblety is the Ripper! I have no doubts about it!"

Rob also agreed with him. Stephanie looked into Ed's eyes as he waited to hear her opinion on what to do next.

"Ed, you make great points and so do these experts about Tumblety. But even if he is Jack the Ripper, what does he have to do with our cases now, besides the victims being mutilated? We have to find out if Dr. Nathan Malcolm is somehow related to him. Tell me everything you know about him up until his death, and then let me check with the head office in D.C. to see if we can find a link between him and Malcolm," Stephanie told him.

Ed smiled and then filled her in on everything he had found on Tumblety. "He might have been born in Ireland in 1833, but we know he was raised in Rochester in upstate New York. He was known to move around from state to state and to Europe, selling his Indian herb remedies and posing as a doctor. He was known to use many aliases and used Dr. Frank Townsend when he arrived in New York on December 3, just as Scotland Yard sent agents to New York to look for him and bring him back to London in connection with the murders. But he gave them the slip. Again he moved around America until he died of heart failure on May 28, 1903, in a hospital in St. Louis. It was reported that among the things he was found to have was a box containing two cheap brass rings identical to the ones that victim Annie Chapman was known to have been wearing the night she was murdered. They were found missing from her middle finger by the police when her body was discovered," Ed finished detailing everything.

Stephanie and Rob were busy taking notes when a knock came at the door. Rob went over and opened it. Rick came in and was amazed at all the paperwork, documents, and books they had compiled. He saw Stephanie wipe sweat from her forehead and the signs of exhaustion on her face. He looked at the clock on the wall and told them they had been locked in there for three hours. It was going on 4:00 p.m.

"Well, looks to me like you guys are really getting Stephanie involved in this opinion of Ed's. But I think you guys need to call it quits for today, and my advice to you all is to go out and celebrate with each other tonight," Rick suggested to them.

Stephanie agreed and admitted she was tired. Ed stated that they would stop and head home for the day. Rick told them to have a good night and that he would see them in the morning. As he closed the door and left, they started to clean up their notes and get their books together. Stephanie told them that before they left she would fax everything they had found on Francis Tumblety to Washington D.C. and ask for everything they had on Nathan Malcolm. She hoped that by this time tomorrow they could find links tying them together.

Rob smiled. He had a suggestion for them. "Hey, it's still early in the afternoon, and I think Stephanie needs a nap now. But Rick was right about celebrating. How about we all get together tonight at my house for dinner? My wife, the great Italian cook that she is, can make you two a nice home-cooked meal. What do you both say?" Rob asked.

Ed smiled and said it was up to Stephanie.

"That sounds very sweet, Rob. Ed and I will be more than happy to have dinner at your home. I am interested in meeting your lovely wife," she said.

Rob looked at his watch and suggested that they come to his house around 8:00 p.m.

Ed thanked him and said, "See you then."

Later that evening, as Ed got dressed in the bedroom, he used his lint brush to remove lint from his expensive black slacks. He then looked at himself in the mirror; he wore his tan button-down dress shirt and black tie. He thought, *Ed, you are one bad stud!* He laughed and then wondered what was taking Stephanie so long in the bathroom. It was going on 7:30 p.m., and he didn't want to be late for dinner at Rob's house. Then Ed remembered Kayla had taken her time getting ready too.

"It must be a female complex," Ed said to himself and then saw Stephanie standing behind him in the mirror.

He was floored by the way she was dressed and how beautiful she looked. She wore an elegant black spaghetti strap knee-length dress. Her hair was soft and wavy, and she had just some lipstick on her lips and blush on her cheeks. The two-hour nap she had taken when they got home seemed to have brought her back to life. She saw the smile on Ed's face, twirled for him, and asked what he thought of the dress.

"It's not the dress that's catching my eye right now. It's the very beautiful woman who is wearing it and who I love very much who has caught my eyes and heart."

Stephanie slowly walked over to him, and they shared a soft, passionate kiss. Ed gently brushed his hand across her face. Then he told her they needed to get going. Stephanie said she knew. After they kissed again, she whispered to Ed, "I love you too."

They arrived at Rob's house shortly after 8:00 p.m. Rob lived in the North Clairemont area. He and his wife, Antonella, were also dressed elegantly. Antonella took Stephanie on a small tour of the house, as Ed has been a guest of theirs many times before. Ed and Rob sat in the living room and shared a drink. Antonella told Stephanie that their daughter, Megan, was sound to sleep in her room as she took her around the two-level Spanish style home. Rob admitted to Ed that Stephanie was a very beautiful woman for an FBI profiler. Ed thanked his partner and said he was very blessed to have met her and have her in his life.

As the women came into the living room, Antonella announced that dinner was ready. She had prepared stuffed shells to start, and then she had made veal with vegetables and salad. As they sat in the dining room to enjoy dinner, Antonella asked Stephanie what she thought of San Diego and maybe moving there.

"Oh, I really love it here in San Diego. It has a more relaxed kind of lifestyle, very different than we have in Los Angeles. I would look into moving here after this case is over if a certain someone would like me to," she said and smiled at Ed, who reached over and held her hand and said he would be more than happy to have her here with him.

Antonella asked them how the investigation was going so far. Rob looked at Stephanie and Ed, his expression asking who should answer question.

Stephanie spoke up. "I feel the three of us, along with the other good detectives who make up the task force, are heading toward a big lead into the cases soon. But we don't know anything about this new suspect just yet," she said softly, knowing she could not mention anything about Jack the Ripper to Rob's wife. She added that no matter what, the case had brought her and Ed together.

Rob and his wife admitted they were happy that Ed had another woman in his life. As Ed kissed Stephanie on the cheek, Rob's home phone rang. When Rob got up to answer it, Stephanie told Antonella what a nice guy and great detective Ed was. "And besides, he is very handsome, just like Rob."

As Antonella thanked her for the nice comment about her husband, they overheard Rob talking on the phone. He told the caller that Ed and Stephanie were there at his house having dinner with him. They stared at each other, knowing something had happened. Rob hung up the phone and walked back to the table.

"What's wrong, Rob?" his wife asked.

He looked at Ed and said it had been Rick on the phone. "They found another body of a young female on the banks of the beach right near the Coronado Bridge, and she has been badly mutilated. Rick and the task force are on their way there now."

Ed took a deep breath, and he and Stephanie rose from their seats and got ready to go. Rob said he would drive them in his car. When they got to the door, they thanked Antonella for dinner, and she told them to be careful.

Rob drove on Route 75, over the San Diego Bay, and into Coronado. They saw the flashing lights of emergency service vehicles coming from the beach beneath the bridge. When Rob took the first off-ramp, police from Coronado stopped his vehicle, but Ed and Rob showed them their badges, and the vehicle was cleared to move on. Ed looked down at Stephanie's feet and told her the sandy and stone-riddled beach would ruin her nice black heels. The car came to a stop. Stephanie made a face at Ed and told him not to open the door just yet. She kicked off her heels and left them in car. She then crossed her legs and pushed her dress up to her thighs. Ed stared at her amazing legs. Rob also had his eyes glued to the rearview mirror. They watched as she slid her thigh-high stockings down both legs and set them next to her shoes on the floor.

She smiled and said, "We can go see what this is all about now."

Ed smiled back at her. Rob grinned as they exited the car.

Ed and Rob saw Rick talking with the task force team. Stephanie walked gingerly over the sharp rocks and sand, and a male uniformed officer took her hand and helped her peer at the body more closely. She bent down to look at the fatal wound—a single slash across the throat. There was also a major gash in the victim's head and heavy bruising on one side of her body, one of the forensic team members told her. The victim's breasts had been removed and were found with her. The body was encased in a large clear plastic bag that was very bloody. Stephanie looked up at the bridge and then down at the body. She used the forensic team member's flashlight to look at the gash and bruising on the right side of the victim's head.

Stephanie stated to the forensic team, "The murder happened somewhere else, and then the body was flung from the bridge above. That's why there are no tire impressions in the sand."

Just as Stephanie finished speaking, they heard a woman screaming. The team looked up as a woman tried to make her way to the body. Rick stepped forward and caught her in his arms. The woman started to cry, and Rick hugged her. He then called for Julie O'Keefe, to come and help comfort the mother of the victim. As Ed looked on, he felt the pain this poor woman was going through as she found out that her daughter had been murdered. Rick called the task force together around the body. Ed held Stephanie's hand as Rick began to brief them about the victim.

"This young lady's name was Jackie Mays. Twenty-six years old, she worked at the nearby Hotel Del Coronado as a waitress at one of the hotel's restaurants. Her purse was found inside the large plastic bag that contained the body. We found her identification and traced it back to her home address. That is why her mother is here now; she lived with her."

A feeling of sorrow drifted over the entire team at having to deal with another young life that had been taken away for no reason.

"Besides the body being thrown from the bridge, are there any other signals for us to go on here?" Detective Ken Rogers asked Rick, and Rick went over the mutilation wounds, which had been made with a sharp knife to the throat. Rick then asked Stephanie what information she had gathered from examining the body closely.

"We know she worked at the hotel. I say the killer was probably driving a cargo van or minivan. As he watched her arrive in the parking lot, he must have parked right next to it. When she left work, he slowly opened the door to his vehicle, clamped his hand over her mouth, and pulled her inside. He probably already had this plastic bag laid out inside his vehicle for her, and he slit her throat and then cut off her breasts. Her fingernails were not removed like the other victims. He did this so fast that this young woman didn't have a chance to fight him off." As Stephanie finished her statement angrily, she looked at the very pretty face of Jackie Mays.

"So did any surveillance cameras catch anything in the parking lot, or are there witnesses?" Detective Skip Jones asked Rick.

Rick replied that the Coronado Police had checked the hotel's security cameras. As the cameras roved and panned around, they hadn't caught the incident as it happened. As there was only one witness, another female employee who heard a female scream and then a vehicle driving off into the distance a few seconds later. But she didn't see what kind of vehicle it was or anything else at the time.

"He stalked her. He had to be a patron of the restaurant or even a guest at the hotel for him to know where she worked, what time she got off work, and where her vehicle would be parked in the employee parking lot," Stephanie told them.

Rick was once again helpless, with few leads and witnesses to go on. He said he hoped forensics and Dr. Adams would find something, but if the killer had been methodical again and used sterile clothing and gloves, it was likely that very little forensic evidence would be found. As they watched the body of the young woman being placed into a body bag and then into the county coroner's van, Rick told his team to gather back at Central Division very early in the morning. They wouldn't find anything else out tonight. Everyone said their goodnights, and the trio headed to Rob's car.

Ed held Stephanie's hand, and he heard her crying softly. "Are you all right?" he asked.

"No, I'm not. Let's just go right home. Please, Ed?" Stephanie asked, and Ed told her yes.

When they arrived back home, Stephanie went right into the bedroom and closed the door to change. Ed went into his office and made another entry into his file titled *Entity Murders*. He added this latest woman's name and age to his records and then heard the kettle whistling in the kitchen, and he knew Stephanie was making herself either tea or coffee. Ed finished up and planned to join her. After he logged off his computer and turned off the office light, he went into the living room, where he saw Stephanie sitting on the sofa, her knees pulled to her chest and her hands clutching a cup of hot tea. Ed sat with her on the couch and held one of her hands softly.

"Too late for coffee?" he asked.

Stephanie broke into a slight smile and just said tea helped calm her down. Ed asked if she was all right.

"Ed, when I bent down and saw the look on that poor girl's face, it wasn't only that she was too young and didn't deserve this that struck me. But thinking of her mother happily expecting to see her daughter come home after a night at work and then being called to a crime scene to find out her daughter was murdered by some creep . . . This one really hit me hard, unlike the other victims. This girl was innocent and for the most part lived a good life. I don't know if I want to continue on in this case any longer. I'm scared now for some reason. I have never been scared before, not in any of the cases I have worked. And I see your anger every time we are called to a new crime scene. You not only want to catch this guy; you want to kill him yourself. Don't you, Ed?" Stephanie questioned.

Ed knew he couldn't lie to her or try to word his answer in any other fashion but the truth. "You're right. I want to kill him myself for what he has done. And I know he is going to come after me soon. That's why I'm going to ask you to tell Rick and Chief Chase that you want to be released from this case in the morning. Please, Stephanie. I don't want you to be harmed in any way because of me. You know I love you. I couldn't live with myself if something happened to you now."

Stephanie started to cry and rested her head against Ed's chest. He held her warmly.

"I care for you so much, and I know if I asked you to resign from this case, you wouldn't. And if I resign from the case and go back to LA, I don't know if I'll ever see you alive again. So I want to stay here with you and just strive on together so that we can catch this son of a bitch!" Stephanie shouted with anger in her voice.

Ed felt her spirit driving hard, wanting to catch the Entity and be with Ed. They kissed softly, and Stephanie started to undo the buttons on Ed's shirt. Ed did the same to her top and then glided his fingers down her soft bare back. They slid gently to the carpeted floor.

The next day, Rick gathered the task force in the conference room. They were just waiting for Ed, Rob, and Stephanie to join them, but Rick had already had other plans for the three of them. When they came through the door, they greeted everyone and took their seats. Rick was going to be very fast now in handing out assignments in the new murder of Jackie Mays.

"So I got a call this morning from the Coronado police detective who is handling the case of Jackie Mays. It seems a white cargo van was seen driving away from the hotel around 10:15 p.m. last night by at least four witnesses. Ken and Jack, I want you to go interview the witnesses, go back to the hotel and crime scene, get everything you can about a possible make and model, and see if you can tie it to the crime. Also see if maybe the hotel had any outside contractors that would need a van like that to be on-site last night.

"Julie and Skip, I want you two to go interview this girl's mother again, along with her friends and co-workers. See if she mentioned to them anything about a possible ex-boyfriend, a co-worker she maybe complained about, or maybe a person she felt was following her. We need to try to find something. I myself am now getting involved here. My wife and I are going to go over the DNA evidence of all the victims, and I will talk with Dr. Diana Farrell, who did the autopsy on Nathan Malcolm. She may provide some answers as to why we have so little forensics to go on here."

Rick then told them to get a move on. As the others left, Ed and his partners looked at Rick, wondering what he wanted them to do this morning. After waiting for the others to leave, Rick produced a large folder of paperwork, and judging by the serious look in his eyes, he was about to explain what it was all about.

"Just about an hour ago, the FBI office in D.C. faxed all this over here, but it was for Stephanie only. I didn't look at it and made certain no one else here looked at it in order to keep your side of the investigation quiet for now. I will leave you guys alone and suggest you work in the same secured office again. I'm going to go meet with Cate now. You can reach me on my cell phone if something turns up," Rick told them and handed the folder to Stephanie.

She looked through it quickly and saw something that caught her eye. She smiled at Rick and thanked him and then told Ed and Rob to hurry into the secured office. They made their way to the office, and Ed locked the door behind them. As Rob turned on the computers, Ed asked Stephanie what she had found that stood out.

"Listen to this. Dr. Francis Tumblety, who was married but is not known to have had any children of his own, had up to eleven siblings, some of whom in turn got married and had families of their own. Like Francis Tumblety, they moved away from Rochester, New York, and settled down around the country. One of the last few surviving relatives of Francis Tumblety was a younger brother named Jessup Tumblety, who was married and had children. He lived in the small town of Marion, Iowa. In 1903 he was contacted by the hospital in St. Louis where Francis Tumblety passed away. Jessup Tumblety ventured to the hospital and claimed his brother's body and had it taken to Rochester, New York, for burial in the family's plot. He then took possession of the belongings Francis Tumblety had with him when he passed away and from a small house he had been staying at, at the time of his passing," Stephanie read from a document the FBI investigative team had found.

Ed shrugged and asked her, "What is so significant about that to this case now?"

Stephanie smiled and answered, "Soon after Francis Tumblety's burial in Rochester, New York, in 1903, Jessup Tumblety returned to Marion, Iowa, and legally changed the family's last name from Tumblety to Malcolm."

Ed and Rob raised their eyebrows and looked at one another.

"So his brother Jessup must have found something that belonged to Francis that would not only have caused him to change his family's name but that would also prove that Francis was Jack the Ripper," Ed said with heated eyes, knowing now that they were on to something that could finally tie Francis Tumblety to Jack the Ripper.

"We may need to go to Marion, Iowa, to search for any family records of the Malcolms and see if there is any known next of kin still living there," Rob suggested to them, and Stephanie agreed. She looked at Ed to see what he wanted to do, being that he was the lead detective on the case.

"Rob, Stephanie and I will head to Marion, Iowa, to check this all out. You team up with Rick and work on any leads that come up in the Mays girl's death. Stephanie and I need to go home and pack; we have a plane to catch to good old Iowa."

Stephanie smiled and said she was ready to see the good old heartland of America.

Rick and his wife, Dr. Cate Adams, met with Dr. Diana Farrell. She had agreed to show him all the findings from the autopsy she performed the day after Nathan Malcolm died in a house fire four years ago. As Cate and Diana talked, Rick intently read the cause of death and the areas of the body that had been outlined in Dr. Farrell's report. She was in her late thirties and a very educated and accomplished biologist and criminologist forensic scientist. She held degrees from MIT University and Duke University School of Medicine. Cate had praised her work to Rick on a few occasions, and law enforcement agencies around the country consulted Dr. Farrell to work with them on complex cases.

Dr. Farrell, like Stephanie, had been an accomplished college athlete in swimming and track. She still jogged up to two miles every morning and did yoga and weight-lifting routines. She even had a picture in her office of her completing a long distance marathon held recently in San Diego. She was about five foot five with shoulder-length blond hair and crisp hazel eyes. Rick found her very attractive but knew to keep his eyes glued to work in the presence of his beautiful wife.

He then questioned Dr. Farrell, "Diana, you state here in the autopsy that Malcolm died as a result of the massive burns he sustained in the fire, as well as smoke inhalation. Were there any other sufficient injuries he could have sustained when he had that violent encounter with Detective Ed Brooks right before the fire overtook the house?" Rick asked her.

She looked at the autopsy results and answered him, "As I can recall, the body was so badly burned and charred that if there had been any open wounds or even broken bones, I wouldn't have been able to see them on him. The smell of burnt flesh was so hideous that Cate and I couldn't even get close enough to the body to take the forensic photographs. As you see in the report, his flesh and hair were badly singed. He even had several teeth that had decayed and fallen out of the gum line because the fire had destroyed the flesh and bone to the point that not even basic cells could live."

Rick looked at another photograph of the body. The intense heat had even caused Malcolm's eyeballs to melt out of their sockets.

"Rick, don't forget that he was using alcohol as an accelerant to start the blaze, and the gas leak exploded, adding to the tremendous heat. It would have taken a huge toll on human flesh, which is very fragile to begin with," Cate added, and Diana nodded.

"He may have a child from his previous marriage, but we were unable to confirm that, and his ex-wife passed away in 1988 as a result of Alzheimer's disease. No next of kin claimed the body, so the judge ordered it to be cremated once you signed off on the final results of the autopsy, right?" Rick asked Diana.

"Correct," she told him.

"May I take the autopsy report? I feel it might help us in our investigations into these recent murders," Rick asked Diana.

She told him of course, but she didn't know how it would help them now. She then asked Dr. Adams if she had made any progress with the most recent body. Cate told her not so far, but she hadn't completed the autopsy just yet. Diana offered to help her if she would like the assistance.

"Sure, that would be great. A second pair of eyes to help me from the great Dr. Farrell," Cate praised her counterpart, and they agreed to work on the autopsy together.

Rick then received a call from Ed, who informed his boss of what they had found. Rick walked to the side of the room to be away from the women, not wanting them to hear his very confidential call.

"Ed, this is great news you and Stephanie have found. Dr. Farrell is going to assist Cate with the autopsy on Jackie Mays. I'm sure they will find a mistake this killer has made in his crimes. In the meantime, Rob and I will go over Nathan Malcolm's known contacts with a fine-tooth comb while you're in Iowa with Stephanie."

Ed told Rick that he and Stephanie would book a flight to leave for Iowa that evening. Rick said he would will meet up with Rob, as he was about to leave with Cate and Dr. Farrell. He rejoined the two doctors, and Cate agreed to have Dr. Farrell drive her back to the county coroner's facility to begin work on the autopsy.

As the three of them headed to the parking lot, eyes from afar watched as Rick got into his car, waved good-bye to his wife, and drove off. Cate got into Diana's Lincoln SUV, and they drove off together. The watcher started up his vehicle and decided to follow the women to try to find out what they were working on together.

A little while later, the two doctors changed into their scrubs and sterile attire and began the slow and very detailed autopsy of Jackie Mays. Cate filled Dr. Farrell in on the details of the murder. Jackie had been pulled inside a white cargo van, and the killer had slit her throat and then removed her breasts. Her fingernails had not been removed like with the other victims. As Dr. Farrell listened to Cate talk, she directed a beam of sharp blue florescent light on the body in the dark as the lab. The bright light would reveal spots of blood invisible to the naked eye.

Dr. Farrell spotted something in one of the victim's right fingernails as the light showed a spot they had not seen before. Cate asked her if it was blood, but Dr. Farrell answered that it didn't appear to be. She used a pair of metal tweezers to grasp the unknown material from underneath the victim's right index fingernail. Diana held the light very close to the material and said it was a piece of carpeting, possibly from inside the cargo van. Diana went over the entire body again twice with the blue light, but she did not see any other unknown evidence and asked Cate to turn the lights back on.

"It looks like a piece of light gray carpeting that is used to line the floor and inside wall panels of vans. Jackie must have torn a piece of the side panel off when the killer forced her into the van," she suggested to Cate, who was astonished by this find.

"So the killer possibly rented a cargo van that now has physical damage to it. If he didn't know about it before he returned it to the rental company, Rick and his team have an opportunity to track down the person who rented it!" Cate said, and Diana told her to call him quickly to inform him of this finding.

As Cate and Diana performed the autopsy on the Entity's latest victim, Rick and Rob went over Nathan Malcolm's personal records. They read Malcolm's medical background and the history of the schools he had attended. He had graduated from UCSF medical school of California in 1982 at the age of twenty-eight. He had divorced his wife, Jane Malcolm, in 1984, just two years later. There was a mention of a child in his personal records, but no records declared his child's whereabouts after 1984.

Rob commented to Rick, "He was born in Marion, Iowa, and he then came to San Francisco to attend school in the 1970s. So he settled out here and married his wife in 1978, and she was from San Diego. It doesn't tell us if they met in medical school, but we can assume that. Then she passed away from a rare form of familial Alzheimer disease. 'A person between the ages of thirty and sixty can be diagnosed with this rare form of Alzheimer's," Rob read.

Suddenly, Rick's cell phone rang; it was Cate wanting to tell him about evidence they had found. Rick informed her that they would come right over. He told Rob of their find, and the two men hurried to meet them at the county coroner's facility.

The watcher saw the headlights approach his location in the dark parking lot. It was now 10:00 p.m. He saw the two policemen get out of their car quickly and go through the secured double doors of the main entrance as the security guard buzzed them through. The watcher knew they were cops because he knew the taller one was Ed Brook's partner. He concluded that the two doctors had to have come up evidence for them to still be working this late into the night. He knew he had to get it away from them somehow, and now. He needed to stop watching and become the Entity.

He paused and waited for a moment. He needed to come up with a silent and stealthy way of getting into the facility, which had security at the main entrance. He looked at the back loading dock and saw a surveillance monitor pointed toward the incoming traffic lane. He knew this would be his way into the complex. His black mask and hooded long black coat would hide him from the camera.

He had his tools in his pocket, and as he looked around the area, he didn't see a soul. He made his way slowly to the back door, which was secured. It needed an employee access badge to open the door. The Entity took from his pocked a very thin piece of metal and placed it between the door latch and its lock. He then took out a fake identification badge that he had modified with a magnetized access swipe, and he swiped it against the square panel on the wall. The latch unlocked itself. He slid the metal strip between the latch and the lock to keep the door open. Then he made his way upstairs to the second floor, where the lights were still on in the three-story building.

"Hey, guys. Look at what Diana found," Cate told Rick and Rob as they showed them the piece of material found under the victim's fingernail.

Diana explained what it was and how they had found it. Rick told Rob they could now check out white cargo vans with light gray interiors that had been recently damaged. Suddenly they heard the sound of glass shattering from the outside hallway. They all look up at once. Rob told them he would go and see what the noise was. He walked out of the lab and turned right down the hallway. He didn't see anything at first, but at the end of the corridor, he spotted the outside light reflecting from the floor. He knew the large glass window had been shattered, and he walked over to investigate what had caused it to break.

Inside the lab, Rick, Cate, and Diana had an eerie feeling; something didn't feel right. Rick called out to Rob, and Cate softly asked if they heard a noise coming from inside the room. All of a sudden the lab lights went out, and the room fell into darkness. Rick told the women to get behind him and took his gun out of his side holster. Diana grabbed the blue light from the table next to her and turned the beam on. She flashed it to her left and then to her right and then in front of her, illuminating the bright face of a masked, hooded figure. The Entity hit the light from her hand and then slashed Diana across her left forearm with a sharp knife. She screamed in pain and fell to the floor. Rick pushed his wife to the floor and started to shoot in the Entity's direction.

As Rick screamed at the women to stay on the floor, he cautiously looked for the light on the wall. He was hit hard from behind. Rick discharged a shot and then dropped his gun. The Entity kicked Rick in the back while he was on the floor. The Entity hadn't found anything useful here. As he started to run down the hallway, Rob was running full speed in his direction. The two men collided. The impact threw Rob off his feet. The Entity staggered and hit the wall to his left, but he was able to regain his balance and kicked Rob hard in his chest. He sprinted down the corridor as Cate turned the lights on.

She saw Dr. Farrell crying in pain and blood running out of the open wound on her left arm. Rick got to his feet and ran out into the hallway, where he found Rob struggling to get up. They again heard the sound of glass breaking. Rick ran down the hallway as the building's security team was coming up the stairwell. The men began to look around the rooms on that floor, and they heard the sound of a vehicle driving out of the parking lot at high speed. Rick took a deep breath and ordered one of the guards to call the police right away. Rob came running toward him, blood trickling from his mouth. The two policemen returned to the lab just as Cate was securing a sterile dressing on Diana's arm. The security guard informed them that he had called for an ambulance as well.

Rick reholstered his sidearm, and Rob cleaned his own face with tissues. They looked around to see if anything had been taken. Cate informed them that the piece of gray material was still in its plastic container on the table. Rick wondered why the killer taken such a risk to accomplish nothing except expose himself to the police and possibly getting killed or apprehended. Rick leaned on the table to regain his composure from all the excitement. After running through the scenario in his head, he went over and hugged his wife and asked Dr. Farrell if she was all right.

"I'm fine, thank you. But I am very scared now. He knows who we are, and he could be watching us at this very moment," she told them.

Rob told her to relax and applied pressure to the knife wound to try to stop the bleeding. Just then they heard the sounds of sirens approaching.

Rick talked to the uniformed officers taking the report, and Rob huddled with the task force, telling them what had happened. The laceration on Dr. Farrell's left forearm required stitches, so Rick's wife accompanied her with a police escort to the hospital. The fellow detectives asked Rob if he or Rick could give a description of the assailant.

Rob just told them, "The guy was tall, strong as hell, and dressed in black. None of us could make out anything about him when he shut the lights off. But when I ran into him head-on in the hallway, I could tell he was wearing some kind of jacket made from the nylon material." Rob then briefed them on all he could remember, and the team took notes.

Rick came over to them. "Well, I just talked to the forensic team here. I took four shots at the suspect in the dark here in the lab. Two shots hit the far wall and are still lodged there. My other two shots hit the medicine cabinet over there, shattering the glass and breaking some expensive medical stuff that will have to be replaced. I just called Cate at the hospital; she said Dr. Farrell received sixteen stiches to her injured forearm, and she is a bit shaken up. She will be staying with some relatives of hers for the night," Rick explained and added that they didn't know what the Entity had been looking for, as the only find the two doctors made was the small piece of carpeting fiber stuck underneath the girl's fingernail.

"Look, guys, I know it's late, but we have to get a move on this lead now. All of you are going to call every rental agency around western San Diego and find out who they rented a white cargo van with light gray carpeting to within the last three or four days and if it was returned with any damage to its right panel. Let's move on this, people!" Rick shouted.

The team went to make phone calls and research all they could find on the computer at 11:30 p.m.

"Do you think they will find out anything by morning?" Rob asked Rick, and Rick replied that if the rental companies still had the name of the person who rented the van in their system, they could track him down easily because car rental agencies only accepted credit cards as payment. So they could track him down that way, even if he used a stolen credit card.

"Just like the CSI shows," Rob told his boss.

Rick smiled and took out his cell phone. He told Rob he was going to call Ed and tell him what happened. Rob stated that he and Stephanie might be sleeping.

Rick looked up at Rob and said, "Believe me, Ed and his new lady friend are not sleeping right now."

Ed and Stephanie had checked into the Days Inn of Marion, Iowa, around 9:35 p.m. central time. When they went out for dinner, they had noted where the town library and town hall were located so they could begin their search of the Tumblety and Malcolm family history early the next day.

Now the television was on very softly in their room. Ed was on top of Stephanie as they made passionate love. Ed's cell phone suddenly began to ring. When he looked up at it on the side table, Stephanie tried to pull his attention back to her.

"Ed, don't answer it just yet. Let it go to voice mail first. Come on now," she said softly, and they kissed deeply.

Ed reached over, brought his phone to his left ear, and said, "Hello?"

Stephanie made a face and closed her eyes, disappointed that they were being disturbed at that very moment. Ed's demeanor became very serious, and Stephanie heard him ask Rick if he was all right. She sat up next to him on the bed and covered herself with her pajama top. Ed told Rick thank goodness none of them had been hurt and that he and Stephanie would try to finish up their investigation in Marion in one day and be back in San Diego late tomorrow night. After hanging up, Ed looked over at Stephanie and told her what had happened with the team.

Stephanie looked sadly into Ed's eyes as a somber feeling overtook her. "Ed, this person—no matter who he is—wants to kill your friends now. I'm surprised he didn't kill Rick or Rob or even one forensic doctors. I have a feeling he knows we are here, and he will strike at you or me when the timing is right for him," she said softly.

Ed touched her face with his right hand. "Hey, I told you I'm not going to let anything happen to you or anyone on my team. Got it? So we finish up here early tomorrow and get back to San Diego. I want to teach you a few things when we get home, all right?" Ed told her.

Stephanie smiled at him and said, "Okay."

They kissed gently, and Ed shut off the LCD television with the remote and told her they needed to get some sleep now. They lay back in the bed together. Stephanie rested her head on Ed's strong chest and felt very safe with him. Ed shuts off the lights and held her in his arms, praying to God to help him keep his word and make sure he could keep Stephanie and his friends safe from harm.

It was now just past midnight California time. Charles Neast and his wife, Kayla, were relaxing at home in their large bedroom, just about to get ready for bed. John was lying in bed, watching the late news on their large LCD television. Kayla walked into the bedroom from the bathroom, holding a jar of Ponds cold cream. She wore lingerie under her short silver silk robe, and she sat on the edge of the bed. Charles leaned over and kissed her on the back of the neck gently. Kayla kissed his lips and then crossed her legs and started to apply the cold cream to sooth her freshly shaved skin. Charles was flirting with the idea that they should have sex, but Kayla told him no. She needed to be at school early tomorrow for a teacher's conference, whereas Charles could get to work whenever he wanted because he was one of the head lawyers in his firm.

They heard their dog, Shadow, repeatedly barking from the backyard, where he was chained next to his doghouse. Kayla asked her husband what he was barking at.

"I don't know. German Shepherds don't usually bark unless there is a reason. Let me go find out what's wrong with him. I might have to bring him inside for the rest of the night if it's going to keep him quiet."

"Just do whatever it takes, Chuck. We don't want the neighbors complaining about our dog now," Kayla told her husband.

Charles put on his long plain bathrobe over his pajamas and headed downstairs toward the back door, which led to the backyard. After Kayla finished applying the cream to her left leg, she crossed her legs the other way and started to spread the cream up her ankle to her inner thigh. As she massaged it in deeply, she gloried in the thought of how good it felt. Suddenly she heard Shadow yelp and then begin to howl. Kayla looked up and wondered what was taking Chuck so long. Then she felt a hand on her shoulder.

"What took you so long? And what was wrong with the dog?" she questioned.

"So pretty you are, Mrs. Brooks," the voice from behind her said.

Kayla, stunned by the unfamiliar soft, raspy voice, started to turn her head to see who the intruder was, but the hand shoved her down onto the bed forcefully. Kayla was about to scream, but the gloved hand covered her mouth. The intruder, who was dressed in all black, made a soft *shhh* sound, encouraging her to be quiet. Kayla relaxed a little bit, hoping that if she did what he wanted, he would not harm her.

The Entity began to talk to her very softly. "It's a shame, Kayla Brooks. You are so pretty indeed. Too bad that because of your ex-husband you have to die now, just like your present husband did."

As Kayla tried to scream beneath his gloved hand, he slit her throat very quickly and then again from the opposite direction. Blood gushed all over her neck and onto the bed. Kayla coughed and gasped for air as she took her last breath and closed her eyes. Her head fell to the side. The killer kept his hand over her mouth a few seconds longer to make certain she was dead.

He would not mutilate this body, but he would leave Ed Brooks a very different calling card instead. He dipped his gloved finger into her blood and wrote a message on the large mirror on the wall: *Just for you, Ed Brooks. We will meet again soon, my friend.*

He quickly ran down the stairs and out the back door, passing over the dead body of Charles Neast. Shadow started to bark again very loudly as the Entity jumped over the back wall and disappeared into the night. Shadow fought hard, pulling and tugging on the chain. He finally broke free and ran into the house. He stopped and licked Charles's face and barked again, but he got no response from his master. He then ran up the stairs and into the master bedroom, jumped on the bed, and licked Kayla's face. His long, wet tongue smeared her blood. He then began to cry and howl, knowing his masters were dead.

The couple who lived next door to the Neasts heard Shadow continuing to bark and howl. Bruce Feldman sat up in bed and told his wife this was annoying him now. They turned on the light. His wife asked him what he wanted to do. He picked up the phone and dialed 911. He told his wife he was calling the police to look into a noise complaint at the Neasts' home, as well as a motorcycle driving around their quiet neighborhood very fast at this time of night. When Mr. Feldman finished talking to the dispatch officer on the phone, he thanked him for his cooperation and then hung up. He told his wife that the police were sending a squad car to the Neasts' house to see what the problem was. He then shut off the light, covered his head with his pillow, and went back to sleep.

Chapter 7

E d instructed Stephanie not to unpack their two suitcases because he wanted to be ready immediately when they were done in Marion. They had a quick breakfast together at a local diner and then took a taxi over to the Marion Library. Once Ed and Stephanie proved to the librarian that they were law enforcement officers investigating the Entity murders in San Diego, she gave them access to all films from 1903 to present day regarding anything about the Tumblety and Malcolm family histories in the town of Marion.

When Ed and Stephanie received the discs that had been recently converted from film strips, they sat at a desktop computer together and started to view the earliest disc from 1903. Stephanie read quickly, making notes on her notepad about the local paper from July 1903.

She read aloud softly to Ed, "Local farmer Jessup Tumblety changed his family's last name to Malcolm today, just two months after he saw to the burial of his older brother Francis Tumblety in the family's plot in Rochester's Holy Sepulchre Cemetery on May 1903. No reason was ever given for why Jessup Tumblety changed the family name. His only son, Jessup Malcolm Jr., remained in the town of Marion. He then married and stayed at the family ranch along with his wife and two young sons, Nathan and Peter," Stephanie finished reading.

Ed told her to hurry as he took that disc out of the computer and put in a disc titled "Marion town history, September 1962." Stephanie began to read the third disc of the three that the librarian had given to them.

"On September 4, 1962, tragedy struck the small family of Jessup Malcolm Jr. His youngest son, Peter, drowned after falling into the farm's thirty-foot well while playing with his older brother, Nathan. Tragedy had hit the family two years earlier in 1960 when Marjorie Malcolm had succumbed to cancer at age forty-seven."

That was all the entire disc contained on the family, so they put in the last and most recent disc and read a news article from 2008, four years ago. The article described in detail about how former childhood resident Dr. Nathan Malcolm had been named in the Quasar Pharmaceutical scandal and was killed during the San Diego police investigation into the Entity murders of three prostitutes. Stephanie read the Ed the dates and names of the victims they already had in their files back in San Diego.

"So except Jessup changing the family name two months after he buried his brother Francis back home in Rochester, New York, we still don't have anything here to officially tell us why he did that," Ed told Stephanie, and she agreed.

They returned the discs to the librarian. They were ready to go to the town hall for more information, but before they left, Stephanie asked the elderly lady where they could find some good information about Marion residents from the early to mid-twentieth century. The old lady smiled and advised them to seek information from the caretaker of the town's historic museum, Joel Quinn. She told them he would be more than happy to help them. Ed and Stephanie thanked her and called another taxi to take them from the library to the historic museum.

Rick received a call early that morning telling him to notify his task force and his wife of a murder that had occurred the night before. As they assembled at the home of lawyer Charles Neast, they found out he was married to Ed's ex-wife, Kayla. There was no doubt about it now; the killer had done it as an act of retribution against Ed Brooks. Rob and Rick spoke softly to Dr. Adams away from the others, again questioning her autopsy on Nathan Malcolm four years ago.

"Rick, as God as my witness—along with dental records and a conformation of DNA analysis done by Dr. Farrell—unless Nathan Malcolm rose from the dead, had new skin form over his entire body, and got a new pair of eyeballs, that man was diseased when Diana and I did the autopsy on him. As for the new victims, I told you the knife wounds and slashes are in different and in more sporadic patterns than the wounds Malcolm inflicted on his victims," Cate yelled angrily at Rick and Rob for questioning her autopsy.

Rob rolled his eyes. "So then the only other possible motive we have here is either a close friend or relative of Nathan Malcolm who not only is committing these new murders but has now targeted Ed and his family. Stephanie may be in danger too," Rob said, and Rick nodded.

"We have the team and forensics doing their work here. I will call Ed now and tell him to come directly to headquarters along with Stephanie as soon as they get back to San Diego. Chief Chase and I will tell him about Kayla and her husband. We will place them in guarded protection around the clock and move them to an unknown and secure location for their safety," Rick informed Rob and then took out his cell phone and called Ed in Iowa.

Ed finished his conversation with Rick on his cell phone, and Stephanie asked him who had called.

"That was Rick. He wants us to go to directly to Central Division as soon as we get back tonight, no matter how late it is. Another murder happened late last night, and he wants to fill us in right away," Ed told her as they walked into the town's small museum.

Stephanie saw an elderly man cleaning a glass showcase that contained some historic items and books detailing the town's past. She asked him if he was Mr. Quinn, and he politely said he was. Ed asked if he had any knowledge of Jessup Malcolm and the name Tumblety as it pertained to their history there in Marion, Iowa. Mr. Quinn saw the serious looks on their faces, and they told him that they were law enforcement officers. He smiled and said he would help as much as he could. He told them to sit down at the small square table in the middle of the museum. Then he took an old book from one of the bookshelves and sat with them.

"I do stay up late at night and watch cable news, and I hear you have a new series of murders in San Diego now. So may I ask if it has to do with that fellow, Nathan Malcolm, from four years ago?" Quinn questioned.

Ed responded that they knew Nathan Malcolm was deceased but that they wondered if there could be other family members related to him who also knew of certain family relatives and secrets of Jessup Tumblety. Quinn opened the old book and read from one page; the book was a scrapbook of very old articles about events that had taken place in Marion long ago. He then began to explain the change of the Tumblety's family name to Malcolm in 1903.

"Toward the end of his retirement from town hall, where he worked as the county clerk, my grandfather retold the story of Jessup Tumblety coming back from his brother's funeral in Rochester that year. My father told me the story and said Jessup showed up at the town hall requesting documents to change their name from Tumblety to Malcolm. He also brought back with him certain items in an old box that had belonged to his brother. My grandfather questioned Jessup about changing his last name, and Jessup showed him the box and said all the proof he needed was inside and that he needed to rid his family of the evil atrocities his brother Francis had committed when he was alive. Jessup did not want to his children and their future children to be outcasts because of whatever Francis had done. So he filed to the courts in Des Moines to have their last name changed, and the courts granted his wish because Jessup and his family were regarded as a good church-going, hardworking family." After Quinn told them the story he had been told by his father, he then showed them the article that mentioned the antique box.

"Jessup returned from Rochester with a Calamander wood box, which was locked. Its contents had belonged to Francis Tumblety. I am certain that whoever that box was passed down to knows what it contains and the answers to your questions, Detective Brooks," Quinn told him.

Ed looked at Stephanie, and she nodded.

"So Jessup Tumblety knew the truth about his brother, and being a good person and Christian, he distanced himself and his family from what he found out about his brother?" Stephanie asked.

"Correct," Quinn said.

"Now we have to find out what that box contained—a journal, a map, or maybe a news article about what we think he did," Ed said.

"If I may ask, what is still so important now that can tie Francis Tumblety and his great nephew to his crimes and the recent crimes in your city, Detective Brooks?" Joel Quinn asked, wanting to know the answer to the century-old mystery his family had kept in the museum.

"All we can say for now is if our theory is correct, this will be an answer and closure for one of the biggest mysteries of all time," Ed told the old man. He and Stephanie thanked him for his time and help. They then got ready to return to their hotel and get their things together for their return flight back to San Diego.

Rick got off the phone with Ed and told Rob, who was seated in front of him in his office, that Ed and Stephanie were in the air and would be landing in two hours or so. Rick looked at the clock on the wall and told Rob that meant they'd be at the headquarters around 11:30 or so.

"Rob, we will take Ed and Stephanie into the conference room and tell him about Kayla and her husband. I'm pretty sure he will be stricken with grief and then rage, so Chief Chase will advise him that he will be removed from this case for his safety and placed under protection," Rick said.

He sat down behind his desk and looked over the records of all the known rented white cargo vans from various car rental agencies around the city. None of the team members had been able to come up with a vehicle that had interior damage or was returned the day after the murder of Jackie Mays. Rick flung the file to the ground. Rob walked over and picked it up slowly.

"It's been almost a month since the first murder happened, and all we know so far is that Cate and Dr. Farrell both agree that the killer is copying the same patterns and wound inflictions as Nathan Malcolm. But we know for a fact that it's not Malcolm because we have positive DNA evidence that he died four years ago," Rob said to Rick.

Rick ran his right hand through his short hair. At that moment, Julie O'Keefe knocked on the door and said Chief Chase and his staff members had arrived. Rick thanked her and instructed his team to gather in the conference room. He then took a small brush from his desk, brushed his hair back, and said they needed to hold a press conference that night and ask Chief Chase to appeal to the citizens of San Diego to come forward and help break the case and offer a huge reward to any lead that provided useful information on the killer.

The late unscheduled press conference had ended forty minutes ago, and it had been aired on the late evening local and cable news outlets. In the conference room, Rick, Rob, and Police Chief John Chase broke the news to Ed about the murders of Kayla and her husband, Charles Neast.

Ed just sat in the chair at first, stunned, and then broke into tears for Kayla. Then he became enraged that the Entity had singled him and his family out. He stood up and threw a chair against the wall, breaking it into pieces. Stephanie came over to him and hugged him to console him. As Ed hugged her back, she whispered that she was very sorry. Rob told Rick he would take Stephanie to his office and talk to her so Rick and Chief Chase could talk to Ed alone. Rob took Stephanie's hand and asked her to come with him. She nodded and told Ed she would be right back.

As Rob closed the door behind them, Stephanie wiped the tears from her eyes. She couldn't explain the amount of grief and sadness she felt for Ed in that moment. She also knew she could have been the intended victim rather than Kayla. She sat down, and Rob handed her a cup of coffee and sat next to her.

"Stephanie, the chief and Rick are going to suggest to Ed that you both be placed under round-the-clock protection. And they are going to suggest that you both be removed from this case, as the killer knows everything about you both now," Rob told her.

Stephanie looked into his eyes as she took a sip of the hot coffee. Then she said, "Rob, we were getting closer on this. We just need to find some particular items that Malcolm passed on to a family member or close friend. They will tie him to his grandfather's brother Francis Tumblety. Ed was right all along. At first we doubted him, but he proved that even I was wrong. We can't give up now. I know we can close this case within a few days' time. Please, Rob. Try to convince Rick and the chief to let us continue. Because now more than ever, I want to see this bastard burn for everything he has done," Stephanie finished quietly as Ed and Rick entered Rob's office.

Stephanie handed the cup of coffee back to Rob. She and Ed kissed and hugged each other warmly. Rick gave Rob some instructions. The task force was outside Rick's office, waiting to hear the chief's decision.

"Rob, you along with the team and eight uniformed officers are to escort Ed and Stephanie to a safe house in Ocean Beach. The house is three stories, and it's used for witness protection, so it's already prepped for us with communications and computers so we can stay in constant contact."

Rob acknowledged Rick's orders. Ed and Stephanie thanked Rick. Ed grasped her hand, and they walked out into the hallway to find four uniformed officers holding twelve-gauge shotguns at the ready. The officers led the couple out the back doors and into the parking lot, where four patrol cars with drivers were ready to move them out. Ed and Stephanie got into the middle squad car. Rob told his team members to follow in their unmarked vehicles.

The convoy of vehicles headed out to their undisclosed location. As they drove, Ed looked out the window to his right and remembered the happy times he had shared with Kayla; she had been his first love. Stephanie still had ahold of his hand. She wanted to comfort him. She laid her head on his left shoulder. Ed kissed her cheek.

"I'm so sorry, Ed. Kayla and her husband didn't deserve to die like that," she whispered.

Ed just kept staring out the window.

Once the team had them inside the large house, Rob explained that the first floor was living quarters for the uniformed officers and communications room. The second level was for Ed and Stephanie, and it was equipped with a large master bedroom, a bathroom, a gym, and a living room. The third level was living quarters for the task force, and two partners would be assigned along with eight different officers to watch them on eight-hour shifts around the clock until this was over.

Ed and Stephanie looked around their living area. Ed didn't care for the idea of being contained when he wanted to be out there tracking the Entity down. Rob told them they had spare clothes in the closets and new clothes would be brought for them tomorrow. It was now late at night, so Rob informed them that Ken and Jack would take the first shift together and that Julie and Skip would relieve them in the morning. Ed and Stephanie thanked the crew, and they all hugged Ed and gave him their condolences for Kayla and her husband.

Ed watched Stephanie walk them to the door and close then and lock it behind them. When she looked back at Ed, he was peering out the living room window, lost in deep thought. She didn't want to bother him right now, so she picked up her bags, which Rob and the others had brought with them, and went into the bathroom to freshen up and shower. Ed walked into the weight room, picked up a thirty-five-pound dumbbell, and started to curl it in his right hand. He thought about Nathan Malcolm and Jack the Ripper. He thought about all the innocent lives that had been taken away for no damn reason. He knew he had to stop this new killer just like he had killed Nathan Malcolm four years ago. Ed wanted to take the dumbbell and hurl it through the window with a vengeance, but he just kept curling the weight in his hand.

"You stole a precious person from my life. Now I'm going to send you to hell with the rest of your family, you bloody bastard," Ed whispered as he continued to work out.

A little while later, feeling refreshed from her shower, Stephanie lay in bed watching the late news. It was 3:30 a.m. She heard water running in the bathroom; Ed was taking a shower after his long workout. They hadn't talked since their arrival at the safe house more than four hours ago. When Ed came out of the bathroom, he was bare-chested and wearing his striped pajama bottoms. Stephanie smiled at him, and he came over to the bed and lay down next to her. She moved closer, and he wrapped his strong arms around her from behind. They kissed gently.

"Thank you for helping me through this tonight. I don't think I could handle it without you being here for me, Stephanie," he told her.

She held his hands in hers gently as she shed a tear for him. "Ed, please don't let your anger get in the way of what you know is best for us. Regardless of what happens from this point, he wants to kill you or make you suffer very much," she said.

Ed laid her back on the bed so he could face her, and Stephanie softly touched the massive scar on his left side with her fingertips.

"He is going to try to hurt me, if not kill me, to get back at you. You know that, Ed?" she said softly.

130

THE RECKONING OF JACK THE RIPPER

Ed covered her lips with a finger, wishing she hadn't thought of that right now. "He can think that way all he wants, Stephanie, but the reality is that I'm not going to let him hurt you or anyone else who close to me, because I'm going to kill him. I swear it," he told her and then kissed her deeply while undoing the buttons to her top. Then he turned out the bedroom light.

Stephanie's eyes slowly fluttered open as she heard music coming from the other room. She saw sunlight streaming through the long drapes of the bedroom window, and she knew it was early morning. She heard footsteps above and below them and sounds of car doors opening and closing outside. She remembered that she and Ed were being guarded at the safe house on the beach. She knew she had to get up and get changed in case Rick and Rob and the others came by. As Stephanie put on her top and long bathrobe, she recognized the guitarist Ed was listening to. *Jimi Hendrix, Ed's favorite.* She smiled at the thought as she went into the bathroom and closed the door behind her.

She turned on the hot water in the sink, bent over it, and splashed warm water on her face to wake herself up. She thought this whole ordeal seemed like it had been going on for a year already. As she looked up, she saw Ed standing behind her in the mirror, and she screamed, startled by his silent approach. Ed grabbed her around the waist, and she relaxed in his arms. They shared a deep kiss, and Ed smiled and glanced to his right. Stephanie looked over and saw the shower. She knew what was on his mind.

"Well, it has to be a fast shower, since we are not alone anymore," she told him.

Ed opened the glass door, and they both entered the marble-tiled shower. Stephanie turned on the water and again screamed that it was cold.

Just after 11:00 a.m., Rick and Rob met with Ed and Stephanie, along with Skip and Julie, who were on duty in addition to eight new uniformed cops. As they sat in the living room, Rick and the others again expressed their condolences to Ed. Rick then briefed them on what had happened at the county medical examiner's office after they discovered the gray piece of material from the cargo van, but they had no records of any type of van being rented that day or the day prior to the murder.

"So after all this, we are back to square one again. This copycat killer has murdered six victims. We asked the FBI for help, which is why Stephanie joined our team, to create a detailed profile of the killer. We have no DNA evidence, and we can't use undercover female officers. He has now moved away from killing escorts, and he is killing random civilians. The only thing we have to go on is a scrap of gray material stuck underneath a victim's fingernail, but we can't track down the vehicle it came from. I say if there was ever a perfect killer, we are up against him right now," Rick told them.

The team's mood was somber, like the killer had broken its spirit.

Stephanie thought for a moment. If this killer was a step ahead of them all the time and he found out where Kayla lived with her new husband, he had to be getting inside information on Ed and the others. *The cargo van*, she thought. *The medical examiner's cargo van is white. There has been no DNA evidence left behind on the victims. It could be an inside medical person with whom Cate Adams works.* She spoke up and explained everything she'd just been thinking about. Ed and Rick stared at her. Then Ed realized she was on to something.

"If not a person who works with Cate, then how about someone on the forensic crew that gathers up the crime scene evidence after a murder? The person acts like he or she is doing a thorough search as he or she gathers all trace evidence. Then instead of bagging it and labeling it, he or she discards it without anyone's knowledge," Ed suggested.

All eyes fell on Rick because Cate was his wife and they thought he should be the one to confront her with this theory.

"Okay, look, let's not jump ahead of ourselves now. Let me talk to Cate and interview her staff with Rob. Maybe we are finally on to something here. Skip and Julie, keep them company and safe," Rick said. He smiled and told Rob to come with him.

They get to work on the case that I'm in charge of, and I have to stay here and just sit back and wait for something to happen, Ed thought as he sat next to Stephanie on the couch. He turned on the television.

"Cable news or soap operas. Take your pick, guys," Ed told them, feeling bored already.

Rick and Rob took different parts of the investigation at the county medical examiner's facility. Rick, along with Cate, questioned her three-man team of crime scene technicians, while Rob and the lead analyst looked at the two white vans the team used. Both vans were white with gray carpet-lined floors and side panels. There were side draws to contain evidence-gathering equipment, but there was still room enough for the van to hold a body on the floor. Rob searched both vans' inside doors and wall panels. He looked for damage or carpet patches or signs the carpet had been replaced, but both vans seemed fine to him. He closed the back doors of one of them. He then looked at the exteriors; both vans had *County Examiners Office* painted on their sides in black lettering. He looked for any sign that the lettering had been covered or taped over; otherwise, these vans would have stood out to witnesses who might have seen them. Rob sighed in disgust. He knew that even with this good theory of Stephanie's they had hit another brick wall. He told the technician that was all for now, and they went back inside to Cate's office.

As Rob opened the door to Cate's office, Rick was talking to the forensic team members. He looked at Rob, but Rob shook his head to let him know they had no leads. Rick thanked the men for their time, and they said they were happy to cooperate in any way possible with the investigation. After the men left the office and Rob closed the door behind them, Rick flung his clipboard of notes on Cate's desk in anger.

"Nothing. No torn material from the vans. They are perfect, inside and out. So I guess the crew's alibies check out too, huh?" Rob asked, and Rick replied yes.

"The men all recounted the same thing: they gathered the DNA swabs, labeled them, and placed them inside the brown paper bags for either Cate or Diana to work on. Everything they logged corresponds with Cate's and Dr. Farrell's autopsy notes, so there are no leads here either," Rick said.

Cate smiled at her husband and told him, "Told you so! I have been working with this crew for almost twelve years now, and I have known Diana for eight years. Do you think we wouldn't suspect if something was wrong with the people we worked with? Women's intuition, Rick. We know when something is wrong."

Rick smiled back. "Well, you know what? Since I'm mentally exhausted from this whole case right now and the whole day has gone by without an incident, I say Rob and Antonella should join us out for dinner tonight at Clover's restaurant. We all deserve a break from this case. What do you say, Rob?" Rick suggested.

"Only if we can bring Megan. My mother-in-law doesn't like babysitting duties dumped on her at the last minute," Rob told them.

Rick said it was fine to bring their daughter. They needed to get out and have fun after all this hard work.

At the house on Ocean Beach, Ed was fulfilling his promise to Stephanie. They were in the gym together. Ed had made room by pushing some of the equipment out of the way and laid out one of the large thick mats on the floor to prevent them from getting injured. He showed her some self-defense moves and counter holds in case she found herself cornered or the killer had a knife or other sharp weapon he intended to use on her.

Ed pulled her around the waist from behind and held a fake plastic knife to her throat. He instructed her to hold his hand tight to her chest and then bend down and twist out of his grasp while holding onto his hand to control the knife and either take it away from him or throw it far beyond his reach. Stephanie understood his instructions, and they went into the full exercise. Stephanie surprised Ed and took him down to the mat. He started to get up, but Stephanie took hold of his right arm, stepped in close to him, and then flipped him over her shoulder. Ed lay flat on his back, angry now, and started to get up fast. As he got to his feet, Stephanie bent down low and swept her right foot into Ed's left foot, kicking his foot out from under him. He fell to the mat again. She quickly picked up the fake knife, sat on top of his chest, held the blade to his neck, and smiled.

Ed just raised his hands and said, "Okay, I give up now."

Stephanie continued to smile at him as she threw the knife to the side and kissed him gently on the lips. "You didn't ask me if I had any martial art's training there, Mr. Ed. I'm a first-degree brown belt in Kenpo karate. I have been taking it for the last few years, but because I have been busy with various cases, I haven't been able to reach my black belt status just yet," she told him.

Smiling, Ed told her she would reach it in no time. He softly slid his hands up and down her bare thighs. Stephanie wore white shorts, a sweatshirt, and sneakers, and Ed wore a full jogging suit and sneakers. Ed pulled her all the way to the floor with him, and they kissed deeply.

"Ed, we are not alone here, remember? We can't be acting like this right now," Stephanie told him softly.

They heard Skip and Julie on the top floor and the policeman on the floor below them as they ordered pizza and cheered at the Padre's baseball game. Stephanie suggested that they go upstairs and see what plans Julie and Skip had made for dinner and then join them. Ed made a face and said he felt safe here but wanted to get out to be alone with Stephanie, even if only for a few hours. He reminded her that Rick and Rob were having a dinner date with their wives and then suggested that they sneak away and have dinner together.

"Ed, we can't do that! What if something happens tonight and, God forbid, he comes looking for us? We need to be here right now for our protection," she told him.

But Ed protested. "Stephanie, first, we are right on Ocean Beach. Even though this house is set far away from the others, there are so many civilians around here that he would be crazy to come here and try anything, even if he did know we were here. Secondly, I don't like being watched over when this is our case, and now it's a personal vendetta between him and me. And third, it's a Friday evening, just after 5:00 p.m. I want us to try that new Italian restaurant in Little Italy called Carmine's. Rob told me they have the best brick oven pizza there, and it's very close. We can shower, change really fast, zip there, and zip back in Julie's car. I know she will do it for me and you. And we'll come right back before 10:00 p.m. for some final dessert together. What do you say, karate girl?"

Stephanie smiled at Ed; she also wanted to be alone with him tonight. So she told him dinner only and right back to the safe house for dessert. Ed told her that was his plan.

"Let's do it," she told him.

Ed told her to start the shower with warm water. He would tell Julie and Skip and get Julie's car keys. As they got up and Stephanie started toward the bathroom, Ed told her there was a present he wanted her to wear tonight hanging in her closet. She smiled and told him she would. Then Ed headed upstairs to make plans for them to sneak away for a few hours.

He got the keys to Julie's Mazda 6 because Julie felt bad for them and agreed they needed to get out for a while to be alone. Skip was very against the idea at first because he felt their safety was in jeopardy and wondered what would happen if something happened and Rick or Chief Chase found out about this. But he changed his mind when Ed told them he had big question to ask Stephanie tonight. Julie surmised what it was, and then Skip gave into Ed's plan, but they all agreed that Ed and Stephanie needed to be back at the safe house by 10:00 p.m. sharp.

Skip suggested they use the handicap ramp, which connected to each outside terrace of the house. They could then access Julie's car, which was parked in the back, and the team of cops on the first floor would not spot them leaving. Ed told them that the officers were so focused on the ball game that they would not see or hear him or Stephanie leave. Ed kissed Julie on the cheek and hurried back downstairs.

He walked into the bathroom. Stephanie had covered up with a white towel. She told him to hurry and that she was going to get changed. She went into their bedroom, opened the closet, and saw a black garment bag from Nordstrom's hanging there. She removed it from the hanger and laid it on the bed. She unzipped the long zipper and was stunned at the beautiful royal blue V-neck dress that was revealed. Ed had also left a shoebox with matching blue heels on the bed.

Stephanie quickly dried and fixed her hair nicely and then slipped on the dress. It was an off-the-shoulder style with an open back. After Stephanie stepped into the heels, she looked at herself in the mirror and adored the dress and shoes. She placed her hands on her hips and smiled. The hem of the dress was about five inches above her knees. *Ed's definitely a man who loves women's legs,* she thought as Ed whistled behind her. He was already dressed in a black-and-blue stripped dress shirt, black slacks, and black shoes.

He smiled at her and complimented her on looking so fine. Then he joked, asking Stephanie, "Now where do you suppose you are going to hide your gun now?"

Stephanie winked and came over to kiss him softly. "Ed, you didn't need to do all this for me. I feel bad now because since we have been together, I haven't had a chance to get you any gifts," she told him.

Ed told her not to worry about it. He had printed out the dress from the computer, and Rick had had one of the oncoming cops pass by the mall and get it for him. She asked him what was the occasion was for them to get all dressed up. Certainly not just to have pizza for dinner. Ed told her it was to make sure they enjoyed a very special evening together.

He put on his shoulder holster and checked his silver Smith & Wesson 9mm. He knew it was fully loaded, and he had another two full clips inserted on the holster. He then picked up the car keys and told Stephanie, "Now, let's sneak out of the house." He opened the sliding door, and they walked down the ramp quickly but very quietly. Then they got into the black Mazda and drove off to the expressway.

A little while later, they were seated in a cozy booth in the back of Carmine's. As their waiter brought their plain pizza and ice teas out to them, Stephanie admitted to Ed that she felt a bit overdressed for the family-style restaurant. Ed told her not to worry and that people in San Diego loved to dress up on a Friday evening and spend a lot of time in the downtown district. The very nice and lavish Westfield Mall was also close by. Stephanie asked if that was where he had purchased the dress and shoes for her. He told her yes, and she asked if they had cost him a fortune. She would feel very bad if he had spent that kind of money on her.

Ed looked around the restaurant and saw there weren't many people sitting near them. He reached into his jacket pocket and handed her a small black gift box with a very small red bow attached to it. Stephanie looked at him, puzzled, and took the box. As she began to undo the gift wrapping, she told Ed that it wasn't necessary for him to do this.

Ed just smiled and said, "Well, the dress and shoes were a lot cheaper than this little gift I got for you."

She smiled, removed the paper, and saw it was a velvet box. As she opened the cover, her mouth dropped open and her eyes gleamed at the breathtaking engagement ring inside. A small note in the inside cover read, *Stephanie, will you marry me?*

"Well, will you?" Ed asked.

Stephanie removed the ring from the box. It was a 1.5 karat three-stone princess cut diamond ring set in 14 karat white gold with two rows of smaller diamonds on either side. Ed told her to hurry up and try it on for size. She slipped it on her left ring finger and held it out for him to see. As Ed smiled at her, Stephanie had tears in her eyes. She looked overwhelmed, as if she didn't know how to respond.

Ed asked her, "Well, I do need an answer from you." He held her hand and asked her himself. "Stephanie Morgan, will you marry me?"

She looked at him with a full smile on her face and shouted, "Yes!"

He reached over and kissed her gently. A few people in Carmine's saw them embracing and started to clap for the happy couple.

"So now we should wait for the case to be over with, and then we can break the news to all our friends on the force and our families," Ed suggested as Stephanie took her cell phone out of her purse. Ed looked on and thought, *Oh, women just can't hold good news in.* Stephanie called her mother at home and told her the news, crying while describing how Ed had proposed and she had accepted. Ed instructed her not to tell the whole world just yet. They held hands, and Ed heard Stephanie's mother's elation for her daughter.

He watched from the rooftop of the apartment building twenty yards away from the three-level beach house. Using night scope binoculars, he looked for Ed and Stephanie on the second level but didn't see any sign of them. Only the television was on in the living room. He knew they had gone out for the night. He looked at the top floor and then down at the first floor, part of which he could see. He saw Skip watching the ball game, and Julie was in her bedroom on her laptop.

As he peered into a window that had its curtains drawn back on the first floor, the Entity knew where to start his attack. He opened his large black duffle bag and took out a black carbon bow. He assembled it and armed it with a black steel-tipped arrow attached to a cable. He looked around as he aimed and then fired the arrow into the home's rooftop. The steel found its target and lodged firmly into the stucco wall. He anchored the steel cable tightly around the chimney of the rooftop he was on, and then he pulled and tugged on it hard. Once he knew it was secure and able to support his weight, he took out a small black pulley wheel and placed it on the cable.

He looked across gap between the buildings; he would sail about sixty feet above the ground to the reach home's rooftop, which was not as high as the building upon which he was standing. It would be perfect. He would come over the sand and the back of the house disguised by the night and would be able to take them by surprise. He flung the bag over his shoulder and stepped up on the roof's retaining wall. Then he cast himself down on the cable; the well-oiled wheel didn't whistle as he sailed through the air so fast that he felt a breeze against his face through the dark black sterile hood he wore. The hood had no slits for his mouth or nose, just cutouts for his eyes. He also wore night vision goggles so he could see in the dark—another thing that would allow him to take them by surprise. When he was above the home's roof, he quickly disengaged from the wheel before he collided with the wall.

The wheel hit the wall hard and made a thud. The sudden noise caused Julie to look up from her computer screen. She shrugged it off and continued to work. Skip didn't hear a sound; he was glued to the baseball game, just like the cops below him.

The Entity was dressed in black ninja style outfit and black rubber-soled ninja shoes; they were made of thin black polyester and went up to his ankles. He took out a pair of wire cutters, went over to the fuse box, and cut the power and the phone line. He quickly went into the duffle bag and took out two samurai short swords and placed them in the black sash at his waist. Then he equipped his black crossbow with an arrow and holstered several more arrows in his belt. As he waited near the door, he heard voices coming up from the stairs as Skip spoke to the officer in charge of the home's security. They agreed that they would investigate the cause of the power outage. The roof door opened slowly. Both men had their guns in hand, and Skip told Julie to call Rick on her cell phone and tell him about the home losing power and phone service.

As the men split up, Skip took out his small flashlight to look at the circuit breaker and saw its door was open. As the lead sergeant moved around the roof very cautiously with his gun and flashlight in hand, Skip yelled over to him and said the power line had been cut. But before the sergeant could respond, an arrow penetrated his left eye. He sailed off his feet and hit the ground hard.

Skip stood when he heard the sound of something sailing over his head. He flashed his light in the policeman's direction and saw the arrow protruding from of his eye. He was about to yell when a hand covered his mouth from behind and the blade of a short sword drew deeply across his neck. The Entity removed his hand from Skip's mouth and used both hands to grip the sword as he again slashed Skip's neck deeply from behind. Blood jetted out of the detective's neck, and he fell to the rooftop dead.

The Entity quickly rearmed another arrow and made his way to the door and down the stairwell. He knew Julie was alone. He would leave her for last, as he knew he had seven men left to kill. He stopped on the top floor as he heard voices coming up the stairs, yelling. The light from their flashlights brightened the hallway. He had to kill them now before they saw him. He took a knee, aimed the crossbow, and fired even before the first man came around the corner. The arrow struck deep in his neck, and the force knocked him backward into his partner, who fell to the floor. The Entity jumped on top of the helpless man as he drew a short steel dagger and stabbed him hard in the throat. He left it imbedded in his throat and then stood up and slashed his neck with his sword, decapitating him.

Julie heard the noise as Rick questioned her on her cell about what was happening. When she saw the man in black standing outside her door, she slammed it, shut, and locked it.

"Rick, he's here! The Entity is here!" she screamed into her phone as she ran to her bedroom to get her firearm.

On the other end of the line, Rick shouted to Rob that they had to go, and both men shot out of their seats, leaving their wives stunned. They ran to Rick's car in the restaurant parking lot and drove off to Ocean Beach. As Rick told Rob what was happening, he used his phone to call Western Division and instructed them to get as many officers as they could over to the safe house as quickly as possible. Rob took out his cell phone and called Ed to see if he was all right.

Ed was eating a slice of pizza. Stephanie had called her brother and her close female cousin to tell them she had just gotten engaged; she was still on the phone with her. Ed just wanted Stephanie be happy and enjoy this moment. He said they would take the rest of her pizza home. Then his phone rang, and he answered it.

"Ed! Are you all right?" Rob asked.

"I'm fine. I'm with Stephanie in Little Italy having dinner. I snuck her out to pop the question to her. She said yes!"

Stephanie smiled; she knew he was talking to Rob. Ed's face suddenly went from happy to very serious as Rob told him that the Entity was in the beach house, killing their team and that Julie was trapped. Ed put down his phone, dropped his pizza, got up, and grabbed his leather jacket.

He grabbed Stephanie's hand and pulled, shouting, "Come on! He's at the house now!"

Stephanie grabbed her purse and shawl and ran with Ed to the Mazda; everyone in the restaurant looked after them, stunned. Ed fired up the engine and pulled out of the parking lot at a high speed. Stephanie fastened her seatbelt tight and asked what was happening.

"Rob just called me. The bastard is at the house, killing off our men! He no doubt came to kill us too. But tonight it's him who is going to die!" Ed screamed, making a hard right onto the San Diego freeway and flooring the gas pedal to speeds exceeding eighty miles per hour.

He held the wheel with one hand and called Rob again on his cell phone. Rob said they were about fifteen minutes away on the freeway themselves and that the patrol cars should be getting there soon.

The Entity kicked the door to Julie's apartment open, and she heard him from her locked bedroom. She had her 9mm ready in her right hand, and she screamed into her cell phone to Rick, "Please get here, Rick! He's in the house!"

Julie heard gunshots from outside her bedroom. Two more men had come into the apartment. The Entity stabbed one in his back, and the blade came out through his chest. The man screamed in pain. As his partner turned to shoot, the Entity slashed the officer's right hand off with his other sword. Still holding the gun, the hand fell to the floor firing rounds. The Entity then slashed him across the neck as the remaining three cops came into the room. They opened fire in all directions, flashing their flashlights all over the room until there was complete silence. Julie crouched behind her bed and listened. She heard the men ask each other if they got him.

"Please, kill him. Please, God, I don't want to die," Julie said as Rick screamed at her on the cell phone, asking what was happening.

As the men moved farther into the apartment, they saw the bodies of their friends on the ground. Suddenly an arrow flew across the room and found its mark in the center cop's forehead. As he flew off his feet and onto the floor, the Entity rose from the floor, slashed one cop across the neck with his sword, and then ducked to avoid the gunshots from the other policeman. He stood up and stabbed the officer beneath his jaw and into his skull with a short steel dagger and then slashed him across the neck. Then he did the same to the other policeman who was still standing.

The Entity knew he had killed all nine men. He placed both swords in their sheaths and, holding the steel dagger, made a running leap and kicked open the bedroom door. Julie stood up and fired her gun. The Entity fell to the floor, jumped, rolled on top of the bed, and kicked the gun out of Julie's hand. He flung her hard onto the bed, jumped on top of her, and covered her mouth with his gloved hand.

"Quiet please, my dear Julie. Just four years ago, in another capacity, you lived. This time you don't have that chance with me," the Entity said to her.

Julie was stunned by his words and voice. He used the dagger to slash her throat deeply once and then again. He watched her gasp and choke on her own blood as she slipped into death. Then he quickly gathered his weapons, returned to the roof, and placed the swords and crossbow into the duffle bag. He heard the sirens of the police cruisers coming closer and could see their flashing lights in the distance. Standing at the edge of the roof, he took hold of the steel cable he had used to make his way onto the roof, cut the wire with his sharp blade, and sailed through the air. He came back to the apartment building and dropped himself down on the cable to the ground.

He replaced his soft shoes with black sneakers and placed a black motorcycle helmet over his head. Placing his night vision goggles in the duffle bag and flinging it over his shoulder, he ran to his Suzuki Hayabusa, kick-started the motor, cranked the throttle, and sped off into the night.

Rick and Rob were coming up on the exit to Ocean Beach when they saw the flashing lights a mile ahead to their right. In the opposite lane, they spotted a black sports bike whizzing by at a high speed. Both men commented on the bike.

"The rider is in black. The bike is black. That's got to be him!" Rick shouted. He made a fast hard right turn onto the off-ramp, gunned their vehicle through a red light, and made a left-hand turn onto the freeway on-ramp to follow the motorcycle.

Rob called Ed to alert him that they were following the black bike. Ed, who was busy driving at a high speed, handed his phone to Stephanie to answer. Rob informed her that they were following the presumed suspect on a black sports motorcycle. Stephanie told Ed. Ed looked to his left and saw the bike passing them in southbound traffic at least eighty miles per hour. He noticed a break in the freeway median ahead, sped up, and just glided over from the right lane to the middle and left lanes, cutting off a few vehicles. Then he made a hard left turn into the southbound freeway lanes and hit the gas hard. He and Stephanie flew back into their seats. Ed took the cell phone from her to advise Rick on how to box in and stop the suspect.

"Rick, get a hold of dispatch and advise them to have multiple cruisers and spotlight helicopters box in the cross points at Martin Luther King Freeway and John Montgomery Freeway. We can stop him there!" Ed shouted the instructions, and Rick told Rob to call Western Division dispatch and get the vehicles at the intersection right away.

Ed pushed the gas pedal all the way down and kept pace with the motorcycle. He watched the suspect dip very close behind cars and trucks as he passed them and zigzag in and out of all three lanes. Ed, an experienced motorcycle rider, knew the driver couldn't brake fast on a turn or he would fly off the bike, especially riding a bike with six speeds to shift. He knew the intersection would be the point of impact for them to stop him. He told Stephanie the plan he and Rick had set. Stephanie's phone rang, and she answered it. Ken Rogers had called to alert them that he, Jack Kerns, and multiple uniformed officers were at the beach house. He told her all eight officers were dead, along with Skip Jones and Julie O'Keefe. He said they had searched every floor and room with their flashlights, and the crime scene was a bloody massacre. Stephanie told Ed softly about their friends and the eight cops.

Ed looked over at her and then back at the bike ahead and cursed to himself. "You son of a bitch bastard! What the hell do you want?" Ed shouted as they came up fast on the intersection. The police cruisers were just now getting onto all three freeways to box the suspect in and divert civilian vehicles out of harm's way.

Rob called Ed again. He had gotten word from dispatch that they had cruisers on every main freeway and intersection. They also had two helicopters in the air that should pick up the motorcycle within moments. As Ed acknowledged Rick, he spotted them in back of him, speeding up to his position in the middle lane. Ed then looked ahead as they approached the three-way junction. Rick asked how they were going to do this. Ed thought of a quick plan as he noticed the flashing lights of the police cruisers in all directions up ahead.

"Rick, close in tight on my left side now. We will give him no shot of escaping. Tell Rob to tell dispatch to have all the cruisers on the John Montgomery Freeway come straight at him and the other cruisers combine and form a roadblock to keep him from exiting the off-ramps!" Ed yelled the plan, and Rick told Rob, who conveyed the interception plan to the dispatch office.

The black motorcycle had now reached speeds of ninety miles per hour, squeezing between two SUVs in the middle and right lanes. The Entity looked back and saw the fast Mazda and another car close behind him. Then he saw the lights of the police cruisers coming at him straight ahead and realized that the east—and west-bound ramps at the intersection were blocked. He had no choice but to go straight because he couldn't stop or slow down without being caught. He cranked the throttle, changed gear, and got up to one hundred miles per hour.

Ed and Rick were just fifteen yards behind him, and the cruisers in all three lanes converged to box him in. Chief Chase was now at Western Division's dispatch desk, and he screamed at Rob over the phone to take the suspect out. The Entity stayed straight in the center lane as the vehicles were about to converge on the black bike. He waited until the last second and then banked to his left just a few feet. The driver in the oncoming lane didn't want a head-on impact with the bike, so he steered hard to his right, creating a gap for the bike to maneuver into. As he passed the SUV, Stephanie screamed at Ed to watch out. He steered hard to his left, hitting the concrete center divider hard. Rick yelled at Rob to brace himself, and he slammed on the brakes and steered hard to his right. Their vehicle collided with the lead patrol cars coming from the other three directions.

Rick's vehicle was hit right in the driver and rear side doors by the middle-bound cruiser, and both cars made a complete 360-degree spin and the finally came to a stop. Their airbags had deployed for their safety. The left-bound cruiser caught the tail end of the middle cruiser and flipped into the air with massive speed and height. The vehicle came down on its top and skidded to a halt against the median. The right-bound cruiser hit a large SUV that was stopped in its lane, and the vehicles exploded upon impact. Ed was able to regain control of the Mazda as he bounced hard off the barrier. Stephanie told him the suspect had taken the second off-ramp to their right. Ed gunned the black Mazda down the ramp and told Stephanie to call dispatch and tell them the Entity was now in the downtown district of San Diego.

The Entity rode southbound on Park Boulevard, and the helicopter above picked him up in the darkness of night with its blue searchlight. The bike's driver weaved in and out of traffic as he saw squad cars coming in the wrong direction on the boulevard to once again try to box him in. He saw something up ahead. He changed gears and eased up on the gas while at the same time arching his body backward and steering to his right. He tugged hard on the handlebars and propelled the bike high into the air, jumping over the right medium and landing softly on his rear wheel as the front wheel came down hard to the pavement. He shifted his body upward on the seat to regain control of the bike and heard the loud collision behind him; the cruisers had smashed into one another, unable to stop at their high speeds, and hit the median.

Ed, who had just gotten onto Park Boulevard, slowed down as he lost sight of the fast bike. He soon came upon the accident of the police vehicles. One officer stood beside the cars, pointing Ed in the direction of the street to his left. Ed knew what he was saying and floored the gas again as he yelled instructions over to Stephanie: "Tell them he is on Eleventh Avenue now! He is heading right for the mall!"

Stephanie relayed the information to dispatch. Chief Chase heard the conversation the dispatch officer was having with her and all the other police cruisers. He had them on speaker phone so the control room could hear what was happening all at once. Chief Chase went over to the large map of downtown San Diego and looked at where the motorcycle was going. He said to the other captains and lieutenants that he was heading to the large Westfield outdoor mall. He looked at the clock on the wall; it read 8:30 p.m. The mall had closed a half hour ago, but there would still be shoppers and employees leaving the five-story complex and its large parking garage. The chief ordered one helicopter to position itself right over the mall and the other to monitor East Harbor Drive because that was the only other highway the suspect could get to if he got by their cruisers.

The Entity made a fast right onto First Avenue and watched the crowds of people exiting the mall. He slowed down to avoid hitting them and noticed more police cruisers coming at him from the opposite direction. He heard a car's tires shrieking behind him. As Ed and Stephanie came around the corner on the Entity's tail, Ed slammed on the brakes to avoid hitting civilians. The cruisers ahead of them also stopped. The Entity stared at Ed through his dark smoked visor. Ed knew the killer was staring at him, and he knew he was going to try to lose them in the five-story mall.

The mall had a long strip running though the center, and on either side were five tiers of stores lined with stairs and escalators. The building was flanked by parking garages. The Westfield Mall had a very upscale and different design. Ed watched as the Entity cranked the throttle and the gas.

"Tell them he's going into the mall and have them close both parking garages to block his escape!" Ed shouted at Stephanie as the Entity made a right turn through the open doors. Ed gunned the engine and followed him.

Stephanie relayed the instructions over the phone and screamed at Ed not to follow him inside the mall. Ed ignored her pleas, and their car was able to narrowly squeeze through the wide double doors. The motorcycle and its rider streamed quickly down the main floor, dodging shoppers and barely avoiding hitting a mother pushing her infant in a stroller. People cursed and yelled at the bike driver, and

Ed slowed down and honked his car horn repeatedly to clear the way for himself. Not knowing what the situation was all about, the people started cursing at Ed and Stephanie. Uniformed police officers filed into the mall on foot with their weapons in hand. They hurried to clear out the mall and keep the citizens safe from harm.

The bike made its way to the very end of the first floor; there were no exits in sight unless he turned around and faced the Mazda head-on. Then the Entity noticed a flight of stairs to his side. He circled around the water fountain in the middle of the floor. The car came at full speed directly at the bike, and Stephanie screamed for Ed to stop. The motorcycle avoided the collision, and the Mazda ran straight into the marble fountain, damaging both the car and the nice statue. The Entity raced up the stairs.

Ed quickly moved the deployed airbag out of his way; the passenger side airbag had also deployed. He asked Stephanie if she was all right, and she told him yes. Ed drew his gun and leaped out of the car, keeping his eye on the motorcycle on the second floor. He ran up the stairs quickly, trying to keep pace with the bike in hopes of getting off a clear shot.

Policemen ran up to Stephanie, who was holding her head, which hurt from the impact with the airbag. She told the officers who she was and that Detective Brooks was in pursuit of the suspect on foot. Four of the six officers ran up the stairs to assist Ed, and two remained behind to assist Stephanie. Ed knew he couldn't keep up with the sports bike, but he kept running as hard as he could, breathing very hard and ignoring the pain in his legs. He spotted the black bike just a few yards ahead of him. Then he heard the rotor blades of the helicopter overhead and saw its light shining down into the mall, searching for the suspect.

Ed watched the bike race up the escalator, making a break for the third floor. He took aim and fired repeatedly at the rider in black. The rounds barely missed him and struck the acrylic glass of the escalator, shattering it upon impact. The Entity reached the third floor and gunned his way down the opposite isle, away from Ed and the police. Ed cursed and noticed the elevator behind him. He ran through the open door and pressed the button for the fifth floor. As the elevator climbed, Ed ejected the empty clip from his gun and replaced it with a full one. He knew the Entity was making his way to the top floor to get away.

The elevator car came to a stop on the fifth floor, and the doors opened. Ed ran out and watched as the bike came fast around the corner at him. He took aim and shot at the rider in black. His first three rounds missed their target. The Entity looked at Ed as he aimed for a direct shot. The Entity leaned back and started to stand up on the bike's seat as Ed was about to fire. He pulled up on the handlebars and hit the brake hard, and the motorcycle was propelled through the air directly at Ed, who leaped to his left to avoid impact. The motorcycle crashed into the wall behind Ed, but the Entity had flipped backward off the bike and then somersaulted himself to a stop on the floor.

He took out one of his sharp samurai swords to confront Ed. Ed got to his feet and noticed he had lost his gun when he leapt to avoid the motorcycle. He braced himself as the man in black ran at him, swinging the steel blade. He dropped to the floor to miss the swipe of the blade, spun on the ground, jumped to his feet, and grabbed the hands of his opponent right before he could swing the blade again. Both men pushed hard against one another to gain control of the sword. Ed forced the blade down with his left hand and used his right fist to hit the Entity square in the chest with all his might. As the Entity fell backward, Ed made a running leap and kicked him in the chest. The Entity flew backward off his feet and hit the floor hard. He dropped the sword upon impact, along with the black duffle bag.

Ed looked down at the person who had taken Kayla's life. "You son of a bitch!" Ed screamed and rushed his foe, who had barely made it to his feet. Ed swung his right fist in a roundhouse blow, but the Entity ducked, drew a sharp dagger from his inside jacket pocket, and slashed Ed's thigh. Ed fell to the floor, and the Entity kicked him in the face.

Ed coughed for air, stunned by the hard blow, as the Entity reclaimed his sword and hid behind a pillar. Three armed cops rushed toward Ed, but before he could warn them, the Entity slashed and hacked them from behind in a fury of speed. His sword slashed through their necks, and he finished them off with deep stab sounds to their hearts. Within seconds, they lay lifeless on the floor. Ed crawled on his back, trying to reach his gun, which was only a few feet away. But the Entity came over and kicked it well beyond his reach. He pressed a foot against Ed's chest, pinning him hard to the floor. Ed looked at the man in black holding the sword in his right hand and knew he was about to end his life.

Suddenly they heard loud voices of several cops running up the stairs. The Entity looked back at the policeman and then stared at Ed on the ground. He pointed at Ed with his left index finger without saying a word. The short stare and point lasted a few seconds before the man in black ran to the side wall and leaped up to grab hold of one of the store signs. He then climbed up to the roof of the mall and ran down the opposite side. Ed took a deep breath and covered the gash on his left thigh, which was bleeding heavily. When the policeman reached him, Ed told them where the suspect had gone, and the lead officer radioed to the helicopter to look for the suspect on the roof.

The man in black ran very quickly, trying to avoid the search light from the helicopter above him. He ran at full speed and then leaped down to a lower rooftop and knew he was now on top of the parking garage. He looked down and saw squad cars converging from every direction on the street below him. The Entity ran down to the far side of the mall's rooftop and leaped again down onto the last low roof, but it was still too high for him to leap to the street below without getting seriously injured. He ran inside the parking garage and saw he was on level 3. He quickly looked around, trying to think of a way to escape, and saw a large dumpster next to the side elevator and stairwell. He quickly jumped inside the dumpster and closed the lid. He then lit his flashlight and started to remove his black ninja outfit and helmet.

Back in the mall, Stephanie made her way up to Ed on the top floor. Many policemen flanked them, and the head captain of the SWAT team unit ordered them to sweep the parking garage levels from top to bottom. He then ordered another heavily armed team to sweep the interior of the mall from the ground floor up because the two helicopters above and the units surrounding the entire mall at the street level had not caught the suspect leaving the grounds of the mall yet.

Rick and Rob had just reached the mall. Ed and Stephanie were taken to a waiting ambulance to receive medical treatment. Rick and Rob also had bruises and cuts from their accident. Ed's knife wound was cleaned and dressed, and Stephanie held and ice pack on her bruised left shoulder. Rick stayed in constant contact with the SWAT team's captain as his men continued to search the mall for the suspect. Rick then went to the mall's security office, and detectives searched surveillance monitors for the suspect.

"Are you all right?" Stephanie asked Ed as the paramedic finished dressing the knife wound; it hadn't required any stiches.

Ed smiled and said that except for ruining a good pair of pants and hurting his pride a little, he was all right. Rob made a call to his wife and told her what had happened at the safe house and the mall. Antonella, along with their daughter and Cate, had been taken from the restaurant to Central Division by a police escort to await Rick and Rob's return as soon as the search was over at the mall. It was now 10:30 p.m.; it had been nearly an hour and a half since the Entity had last been seen on the mall's roof, and there had been no sign of him since.

The Entity had waited in the dumpster for a long while after removing his ninja outfit and putting on a black sweatshirt, black sweatpants, and a ski mask that covered his face and neck. When he thought the coast was clear, he moved to the stairwell and positioned himself up on two large lead pipes that carried water for the parking garage's sprinkler system. He was turned on his side, and his slender body was covered just right. He was now concealed way up on the ceiling of the stairwell, waiting for the right moment to make his escape.

He heard their footsteps approaching and their soft voices getting closer, and soon the Mag flashlights attached to their guns illuminated the stairwell. The SWAT team of five men walked right under his position as the team leader radioed to his superior and said the ground floor was all clear. The Entity heard their superior tell the team, "Ten-Four," and the team leader told his men to move straight forward.

He waited until he knew they were far enough away from his area, and then the Entity very quietly lowered himself to the floor. He looked around the garage and saw no signs of policeman or civilians, but there were two surveillance cameras positioned up high on the ceiling. One was pointed away from him, and the other was pointed toward the area where he needed to make his escape.

When he saw the grand opportunity he needed, he crawled quickly on his hands and knees and was able to take cover behind a large SUV parked directly in the camera's line of sight. It gave him cover as he pulled open the steel grate of a sewer cover, lowered himself inside, and stepped down onto the ladder fixed on the wall. He closed the grate quietly and then stepped down all the way until his feet touched the dirty sewer water. He took out his small flashlight and looked around to see if he could get a bearing on his position. He knew he had to be right under the main part of the mall on First Avenue. He walked to the three-way intersection of the sewer system and figured that if he traveled along the right tunnel, it would take him due east and he would be able to find a manhole cover under Fourth Avenue. He quickly but quietly walked in that direction and knew that he had once again outsmarted the police.

He climbed the steel rungs of a ladder and heard the rushing sounds of vehicles above him. He looked up as he used enough strength to push the steel cover up and confirmed that he was on Fourth Avenue. Other than the rush of cars, he didn't see or hear any people passing by even though he was directly under a pedestrian sidewalk. He pushed the steel cover away from the manhole and climbed out. He then rolled to his left side and placed the cover back into place. He stayed low to the ground, rolled again to his left, and found himself hidden behind a group of bushes in front of a tall commercial building.

He took off his ski mask, placed his flashlight in his back pocket, and dusted himself off. He then calmly strolled out from behind the bushes and started to walk at a slow pace as two police cruisers whisked by, heading in the direction of the mall. He laughed to himself as he saw a yellow taxi parked on the side of the street. He very politely asked the driver if he could take him to National Avenue. The driver obliged, and the Entity sat in the backseat and smiled again to himself. *The fools. I evaded them again, and I took out so many of their elite team members. But I didn't get to kill you just yet, Brooks! But I will wait for the right moment; I want to face you in person alone so I can kill you, along with your precious Stephanie,* he thought as the taxi made its way to the address he requested.

Chapter 8

It was 1:00 a.m. by the time all the teams completed the search of Westfield Mall. The only items they found were located in a garbage dumpster on the top level of the parking garage. They had found the Entity's ninjalike uniform and both of the swords he had used in the fatal attacks upon his victims. Any other small daggers or tools he had taken with him as he made his escape.

Chief Chase briefed Rick in Rick's office. He asked if the team was assembled in the conference room. Rick picked up the phone and called the room's extension. Rob answered and told him the team was present and waiting for the chief and his staff to brief them on the bloody night of Friday, August 19, 2012—a date that would be marked from now on by the massacre and other fatal accidents that had taken the lives of sixteen policemen and civilians in the city of San Diego.

Rick and Chief John Chase entered the conference room, and Rick closed the door behind them; his deputy chief was already present, along with the remaining members of the task force and Stephanie. Chief Chase sent a dirty look at Ed and Stephanie, who were seated next to one another. The entire room was dead silent, and there was a feeling of shock and sadness among the remaining team members. But they all knew the mood was going to turn to heated anger as Chief Chase prepared to speak.

"I want to first say that I thank God that my remaining team members were not killed or seriously hurt. But we lost our good friends and exceptional team members Julie O'Keefe and Skip Jones, along with thirteen other policemen and one civilian, who was killed on the freeway during the vehicle chase," the chief told them as he read from his briefing report. Then he threw the folder down on the table.

"So now we are more than a month's time into these new serial slayings, and from what Rick has told me, we are no closer to solving this case on forensic evidence or even naming a suspect at this time, which has resulted in a total of twenty-three deaths in my city—the largest number of serial slayings in the shortest amount of time in not just our country's history but the whole damn world's!

"Even with the help of the FBI, who gave us the assistance of Miss Stephanie Morgan, their best profiler on the West Coast, the only thing we have accomplished so far has been a nice love match between Miss Morgan and Mr. Ed Brooks, who are now engaged to be married. Well that's fuckin' impressive, Brooks! Congratulations to you both, because you can now spend as much time with one another as you want! You're both removed from this case, along with this entire team. I am now letting the FBI lead the investigation into this case. Rick will be the only current member staying on to assist the FBI, and I will be picking a whole new team of detectives," Chief Chase shouted at them at first and then finished in a calm voice, letting the team know they had been replaced for not discovering any useful leads or evidence to follow up on.

Ed and Stephanie glared at Chief Chase after hearing his remarks about them. Ed slowly rose from his seat. Stephanie gently reached out and held his left arm in an effort to persuade him not to confront the chief. But Ed pulled away from her grasp, and his gaze fixed upon their boss, burning with rage

"You know something, John? Out of all those victims you just mentioned, I think you forgot this guy killed my ex-wife and her husband, and he was truly out to kill Stephanie and me tonight at your so-called safe house. How did he know we were staying there?

And you think we have no new leads or connections or evidence. You're wrong, because Rob, Stephanie, and I think there is a link between this killer and the Nathan Malcolm killings four years ago, along with another big link. No one has put that together except for the three of us," Ed told the chief, referring to the connection to the Jack the Ripper murders more than a century ago.

Ed went into the gory details about how the Ripper's five victims had been mutilated and the similarities to the murders four years ago and more recently. He explained the ties between the main Ripper suspect, Francis Tumblety, and his relation to Nathan Malcolm. The chief stood in place, staring in disbelief. He then turned to look at Rick, who admitted he had known about Ed's theory from the beginning but that they decided to keep it classified so it would not leak to fellow officers or the media. They hadn't wanted the story to break until they were absolutely certain they were right about this.

Ken Rogers and Jack Kerns turned and look at one another, because for four years Ed and Rob had kept them in the dark about this. Chief Chase, still mystified by what he had just heard, ordered Rick to have them bring all their files into the room. Rick also arranged for food and coffee to be sent in, and the chief said it was going to be a long night and very late morning as the team went through all the files and evidence.

For the next four and a half hours, Ed and Stephanie went over everything they uncovered about Nathan Malcolm: how he had grown up in Marion, Iowa and how his grandfather had claimed the body of his great uncle, Francis Tumblety, in St. Louis in 1903 and then changed his family's name to Malcolm a short time after he saw to Francis's burial in Rochester, New York.

Chief Chase read all about Francis Tumblety and how not only Ed but other historians believed he was the Ripper. Chase couldn't believe that Tumblety was a blood relative to Nathan Malcolm and that was what had put him over the edge and inspired him to murder those poor women.

As the men kept talking about the case, their sleeves rolled up and freshly made coffee in front of them, Stephanie—who was still wearing her elegant royal blue dress—placed her hand over her mouth and yawned softly. Ed looked up and noticed how tired she was. He got up from where he was sitting, went over to her, and grasped her hand.

"Hey, why don't we get a large number of cops together and have them escort you back to my house so you can get some sleep? I know it's been a very traumatic and sad night for all of us," Ed told her.

Stephanie touched his face and said it had started out a happy night for them when they got engaged. Rick heard them talking and told Stephanie that Ed was right. They would finish up here soon, and then they would break for a few hours and convene again by early afternoon.

The chief gave Rick permission to have ten officers escort Stephanie home; he wanted them heavily armed and in constant contact with headquarters. Ed placed his jacket over his fiancée's shoulders and walked out the door and into the hallway. Five heavily armed cops were ready to escort Stephanie to the parking lot and the awaiting unmarked vehicles. She hugged and kissed Ed gently, and he told her not to worry; she was safe, and he would be home very soon. The cops walked her out the back exit doors, and Ed watched as she got into one of the vehicles and they all drove off together. He overheard Rick telling Rob that he had two units of cops looking after his wife and daughter at home. They would take every precaution necessary to maintain their safety until this whole ordeal was over.

"So we were able to recover the suspect's duffle bag, which contained two short samurai swords, one black crossbow with arrows, a pair of short steel pliers, and an entire black ninja outfit made of black sterile cloth. We shipped the items over to Dr. Farrell's office so she can test them for DNA and fingerprints, but my guess is that we will not find anything if he used gloves and cleaned his weapons good before using them tonight," Rick told John Chase, who nodded.

As he looked at the gruesome crime scene photos from the supposed safe house where his men were supposed to keep Ed and Stephanie safe, Chase felt sorry for the way he had snapped at Ed earlier and wanted to apologize.

"Look, Ed, I'm sorry I lost my temper with you and Stephanie. I was just so mad that we lost so many good men and women tonight, and now their families have lost them forever. I know this piece of crap killed Kayla and her husband just to get back at you, and he was after you two tonight. You saved Stephanie's life by taking her out for the evening, and that was really a brave thing you did confronting the Entity in the mall all alone before backup got there to assist you, just like you did when you went after Malcolm the first time," Chase told him.

Ed broke into a smile and thanked him. After returning their attention back to the case, they were still frustrated that they couldn't find any connecting evidence or suspects who might be related or connected to Nathan Malcolm in any capacity.

Chief Chase looked at the time; it was now 8:30 a.m. "All right, we have been going over this all night, and now it's morning. Let's all break for a while as Dr. Farrell and Dr. Adams do their jobs, and I will have Western Division's detectives check on the sports bike the suspect was using. We know it came up stolen from a civilian the other day. Maybe some witnesses saw the suspect take it from the beach, where it was last parked by its owner. We need to be back here by 2:00 p.m. Ed and Rob need to be escorted to their homes," Chase ordered, and everyone felt a bit of relief that they could finally break for a shower and some sleep.

Ed arrived home shortly after 9:00 a.m.; there were six police cruisers parked outside his housing complex. As he entered his condo, he was met by the lead commander of the SWAT team assigned to his protection. He explained to Ed that he and his four-man team would stay inside the apartment with him and there would be a change of shift of uniformed officers stationed outside the home's perimeter. Even the uniformed cops were heavily armed with M4 machine guns.

Ed thanked him and his men and told them to make themselves comfortable but for no one to touch any of his Jimi Hendrix CDs or his LP collection.

Ed then quietly opened the door to his bedroom. Stephanie was asleep in bed. He walked over to his dresser and took off his shoulder holster and gun. Then he undressed and got into bed beside Stephanie, trying not to wake her. As he lay facing the ceiling, he thought of Kayla, Julie, and Skip—the people he had known the best—along with all the other cops who had been killed. He closed his eyes, not because he was tired but because now more than ever he wanted to kill the new murderer, for he had made it a personal vendetta against Ed Brooks. And Ed was still searching for the reason why.

Stephanie reached over and held Ed's hand under the covers. Ed looked over and saw her smiling at him.

"Please promise me you're not going to do anything crazy to stop this guy, Ed. You may walk right into his trap if you go out on your own to stop him. I can't lose you now that you've asked me to be your wife. Please think of the life we can share together before you go back to Central Division later," Stephanie pleaded.

Ed reached over and pulled her to him. She rested her head on his chest and closed her eyes.

"I promise you I will be all right and make sure no harm comes to you and the rest of our friends. I also promise you we will get married shortly after this is all over with," Ed vowed, and Stephanie felt safer and content being held in his arms. As she drifted back to sleep, Ed softly glided his hands up and down her smooth bare skin, closed his eyes, and dreamed of a new happy life with her.

At 2:00 p.m. that afternoon, Ed and Stephanie were back in the Central Division's conference room as Dr. Diana Farrell presented her DNA findings from the recovered weapons and pair of pliers used by the suspect. Rick read off the findings from the printed report and then passed the folder to Ed and Stephanie to look over. Ed again became very angry and frustrated that the suspect had left no DNA behind.

"Dr. Farrell found no human DNA, fingerprints, blood, or hair on any of the weapons or the pair of pliers. Neither was there DNA evidence inside or outside the black duffle bag or ninja costume he wore. Latent fingerprint experts went over the motorcycle inch by inch, and the only fingerprints they found on the bike were that of the owner's. Both Farrell and the fingerprint experts believe the suspect wears either sterile cloth gloves or latex gloves when handling weapons and clothes. The swords and knives did show that they had all been cleaned with honing oil before they were used last night."

Ed read both Farrell's findings and the handprint examiner's findings and told Rick and Stephanie that the killer cleaned his weapons with honing oil because it kept them free of rust and dirt and made it very unlikely for him to leave any DNA behind. Rick declared that they were dealing with an intelligent person who was aware enough of DNA and forensics to know how not to leave any behind.

"Well, I say the killer has medical knowledge and medical equipment to carry out his work. What if we searched local hospitals and even medical colleges for potential suspects?" Stephanie suggested.

Ed raised his eyebrows at the idea. "That's one thing we haven't looked into yet. He would have access to a hospital's medical equipment and white vans. Medical schools use white cargo vans to teach students what to expect from crime scenes as medical examiners," he said, and Rick picked up the phone and called Ken Rogers and Jack Kerns to get them back to Central Division as soon as they were done following all the stolen motorcycle leads.

"Once they get here, we will brief them on this new possible lead. The three of us are going to look in the computer at all the medical doctors and nurses at area hospitals. There has to be at least one person who has medical knowledge and has broken the law in some fashion that we can follow up on," Rick told them.

The three of them agreed to begin searching hospitals in the area. They worked on separate computers to save some time. When Ken and Jack arrived at the homicide division's office, they told the others that they'd had no luck with witnesses who had seen the suspect steal the motorcycle. Another good lead had turned into a dead end. Rick and Ed briefed them that they were now looking at medical personnel at the area's eight main hospitals, mainly physicians who had criminal pasts that might tie their medical knowledge to the crimes. Ken and Jack took seats and started to look up names and hospitals to help them.

The time was now going on 4:30 p.m., and they hoped to find a good suspect to investigate this evening, as the FBI had informed Chief Chase that they would be sending six top agents to take over the lead of the investigation. Ed and his team did not like the thought of losing control as the lead team, but they all knew they had no choice in that decision.

For four more hours they went over all established doctors, nurse practitioners, and student residents. They eliminated the smaller hospitals and were now looking at the last two major hospitals in the city. Both hospitals were medical centers and universities for student doctors to work on their internships. Ed had a feeling they might be on to something, but time was against them. He encouraged the team to work until 9:00 p.m. Then they would break for dinner.

As Ken looked through last names that began with the letter *P*, he clicked on the next name: Alan Pace. He leaned back in his chair to stretch his arms and legs. He hoped Ed would let them break for dinner soon; he was starving. As he was about to let out a big yawn, the screen brought up Alan Pace's driver's license picture and the medical resident's felony record. Ken held his yawn in, his eyes now locked on the computer screen. He yelled for Ed and the others. "Hey, guys! I think we got something here."

Ed and the others came over to Ken's desk to look at what he found. Ed was the first one there and began to read about Alan Pace.

"Alan Pace, twenty-seven years old, born August 22, 1985, was arrested while in college with others when they were interns at California Medical College. Pace was the lead suspect in an attempted gang rape of a fellow female student at a frat party two years ago. Pace had planned with two other males to lace the alleged victim's drink with sedatives and move her to a secluded location where they would take turns raping her. The men were stopped by the victim's friends before they could move her out of the house and into his vehicle. The police were called to the scene, but after Pace and his two accomplices were arrested, they were released because of lack of evidence. His high-powered attorney claimed the female was just drunk, and no narcotics were found in her system by the urine test." Ed continued to read the whole police report on Pace, which said he was currently a resident at the Regional Medical Center for general surgery. He looked at Stephanie as Ken continued to read more about Alan Pace.

"Hey, Ed, according to this, Alan Pace's father is Dr. Albert Pace, a head member of Quasar Pharmaceuticals here in San Diego," Ken said, and the whole team looked at him, knowing that was where Nathan Malcolm had worked. Alan Pace's father might have been a close colleague of Malcolm, and this guy, Alan Pace, might have some knowledge of that connection and a link to these latest murders.

"Okay, Ed, you and Rob go with Ken and Jack to locate Alan Pace. Stephanie and I will locate his father and find out whatever he knows about Nathan Malcolm and his son. I'm not telling the chief or anyone else about this yet because we are merely going to question these men. Understood, people?" Rick told his team, and they all acknowledged his orders. But as they all headed out to their vehicles, Rob and Stephanie knew Ed wanted to do more than just talk chat with Mr. Pace.

Rick and Stephanie went to the listed home address of Dr. Albert Pace, which was located in one of the very affluent neighborhoods in San Diego. His wife invited them in and was very cordial to the two law enforcement officers, considering they hadn't called beforehand and it was getting late into the evening. Ed and his men went to the Regional Medical Center to see if they could locate and question the younger Alan Pace. As the four detectives walked into the hospital after parking their unmarked vehicles in the front drive, they held their badges out to identify themselves as policemen. The volunteer at the desk paged one of the nursing administrators to come and assist Ed's investigation.

A female nursing administrator came to the main lobby. Ed briefed her on why he and his team were on the premises. She started to make phone calls to different departments of the hospital to try to locate Mr. Pace for them. After a brief time, she was able to find out that he was working alongside a surgical team performing minor surgery in one the OR units upstairs. She escorted Ed and Rob up to the fifth floor, but not before Ed instructed Ken and Jack to stay in the lobby, and Rob told them he would call them on the main lobby desk's extension right away if they had trouble dealing with their suspect. Ken and Jack stated to Ed they would remain in the lobby, and they had a picture of Alan Pace in case he tried to make his way past them.

Ed and Rob posted themselves right outside the two metal doors that led into the OR wing. Then Ed went over to a nearby desk's landline phone and called Stephanie to see if she and Rick had made any progress. When Stephanie answered her phone, she whispered to Ed as Rick interviewed the older doctor and his wife.

"Ed, we just got here, and Rick has been asking him if he has any deep knowledge on Nathan Malcolm. We haven't asked him any questions about his son just yet. He told us that when the news broke that Malcolm was about to be indicted on the illegal steroid charges, he flipped out. He made statements about how he wanted to hurt those who were against him and how his wife Jane had destroyed his life and relationship with their child and how he wished he could have killed Jane himself and how women in general were the cause of all the problems in the world."

Ed was listening to her when he saw the doors open and Alan Pace come out in his blue scrubs. Rob pulled him to the side and started to talk to him. Ed looked back down as he continued his conversation with Stephanie. He encouraged her to press Dr. Pace on whether his son had followed the case of Nathan Malcolm. As he was about to say good-bye, he heard Rob scream his name. He looked up and saw Alan Pace running down the hallway away from them. "Shit!" Ed yelled as he hung up on Stephanie and called Ken and Jack on the lobby's extension to warn them that their person of interest was on the run.

Jack said he would cover the back exits in case he tried to flee to his vehicle. Ed and Rob ran in the direction Pace had gone, and they spotted him running up the stairwell to the top floors. Ed and Rob ran right behind him. They knew the hospital had eight regular floors and that the ninth and tenth floors were mechanical rooms for the elevators and the roof access. Ed called out for Pace to stop running, but Pace passed the ninth floor landing and made his way up the last flight of stairs toward the roof. As Pace opened the door and ran into the top floor mechanical room, Rob reached the door but waited for Ed before proceeding inside. Rob took out his small flashlight. They armed themselves and then very cautiously entered the very dark and large room. The mechanical units for the elevators were in operation, their cables and mechanics functioning loudly. As Ed and Rob passed the units, Ed motioned to Rob to go check the right side of the room as Ed stayed to the left side.

The room was dirty and smelled of oil. Ed noticed a door at the back of the room, which he thought led out to the roof. He moved very slowly along the wet, stained floor. Rob held his flashlight out to peek around the corners he came upon. He knew Pace was still lurking on this floor because he hadn't gotten by him and Ed. Just as Rob came around the corner of a large metal cabinet, a metal crowbar struck the hand holding the flashlight. Rob dropped the flashlight, looked up, and was struck hard in his ribs. He fell into the cabinet and was punched in the face. He fell to the floor. Upon hearing the commotion, Ed ran over to Rob. As he looked up, he saw Pace darting for the roof door. Ed screamed at him to stop running. When Pace threw open the door, its alarm went off very loudly to alert the security personnel.

Ed bent down to Rob, who stated he was fine and ordered Ed to go after their man. Ed ran full speed out the door and stepped out on gravel surface of the roof. He looked around the large rooftop and saw several air conditioning units and alcoves Pace could be hiding behind. As Rob made his way to the doorway, Ed instructed him to stay there; it was the only way for Pace to make his escape. Rob took out his cell phone and called dispatch for assistance stat.

Ed moved with his back against the bricks of the nearest alcove. The light of the half-moon gave them enough light to see by in the dark. Ed kept his finger gingerly over his gun's trigger, not wanting to kill this young man but hoping to apprehend him and question him to gain knowledge about these crimes. Ed moved to the corner of the alcove and was about to peer out when Pace came up behind him and prepared to strike him in the back of the head with the crowbar. Ed heard his feet scrape on the gravel behind him, quickly turned, and bent down, dodging the swing of the crowbar, which struck the bricks. Ed blocked a return swing with his left hand, kicked Pace in the stomach, and hit him in the face with his left fist. Pace flew off his feet and onto the rooftop. Ed called for Rob, who ran toward them with his gun drawn. Pace got up and started to run away.

Ed and Rob followed very slowly, knowing he had nowhere to go. Rob told Ed that units were on the way to assist them. Pace made his way to the far railing and ran out of room. He looked back at the two cops who had him cornered.

Ed said to him very calmly, "All right, Alan, that's enough. You have nowhere else to run. Drop the crowbar and just surrender to us so we can take you in and talk all this over. No harm will come to you, I promise," Ed tried to reassure him that he would be treated very well. He knew Alan Pace must be emotionally disturbed.

Pace dropped the crowbar to the gravel rooftop and threw his hands up into the air to give them the impression that he was about to surrender. Ed told Rob he had him covered. Rob holstered his weapon and took out his handcuffs to secure Pace.

"You think you can help me? You can't! No one can help me. All the best doctors and shrinks have tried, but they can't! I don't want to go back to another mental hospital! I want my freedom and to continue to do what I love!"

Ed and Rob looked at one another. Rob told Pace to move away from the edge of the roof as he moved closer to handcuffs him. Ed whispered to Rob that they needed to get him very quickly, and they started to run toward him. Pace cursed at them. Then he smiled and leaped over the metal fence, hurling himself down ten stories to the ground. He hit the pavement headfirst, killing him instantly. Ed cursed loudly, knowing they had lost a key suspect.

The police blocked off the back parking lot where the body of Alan Pace had landed after his plunge off the roof of the Regional Medical Center. The forensic team removed the body after the team went through Pace's pockets and found a set of car keys and a key to his personal locker in the staff locker room. To save time, Ed and Rob went to investigate his locker, and Jack and Ken went to look through his vehicle—a Mercedes SUV parked in the staff parking lot. Ed and Rob found many *Playboy* magazines in his locker; they also found keys to his apartment, which was located in a nearby complex. The other two detectives donned latex gloves and looked through the SUV. They found some very disturbing items in the center console and glove compartment. Ken and Jack looked at one another and said they needed to bag the items and inform Ed. They then told the forensic team that they could tow the vehicle to the lab for examination and testing for fingerprints.

They met up with Ed and Rob at the Mission Hills Garden apartment complex and entered the apartment, equipped with a search warrant. They began to look around for more evidence and items like the ones found in Pace's vehicle. As Ed and Rob checked the bedroom, Ken and Jack looked through the kitchen cupboards and refrigerator. Rob found a shoe box on the floor of the closet. He opened it and found various styles of knives and duct tape.

Ed called them all into the bedroom. Jack and Ken had found some key items in the refrigerator. They bagged them and went to see what Ed was calling them about. They entered the bedroom. Ed had turned on the television, which was hooked up to a portable recording system. They watched a very disturbing video of a naked girl unconscious in bed. They were able to hear Alan Pace gloating over her; he was very pleased to have another sexy girl as his victim. Ed quickly turned off the television and instructed Jack to get the camcorder and all the discs together. Rob found more CDs and pictures of naked women. Ed informed them that they would bring all the evidence back to Central Division for Stephanie and Rick to view.

Ed called Rick, and Ken came over to him and showed Ed the items he and Jack had found in the kitchen. Ed looked into the paper bag and saw many bottles of liquid ecstasy, a date rape drug. Ed shook his head in disgust as Rick came on the line and briefed him on their findings. Rick told him good job and that they would see him back at the office soon.

Back at Central Division, Stephanie was interviewing Alan Pace's parents in a small office to get more information about him. His parents were distraught over his suicide. They'd had no idea their son had a dark side to him or that he would meet and drug women who declined his romantic advances. Raping them while they were unconscious was his way of exacting his revenge on them.

When the detectives arrived from Pace's apartment, Rick took them to the conference room and got the full story. It appeared to the team and Chief Chase that even if Alan Pace had nothing to do with the serial murders, he was in fact a serial rapist of at least four women, if not more. The forensic team was still going through the CDs they had recovered from his home.

Stephanie came into the conference room. She was holding her notepad, ready to brief them on what she had been able to find out. She took a seat next to Ed.

"Well, from what I gather from his parents, Alan was very smart and very outgoing from his childhood and when he began school through when he started medical school. He was liked by his friends and wanted to follow his father into medicine. He enjoyed sports and traveling, just like many young men his age. But one thing his parents did admit to me, and something they didn't feel was a very big issue even though he kept it a secret from them, was the fact that he had no luck with women. From when he was in high school to even now, he never had a steady girlfriend.

"There may have been disturbing reasons behind why women didn't find him attractive. So in order for him to force himself on unsuspecting young women, he would meet them in a club or a bar, make small talk with them, lace their drinks with the liquid ecstasy, and walk them out of the bar or club while everyone assumed the female was only drunk. He would then take them to his apartment, rape them, and videotape it so he could cherish the act later. He was very sick and disturbed indeed, but after watching three of the rapes he recorded, I don't think he ever killed any of his victims. He never stated in his videos that he wanted to hurt them; he just found that drugging them was the only way to fulfill his sexual desires and fantasies," Stephanie told them.

The men looked at one another and felt sick to their stomachs at what this soon-to-be doctor had been doing to these poor women.

"This guy had the same MO as the famous Andrew Luster case, another sick fuck who's imprisoned for life," Ken Rogers's remarked.

Stephanie stated that she believed Alan Pace had watched the trial of Andrew Luster and got his motivation to act the crimes out from that case.

"So this is great. We were able to stop this piece of shit! But is there any connection at all between this guy and Nathan Malcolm, Francis Tumblety, or Jack the Ripper?" Ed blurted out, angry that after getting into a violent confrontation with Alan Pace that resulted in his suicide, they were once again no closer to breaking open their case and were going to lose their investigation to the FBI tomorrow.

"Ed, if you will let me finish explaining, I will tell you that I did find out a few things from Dr. Albert Pace, who knew Nathan Malcolm from when they worked together at Quasar Pharmaceuticals. He told me he knew Malcolm always worked late in his office, researching the most potent brands of GHB and anabolic steroids, but not just to make a fortune distributing them. Apparently he felt that if he took them himself, they would make him very powerful and even younger in appearance. As we all know, a lot of sports athletes use them to enhance their performance and make them stronger. In Malcolm's case, he did it to fight off and physically control fit young women, and my guess is it helped him elude the police as well," Stephanie told them. "As impressive as this all is, Albert Pace had no knowledge that Malcolm was the killer until he was stopped four years ago. Malcolm never told him whether his only child was a boy or a girl or what became of the child after his divorce."

"So what do we do now? All of our solid leads have turned out to be futile. It's obvious from the safe house attack and the attack on Dr. Farrell and Dr. Adams that the killer has inside knowledge of our doings and investigations. So what if the killer is one of our own? A cop or another forensic investigator we missed, or even an FBI agent?" Rob expressed his belief.

When he said *FBI agent*, they all looked at Stephanie. Ed's eyes locked on her, and he thought, *Why couldn't the killer be female? Stephanie is strong, in great shape, and has martial arts training. Could she be the daughter of Nathan Malcolm?*

As Ed thought this crazy scenario over, Stephanie became red in the face. She knew what Ed and the other men were thinking. "What? Are you crazy? To think I'm the killer! Ed, what's wrong with you? I was with you the whole time during the murders at the house and when we chased him into the mall! I'm your fiancé! How could you all think this about me?" Stephanie screamed at them, getting up from her seat, storming out of the conference room, and running down the hall.

Ed ran after her, and Rick and the rest of the men felt embarrassed and rotten for even considering the idea. Rick told them to break for the rest of the night—it was after 11:00 p.m.—and instructed them to be back early in the morning.

As Stephanie ran into the parking lot, she saw a team of uniformed cops around their squad cars. Just as she asked them to take her home, Ed caught up to her and told the cops to forget about it and that he would take her home. Stephanie broke away from his grasp and walked fast toward Ed's SUV. Ed called to her to wait, but Stephanie just yelled at him to unlock the door. When Ed caught up to her again, he placed his hands on her shoulders. Stephanie demanded he take her home now and shouted that she was going to pack her things and book a plane back to LA tonight.

"Hey, I'm sorry, Stephanie. The guys are sorry. I know you could never hurt anyone. I know how you feel about me," Ed told her.

Stephanie continued to stare at him angrily, still very upset with Ed and his friends. "What on Earth would make you think I could be involved with harming any innocent person or be related to Nathan Malcolm? Why? Just because I know karate and kicked your ass one night? That makes me a prime suspect for murder?" she shouted at him and then started to cry. She yelled at Ed again to open the door and take her home now.

Ed gently took her in his arms, and Stephanie tried to break away from him. He kissed her softly on the lips, and she calmed down and eventually returned his kiss. Ed lifted his head and held her tightly in his arms, whispering to her that he was sorry and knew he was a jerk for thinking that about her.

"No, Ed, you're not a jerk. You're an asshole, like the rest of your friends, for thinking that about me," she told him.

Ed broke into a soft laugh and asked her if he could take her home now and if she could forgive him.

"Yes, Ed, take me home now, but you're sleeping on the couch tonight," she said, and Ed told her that was fine. They got into his Envoy and headed home, escorted by the two squad cars.

Once home, Ed ate a quick sandwich, and Stephanie had a ready-made salad. She hadn't said a word to him since they arrived.

Ed showered and changed into his pajamas. As Stephanie waited for him to finish in the bedroom, she left him two blankets and his pillow on the edge of the bed to take to the living room couch. When Ed noticed the pillow and blankets, he thought she was kidding. But she wasn't. Not wanting to anger her further, Ed took the items, walked out to the couch, and made himself comfortable. He used his remote and started to play a Jimi Hendrix CD on his stereo system. *Well, at least I got you, Jimi. Women! I wish I knew what it is that make them so sensitive to everything,* Ed thought, turning the television on but keeping the sound off so he could hear his music.

Stephanie finished her shower and put on an elegant cream silk slip and then her long bathrobe to cover herself. She heard the music coming from the living room and thought about Ed and his favorite musician. She wondered how she was going to get any sleep tonight listening to Jimi Hendrix songs. She walked to the door and looked out at Ed, who was watching the late news cast about the death of Alan Pace.

"Ed, please can you turn that music off? I want to try to get some sleep now if that's all right with you," she told him.

Ed stared at her. He was about to say that this was still his house, but he knew Stephanie would probably pack her things and walk out that very minute if he said that, so he shut off the CD player. She thanked him and closed the door to the bedroom. Ed then shut off the television and picked up a book Rob had lent him. As he was about to start reading the first chapter, Stephanie opened the door and came out of the bedroom. She asked if she could sit with him for a minute to talk. Ed told her of course. Still wearing her long bathrobe, she sat next to him on the couch. She looked at the book and asked what he was reading. Ed told her it was a book Rob had loaned to him a while back. It was based on a true UFO case, and he'd raved about how good it was. Ed hadn't had chance to read it yet. As Stephanie smiled at him, Ed held her hand and looked at her engagement ring, which was still on her finger.

"So it must be a good sign that you're still wearing my ring. Are we still engaged, or are you just going to keep the ring and sell it for money?" he asked her.

Stephanie shook her head. "Again, Ed, you say something that you know is impossible for me to do. I have no plans to end our engagement, and I will never sell this ring. It is my first and will be my only engagement ring, and I still want to be your wife, but I'm still mad at you for thinking that way about me at Central Division tonight."

"Stephanie, I said I'm very sorry, and I know I hurt you. What else can I do to make you forgive me? Let you kick my ass with karate again?" he replied.

Stephanie started to laugh and said, "That will be a start."

Ed laughed at her. He held her soft hands and pulled her toward him, and they kissed. Ed picked her up gently in his arms, carried her to the bedroom, and laid her on his bed. As they kissed passionately, Ed removed her bathrobe and undid the straps to her slip. Stephanie stopped him and asked what had made him think that she could ever be a serial killer.

"Well, I remembered the movie *Basic Instinct* with Sharon Stone, so I thought why not the woman you love as the killer?"

Stephanie called him an ass. Ed removed her slip and kissed her deeply while Stephanie removed his top and bottoms, unaware that they were being watched from afar. The looker also counted the number of policeman gathered around the house in both marked and unmarked vehicles. He looked through his night vision scope, gazing upon Ed and Stephanie through the sheer curtains of their bedroom window, and debated what to do next.

"Twenty cops assigned to protect you two from me, way more than last time. I can have so much more glory and satisfaction killing all of them now and then you, Ed Brooks. But I'm experiencing such delight watching you make love to your dear Stephanie. I have elegant plans for this beautiful woman of yours. I will wait for the right time to kill you, Brooks, along with the rest of your friends. The time is sooner than you all expect."

He laughed to himself as he watched Ed and Stephanie make love from his position on a nearby rooftop. He became aroused as he gazed at Stephanie's naked body. Her figure and breasts and her very good facial features made her the most beautiful woman he had ever laid eyes on. He couldn't kill her. He now wanted her for himself, and he knew she would be his soon enough.

Chapter 9

When Ed awoke the next morning, he didn't see Stephanie next to him in bed. He got up, put on his bathrobe, and went into the living room, where he saw Stephanie working on her laptop. Ed walked over and kissed her good morning. Then he fixed them both a cup of coffee and asked what she was working on. Stephanie told him that with the amount of evidence they had gathered about the suspect and their knowledge of what he knew about the Malcolm killings and the Jack the Ripper murders, she could now formulate a profile of the killer.

She told Ed she had been working on it for two hours now, and she planned to print it out and show the whole team. It summarized the likely suspect's age, height, weight, and ethnicity. She explained to Ed that the work of a profiler was not a science but rather an art. Her task was to outline the traits of the suspect and the path these traits provided would lead the police and investigators to the guilty party. But Stephanie cautioned him that even profilers could be wrong, and the suspect could turn out to be someone they would never have suspected.

Ed tried to peer in closer at the monitor to read at what Stephanie was typing, but she gently pushed his face away and told him she would tell them everything at the office. She believed their suspect's characteristics would allow them to finally identify and arrest him. Ed told her good work, and they shared a kiss. Then he told her they needed to hurry up and get to Central Division before the briefing began.

A little while later in the conference room, Stephanie handed out copies of her complete profile for the team members to carefully look over. Rick had called Chief John Chase to come view the profile for himself. Stephanie used the room's laptop to bring the profile up on the LCD screen so she could outline key points of the suspect profile as she spoke.

"Now, before we begin, let me first say that I can be wrong about this. As I admitted to Ed this morning, a profiler's job is not to say definitively whether a certain individual is the one who committed a crime. My job is to combine all the evidence with the crimes patterns and the known behavior of the suspect to get as close of match as possible," Stephanie explained and then opened the floor for the men to ask her questions.

Rick read the age of the suspect and his physical stature and traits. "So, Stephanie, you concluded that our suspect is a white male between the ages of thirty-four and forty-three years of age. He may have ties to Nathan Malcolm, either as a close friend or co-worker from the pharmaceutical company, or he may just be a person who is very interested in both the Nathan Malcolm killings and the Jack the Ripper murders and wants to be recognized as an infamous sociopath killer like them."

Stephanie told Rick that was precisely what she believed and that there was also a remote chance that the killer was even a blood relative of Nathan Malcolm out to exact revenge on both innocent victims and the policemen who stopped Malcolm. Stephanie referenced the murders of Ed's ex-wife and her husband. Ed looked up at her.

"So you also believe that the killer lives within a certain radius of all the murders, knows the city of San Diego very well, and preselects his victims and the locations where he meets and murders them. In the cases of Lauren Morton, Ashley Cook, and Jackie Mays, he abducted and killed them in different locations and left their bodies in areas people either inhabit or visit often. So he wanted his victims' remains to be discovered and for law enforcement to try to catch him," Rob read back to her.

Stephanie told Rob that this killer, like Malcolm, was not afraid of the police or the FBI, and he wasn't afraid to die. Rob shook his head, knowing that after all the things the killer had done and the big car chase he had led them on, he had no respect for people or life itself.

Ed wasn't one bit surprised by all the things Stephanie had detailed in her profile about the killer, but one thing she wrote about the Ripper murders stood out to him. "You write that you believe that just like the Jack the Ripper suspect who wrote the "From Hell" letter to taunt George Lusk and the police of Scotland Yard, this suspect is trying to do the same thing to us. He wants us to piece this all together somehow, and you think he may be setting a trap for us, if not planning to kill the policeman he has singled out?" Ed asked.

Stephanie looked at Ed sadly and nodded. Rick and the team wanted her to explain this theory.

"After the murders of Kayla and her husband and the massacre at the safe house, which we all know was intended to kill Ed and myself, there has to be a big motivation for this killer to kill Ed Brooks and myself, being that I am now romantically connected to him. But because we are now guarded by the police 24/7, the killer will have to look at exacting revenge on our close friends and families if they are easier targets," Stephanie told them.

Rob and Ed looked at one another and then back at Rick.

"Guys, call your families now and find out where they are and ask them to get to a crowded public place or a friend's home right away if they can," Rick ordered.

Everyone took out their cell phones and began to contact their loved ones immediately. Rob called Antonella at home, Rick called Cate at her office, and Jack and Ken called their wives. Ed picked up the office phone and called Dr. Diana Farrell, being that she had already been a victim of the killer's attack once.

While all the men were busy contacting their families, Stephanie told them that the killer would stick to the late hours of darkness and continue his pattern of concealing himself to make it easier for him to escape if he was cornered again. Rob was still waiting for his wife to pick up the phone. When Antonella finally answered, Rob asked what was she doing and if the two policemen were outside in their vehicle, watching her and their daughter. She told him she had just come into the house after running some errands before heading to work.

"Rob, I just dropped Megan off at my mother's house to babysit. I know you will be working very late again tonight. I have to get back to work for a busy day and a late meeting," Antonella told him. As she talked to Rob on the cordless phone, she looked out the window at the unmarked vehicle but was unable to see the two men in the car. Puzzled, she told Rob she didn't see them.

"Look, lock the doors and stay inside. I'm coming over," was all Rob could say to his wife before the phone line went dead. Antonella quickly dropped the phone and ran to the front door to make sure it was locked. She then hurried to the back door. She was about to pass through the living room when she stopped and screamed as she saw a uniformed policeman sitting on her sofa with his throat slashed open and blood flowing from the deep wound. She turned and was about to run through the living room when she stopped and screamed again. Impaled to the wall with two knives in his palms and two knives in driven deep into his eyes was the other policeman.

Antonella turned around, and standing behind her was the Entity dressed in all black and holding a sharp short dagger. He told her in a soft voice to sit down in the chair, for he was not going to hurt her as long as she did what he said. Antonella knew everything about this killer from what Ed and Rob had told her. She knew she couldn't get away from him, and she knew Rob and Ed were coming to save her. So she complied with his instructions in order to buy herself time until they came.

She sat in the chair, and he told her to place her hands behind her and cross her wrists. As she crossed her wrists, he quickly used duct tape to bind them tightly together and then did the same to her feet. Antonella started to cry softly and begged him not hurt her because she had a young child.

The Entity placed his dagger back in its holder and then picked up a picture of Megan from a shelf. He stared at her innocent young smile and held the picture next to Antonella's face. Then he made a very surprising comment.

"Your daughter looks just like you, Mrs. Cullen. A very beautiful young child and her very beautiful mother," he said, stroking Antonella's cheek with his gloved hand. "You are different from those other foul women I have disposed of, for you are the mother of a child. I will not harm you, my dear, for I need you to deliver a message for me." Antonella listened in horror as he told her his message.

Suddenly she heard sirens blaring and the screeching of tires coming to a stop. The front door was kicked open, and Rob and Ed flew inside with their guns drawn. At the same time, Rick, Ken, and Jack broke through the back door. The men converged upon the living room, and Antonella yelled for Rob, crying. Rob and Ed rushed over to her. Ed took out his pocket knife and carefully cut through the duct tape to free her. She stood up. Rob held her tightly in his arms and asked if she was all right. She told him the killer hadn't harmed her, but he had killed the two poor policemen. Ed and the others looked at the shocking ways the officers had been killed and posed. The killer was openly mocking the police. Antonella called for Ed. He walked over to her and asked if she was all right.

"Ed, he instructed me to tell you this message. He said not only is he going to kill you, but he is going to take away everything you love and hold dear. He said just like he did with Kayla, he is going take away the woman you love now," she told him, crying hysterically.

Ed knew she meant Stephanie. They had left her at Central Division with other policemen in the building, but Ed still ran out the door, followed by Rick.

Once outside, Ed called Stephanie on her cell phone. When she answered him, he asked if she was all right and still at the office. She replied that she was all right and there were many policemen still with her. She asked if Antonella was safe. Ed filled her in on what happened and told her that Rob and his family were going to be moved to a secure location for their safety. Stephanie paused after hearing what had happened to Rob's wife. She knew it was going to be up to her to come up with a lead suspect if Ed and his fellow cops couldn't catch him in the act.

Rob and his family were taken out of the city of San Diego for their protection. In order to keep it as secret as possible, not even Rick or Ed were told where they were moved. Chief Chase agreed with Stephanie and Ed on one point about the suspect, whoever he may be: he could be a local medical doctor who had superior knowledge of the city and police procedures, or he had an inside contact who was leaking him vital information on the task force members, including where they lived and personal information about their families.

Rick and his wife, Dr. Adams, were seated with Ed and Stephanie in the conference room. Cate had joined them at Central Division when she brought over the autopsy results she and Dr. Diana Farrell had done on the last victim. The two couples had ordered dinner and were taking a break. It was 9:00 p.m.

"So do you think Rob will be rejoining us soon, or do you think he will want to stay with his family until this is over with?" Ed asked Rick, who looked over at Cate before he answered.

"I think Rob may want to stay with his wife and daughter and make certain they are safe. I don't blame him one bit. I talked with Chief Chase a short time ago, Ed, and he feels you and Stephanie should be placed into full protection and taken out of the city like Rob and his family. We know the killer has his sights set on both of you, and it's only a matter of time before he makes an attempt at one of you," Rick told them.

Ed knew he was right, but he wanted to stay on the case until he caught the Entity himself. However, he wanted Stephanie off the case and back home in LA by tomorrow.

"Rick, you know I'm staying active on this one until it's over, but I agree with you that Stephanie needs to be taken off the case and moved back home by tomorrow."

Stephanie made a face at her fiancé and was about to argue with him, but Ed cut her off and told her how he felt. "Look, Stephanie, this guy wants to not only kill me but you too. He killed Kayla just to get back at me, and if we hadn't gone out for dinner that night and away from the safe house, he would have killed both of us. So please, I want you back home in Los Angeles tomorrow and placed in around-the-clock protection," Ed said.

Stephanie was tired of arguing with him, and she knew he was right. She was very scared for their safety. Rick looked hard at Ed, and Ed returned his stare. This was a great way to get their families and close friends out of harm's way and concentrate all their efforts on stopping the Entity.

Ed and Stephanie returned home by 11:00 p.m., escorted by a great number of police cruisers and unmarked vehicles. As they entered their condo, Stephanie placed her laptop bag and briefcase down on the couch. She looked tired, disgusted, and angry with the whole situation. Ed saw she was upset, but he didn't know what she was mad about. He went into the bedroom and took off his jacket and shoulder holster. He placed his handgun on the end table next to the bed. When he came back into the living room, he found Stephanie sitting on the couch with a cup of tea in her hands, and he went over and sat with her. He reached out and took her hand, and she smiled at him. He asked her what was wrong.

"Ed, I'm not mad at you or Rick or the cops you work with. I know you are all doing your best to catch this creep and protect me, but I don't like being watched by men I don't know around the clock, even if they are cops and protecting us. Last night when we made love, I felt a little uncomfortable, like we were being watched."

Ed wanted to sound encouraging as he tried to assure her that his fellow police officers would not peer or pry into their personal business.

"Ed, I didn't feel like it was the police. I feel like it's him, and he knows all about us. He may be watching us right now," Stephanie told him.

Ed started to look around the room and at the windows. The curtains are drawn, but he felt she could be right. If he was following them, the Entity might have the upper hand and know all their movements, even when they least expected it. Ed got on his cell phone and called down to the shift commander assigned to their protection for the night. He asked him to make a sweep and look into all parked vehicles up and down the street and on the nearby rooftops because they felt they were being watched by the Entity. The commander thought Ed and Stephanie might just have a case of the eerie chills about that guy tonight, but he complied with Ed's orders and got two teams of four cops to patrol the areas around the complex.

From the same rooftop upon which he had conducted his dark surveillance the last couple nights, the Entity couldn't see them in the living room with his powerful night vision scope. However, he was able to hear their conversations by pointing his portable dish and microphone at the complex. The equipment was so powerful that he could hear them from 300 yards away. As he listened, he heard the squad leader begin the search of the vehicles below and the spot-checks of nearby rooftops.

He knew he had to leave now or risk being spotted by the police. He quickly gathered his equipment and placed it back into his black carry bag. He was once again dressed in a black ninja style outfit with a full black mask. As he heard voices below, he took out his black steel dagger as he moved to the far side of the roof and away from the stairwell door. He suspected that the police were moving in pairs or teams of four, and he had to get by them to make it to ground level.

He heard footsteps coming up the stairs, and the door slowly opened. He watched from around a brick corner. The two cops flashed their Mag flashlights around the roof, and they radioed back that they were now checking the rooftop of the apartment complex across the street.

The Entity smiled to himself and knew this was a challenge for him, but killing Ed's friends would bring another adrenaline rush. He gripped the handle of the knife harder in his right hand as he waited for the cop closest to him to come into view. He then rose from the ground behind the cop, grabbed his mouth and chin with his gloved left hand, drove his blade into the man's throat hard and deep, slicing it open. As the cop yelped in pain, he fired his gun into the air. The Entity threw him to the ground as his partner turned around and started to fire into the darkness, not even knowing what he was shooting at.

The Entity charged at him quickly and made a flying tackle into the cop's chest, throwing him back into the wall. He pinned the cop's right hand and gun to the wall and stabbed him repeatedly in his chest and stomach. With the last thrust, he slit the man's throat. His blood poured through his uniform from of his deep wounds, and he fell to the ground dead. The Entity heard more cops screaming below; the gunshot had alerted them to his location on the rooftop. He ran to the edge of the wall, leaped down to the fire escape, and began to run down the stairs.

Ed, hearing the gunshot ring out, ran to get his gun and then returned to Stephanie, who was standing in the center of the living room. Ed told her to stay away from the windows. There was a loud knock on his door, and a voice identified the knocker as the squad commander. Ed quickly unlocked the door, and the commander entered with five of his heavily armed men. As they secured the apartment, he instructed Ed that the five officers would stay with them for their safety as he and the rest of his team searched for the Entity. He had already called for additional backup.

Enraged, Ed hugged Stephanie and told her he would be back. He then told the commander that he was coming with him to search for the killer. After the two men ran out the door, one squad member locked and secured it behind them. Stephanie didn't even have a chance to tell Ed not to go, and she found herself alone, guarded by heavily armed men. She wrapped her arms around herself and started to cry. She prayed that Ed and his friends could stop the Entity.

The Entity ran down the fire escape until his feet hit the sidewalk. Then he bent down and saw police cruisers going by on the street to the condo. As he ran away through the back alley, he heard voices behind him yell for him to stop. Up ahead he saw the high chain-link fence and jumped to his right. His feet landed on top of a steel dumpster, which he jumped off quickly as bullets narrowly missed him, and he leaped over the fence and down to the ground. He ran very quickly as the cops behind him started to climb the fence and radioed their location back to their fellow squad members, along with the direction in which the suspect was running.

Ed heard the conversation on the team leader's radio. The squad commander told all his mobile units and foot patrol officers to set out and search the area of La Jolla Boulevard; it was the main road in the area of Lower Hermosa. Ed didn't wait. He charged alone toward the back alley where the Entity had been sighted. He ran through the back gates of the adjoining apartment complex and ran into the alley to find five armed cops. Ed asked them where the suspect had gone. One of the team members explained to Ed how they had chased him to this point, but he just disappeared. They had two groups of five-man teams now searching the rooftops of the two buildings on either side of them. They believed he ran up one of the fire escapes to make his escape.

Ed took a deep breath to control his breathing. He checked the 9mm he held tightly in his right hand and prepared to turn and run up the fire escape to his left. Suddenly a black car crashed through the garage door across from them, and Ed dove to the ground to avoid getting hit. The vehicle struck three policemen, who tried to fire at the vehicle. Ed heard their terrifying screams of pain upon impact. He got to his feet and ran after the dark older model vehicle as it drove out of the alleyway and onto the boulevard.

Ed tried to steady his right hand as he took aim while running after the vehicle and fired round after round at the back of the car. One round struck the back window, shattering it. Ed quickly dropped the empty clip to the ground, took his last full clip from his pocket, and rearmed his gun. The old Monte Carlo car made a hard right turn and was hit from the side by a police cruiser. It spun around fast, but it didn't stop as its driver regained control and continued straight on the main road.

But the impact had stalled the vehicle for few seconds and allowed Ed to gain ground on the car. He leaped onto the trunk of the Monte Carlo and grabbed the shattered windowpane. The shards of glass cut his hand as he tried to aim his gun at the driver, who saw Ed in his review mirror. Ed was about to shoot at the dark figure when the car made a hard swerve to the left and hit parked vehicles. Ed quickly braced himself as he almost lost his grip. He repositioned himself on the trunk and fired into the car, but his rounds didn't hit the driver. One round shot through the vehicle's windshield. Ed steadied his gun and aimed again.

Just then, the Entity saw his chance of escape and made a hard right turn at the intersection, avoiding a collision with two police cruisers coming fast at his vehicle. Ed, afraid he was going to get hit by the impact, let go of his tight grasp on the window. He was thrown far by the car's tremendous speed from the turn and flew through the air, spinning like a top, until his body struck a parked car. He hit the pavement.

The Entity drove down Grand Avenue and saw a roadblock of police vehicles ahead of him, and squad cars had begun to chase him from behind. He knew he was about to be stopped, so he countered their offensive by making a hard left turn and driving directly through the guard rail of the overpass. The car sailed through the air, and he leaped from the vehicle just as it was about to hit the water below. He braced himself as he entered the water and dove deep beneath the surface to avoid being seen.

Ed opened his eyes, semiconscious as squad cars came to a stop around his location. Policemen rushed over and asked if he was all right. Ed, who was in a tremendous amount of pain, just closed his eyes and heard the loud voices saying they needed an ambulance right away. After that, he heard nothing but silence.

When Ed opened his eyes, he felt someone holding his hand, and he was able to glimpse Stephanie sitting beside him. He turned to his right and saw Rick along with Rob and a few other cops standing around his bed. He knew he was in the hospital, and he saw a doctor in scrubs and a nurse monitoring his vital signs on the heart monitor and blood pressure machines. The doctor looked into Ed's eyes with his small penlight and explained that he had received a concussion from the hard impact, along with heavy bruising to his left shoulder and ribs, but he should be fine in a few days because he hadn't broken any bones or withstood any deep lacerations. Ed thanked the doctor, and the doctor told Rick to make sure Ed stayed in bed the rest of the day. It was now 4:30 a.m. Ed couldn't believe he had been unconscious that whole time. As the doctor and the nurse left, they informed Ed they would return with some pain medication for him.

Stephanie smiled and asked how he felt, besides being in pain. Ed remarked that he felt like he had been hit by an eighteen wheeler, and Stephanie thanked God that he was alive. She kissed his cheek. Ed gently placed his arm around her and said he had tried to save them all last night. He looked at Rick and wanted to know the outcome of what had transpired.

"After you were knocked off the car, our cruisers pursued him until he came to the vehicle roadblock set up at Grand Avenue. The suspect then flipped his car into the river below. Our divers and search boats scoured the stream and the banks for our man, but we didn't find any sign of him or his body. We did find a black nylon bag that belonged to him still inside the black Monte Carlo when we raised it from the water. The bag contained a few sharp knives, a short sword, a powerful night-vision scope, and a hearing surveillance dish and microphone. He was no doubt watching you both and the squads protecting your place, and he killed two more cops on the apartment rooftop where he had positioned himself to spy on you two," Rick informed Ed.

Ed just sighed in disbelief that he had been unable to get a clear enough shot to shoot the son of a bitch in the head. He asked Rick if they had been able to trace the car back to a suspect. Rick told him the Monte Carlo was an old eighties model, and it was an abandoned vehicle that had been stolen from a local impound. They were still checking for forensic evidence, but they knew their man was too good and too cautious to be caught by leaving DNA behind.

"Ed, just relax now and get some rest. We have this hospital monitored by more than fifty cops, as well as the whole hospital security force. We will be back by noon to see if you will be released by then, and Stephanie will be staying in the same safe house as Rob and his family," Rick explained.

Ed thanked them for coming to see him, and they all left the room so Stephanie could say good-bye to him.

"You know that was the most stupid and crazy stunt I have ever heard of a cop trying to do to stop a crazed killer. But I know it was a very brave thing that you did in order to protect all of your friends, and mostly me. I'm so happy you weren't seriously hurt tonight. Just next time stay with me and hide indoors," Stephanie told him and gently kissed him on the lips as he brushed her tears away. She told him she loved him very much and rested her head on his chest.

Rob opened the door to the room and told her they were ready to move them out. Ed told her not to worry about him and that he would be all right. They kissed again, and Stephanie told him to rest. She would be back with his friends at noon. Ed watched her leave with Rob. The door closed behind them. Ed then turned on the LCD television hanging high on the wall and listened as the newscast talked about how the serial killer known as the Entity had struck again tonight, killing two more police officers and injuring others in the high-speed chase, after which he'd been again able to slip the police's grasp. Ed became mad and shut off the television. He closed his eyes and then reopened them.

"Your chances are getting very slim with me, because the next time we meet, I will kill you, and then we will finally know who you really are," Ed said to himself as he closed his eyes to get some sleep.

He was able to get home under the cover of darkness. He was soaking and wet from the dark, dirty water of the river that had concealed him well. He had swum downstream a few hundred feet until he reached a clearing. Only then had he broken the surface and risen from the water to find refuge in his second vehicle and make it home.

He took off his black outfit to burn in his old-fashioned stove, as he had done to all his others. He placed the clothing into the iron kettle stove and pushed them far down with the iron poker. He then put the lid back on the stove and watched as the very hot flames incinerated his uniform of choice. He was now standing naked in his home. The lights were all off as he made his way to the bathroom to shower and relax.

As the warm water of the shower cleansed him from the dirt and foul odor of the river, he thought back to the night Ed and Stephanie had made love. He couldn't get her out of his mind. He knew he had to stop killing now for a few days to allow the police to relax and set their focus away from him. But he knew he needed to plan this perfectly. He knew Stephanie would almost always be with Ed or guarded by many policemen. He cleaned his body with the liquid soap and scrubbed his skin very hard. He smiled to himself as he thought of a plan. Then he shut the water off, pushed the shower curtain open, exited the shower, and dried himself with a towel.

Then he stepped into his shower shoes, walked into his bedroom, and turned on the light on his mirrored hutch, where he had many pictures of Stephanie taped. He had taken them on his old 35mm camera. He even had a few pictures of his nemesis, Ed Brooks. He had taken them as he followed them all over the city. He stared at the one he had taken of Stephanie in her white dress on her first night in San Diego. She had looked so beautiful that evening.

At first he had thought she would be a prize kill for him. But not anymore. Now he wanted her for his own. He picked up the picture of Ed Brooks and stared at it.

"You think you're going to stop me. You think you can save her from me. I will kill you in due time, as I now know how to defeat you and get Stephanie for myself," he whispered, crumbling Ed's picture in his left hand and staring deeply at Stephanie's picture in his other hand.

Chapter 10

Just before 1:00 p.m., Ed was changed into fresh clothes that Stephanie had brought for him from home. The team and extra cops for their protection were now ready to move Ed and Stephanie out of the hospital to Central Division and then into the new safe house. Ed walked with a slight limp from pain that ran from his left hip down to his foot. He took an Advil and knew this little bruising had hurt his ego more than his body. But nothing was going to keep him from taking down the Entity. He was too deeply involved in the case, professionally and very personally.

Ed and Stephanie walked outside to the parking lot to find three large SUVs and more than twelve police cruisers and unmarked cars waited, ready to escort them to Central Division. As the couple got into the middle SUV with Rick and Rob, Ken and Jack got into the lead SUV. Rick told them that his wife, Dr. Adams, and Dr. Diana Farrell were in the last SUV, along with the FBI agents now assigned to the case. Ed was about to protest to Rick that the FBI was going to oust him from the case, but Rick told him to calm down. They would all be having a big briefing with the FBI about the forensic findings and, most importantly, Stephanie's profile of the killer. Rick admitted to them something was in the works for a counter option.

Once the caravan arrived at Central Division and everyone had gathered in the conference room, Rick let the two female doctors explain their findings of physical and DNA evidence. Next they read Stephanie's detailed profile of the killer, and Dr. Diana Farrell, with her expertise as a forensic criminologist, gave her opinion on who the killer might be. The team listened to her speak. There were also three FBI agents seated in the conference room, one of which was another top profiler.

"From studying how he conceals himself, the way he murders, and his knowledge of how not to leave any of his DNA evidence behind, I have no doubt that this suspect is an experienced medical doctor. Or, judging by the carpet fiber left under the victim's fingernail, he may even be a mortician with skills to cut open a human corpse and remove organs and know exactly where major arteries and veins are located on the body. As a mortician, he would have a commercial van to transport bodies," Dr. Farrell told them.

Rick's and Ed's mouths dropped open, and Rob looked at Ken and Jack. Stephanie told Dr. Farrell that she was absolutely right. Rick ordered his men to hurry up and check all local funeral homes and morticians' names. The FBI agents said they could get more done with the help of the Washington D.C. office, and the team ran out of the conference room to their offices to begin the online searches. Ed asked Rob to stay in the room along with Rick and the women. He wanted to talk to them alone about something.

"Look, guys. We know this killer has an inside person leaking information about us. He gained knowledge of where I live, along with Rob's residence and the location of the first safe house. So if we can't capture him in the act, how about we beat him at his own game?" Ed suggested, and Rick felt he may have a good plan brewing for them to capitalize on.

"You mean devise a plan to leave the door open for him to walk through, and once he's inside, we slam it shut fast and take him down," Rick responded.

Ed smiled and told him that was exactly what he had in mind. Rob and Stephanie agreed, and so did Cate and Diana, though they were not law enforcement officials. They then asked how they were going to pull it off. Diana reminded them that they were dealing with a person who was very smart and dangerous. Ed thought to himself for a few seconds and looked at his watch.

"First, Rob is going to drive me back to my place and leave his car there for safekeeping for a few hours. Then we follow up on all the mortician leads we have here in the city. Then if nothing breaks by 10:00 p.m. tonight, we just head home and call it a day," Ed told them.

They all look at one another, puzzled.

Rick smiled back at Ed and told him, "Let's get the wheels turning on this then."

Ed drove back to his home, and Rob parked his car in Ed's garage, but not before Ed drove his Envoy and Fat Boy Harley Davidson motorcycle out of it. After Rob pulled into the garage and parked his vehicle, Ed secured the garage door and put on his black biker helmet and thick padded leather jacket and gloves. As he handed Rob the keys to his Envoy, he told him they could return to Central Division now. Rob was still confused about what they were doing, and Ed said that he and Rick would explain later in the day.

Dr. Diana Farrell returned to her office, and Stephanie went with Dr. Cate Adams back to the county examiners facility to look at photographs of the wounds to the first victim, Ashley Cook, and compare them to the fatal wounds of the victims of Nathan Malcolm. If Stephanie's theory was correct and the killer was a close friend of Malcolm's, this new killer had to have left some kind of new calling card to taunt the police investigators, just as Malcolm had when he had removed and positioned the victims' organs in a symbolic and mocking way. Cate had told Stephanie and the others that she had found no evidence of that, but Stephanie wanted to check for herself.

Ed and Rob returned to Central Division by 3:00 p.m. As they entered Rick's office, Rick told him where everyone else was and what leads they were following up on. Rob now asked them what this open-door plan was all about. Ed made sure the door was locked so they couldn't be overheard by anyone outside the office.

"Look, we have been beaten by this guy every time we tried catch him or hide ourselves from him, so I know his leak has to be someone within this division, if not one of our own team," Ed told them.

Rob and Rick agreed, but they weren't so sure that the leak was a trusted member of their team.

"So unless we can catch him on the phone, telling the Entity where our safe house is or what leads and suspects we are looking at, how can we catch him?" Rob asked. "Are we going to wiretap the whole phone system in the building and then call every cell phone service carrier to do the same for all our team members in order to spy on them? That would take at least two or three days to cover. We don't have that time on our hands because we are about to lose this whole thing to the FBI according to what Chief Chase told Rick last night," he told Ed, implying that his plans of spying on his team members was very shaky at best.

Ed told him that wasn't what he had in mind at all. "Rick, where is the new safe house we have Rob's family at?" Ed asked.

Rick turned in his chair and pointed to a location on his map of the city. "The safe house is here in North Park. It's a good-sized home positioned near three other homes. We have our team members and surveillance set up all over the safe house and the perimeters of University Avenue. The major street to leads to that location," Rick told him.

Ed's eyes lit up as he stared at the location and the main road. He thought to himself, and Rick didn't yet know what he had in mind.

"Good. We move Stephanie and me there around 10:00 p.m. tonight. We don't mind spending the night with Rob and Antonella and Megan."

Rick and Rob still didn't know what Ed's plan was, so Ed went over to the map, picked up several colored thumb tacks, and stuck them into the location of the safe house and University Avenue. As he turned back to his partners to tell them his full plan for the evening, he asked Rick if they had a female officer who matched Stephanie's height and hair color.

Stephanie and Cate had been going over the crime scene photographs for some time now. Stephanie had even brought with her the photographs of Nathan Malcolm's victims and the five known photographs of Jack the Ripper's victims. Cate became very upset as she looked at the gruesome picture of Mary Kelly's crime scene. Stephanie told her that the photographs belonged to Ed and that he had convinced her and Rob that the murders of Malcolm and this new killer were related to the Ripper suspect Francis Tumblety. As Stephanie explained the whole connection to Cate, they looked closely again at the photographs of the victims, and Cate asked if the Ripper victims had any wound patterns that stood out or personal belongings that had gone missing.

"Victim Annie Chapman had two brass rings taken from her; they were only articles of clothing or jewelry that investigators knew to be missing from any victim. Victim number four, Catherine Eddowes, had deep V-shaped cuts on her cheeks. But Nathan Malcolm made no similar markings, and he didn't take any jewelry from his victims. Neither has our current killer," Stephanie explained to Cate but then stopped and thought to herself for a minute. She was pondering the two brass rings when Cate asked what she was thinking.

"Oh, it's nothing. I was just thinking of those two brass rings. I wish Malcolm had taken jewelry or something of significance from his victims. He only taunted us with the placement of the organs like Francis Tumblety did with Mary Kelly," Stephanie explained as Ed and his team members walked into Cate's office.

The women were surprised to see all the men walk into the room, and Stephanie knew they had some new plan in the works to catch the killer.

"How are you two making out? Any new evidence or leads we are able to follow up on?" Rick asked.

"So far nothing really useful from the photographs of all the victims, past and present, to link them to the original Ripper victims, but sometimes the clue you don't expect will come to you when you keep looking for it," Cate told them, and Stephanie asked Ed what they were planning to do next.

"We are going to set one more sting operation into play to try to lure him out, since we know he has been following us and he has to have some inside source in order to learn all about our private lives and our supposedly secret safe houses. Chief John Chase is only giving us until tomorrow to catch him and try this one last plan to learn his identity," Ed told her.

Stephanie pulled him to the side to talk alone. "Ed, please don't tell me you're going to be in the heat of things again. He wants you vulnerable so he can kill us. Please, we are close to ending this, and then we can be together always. I have never had the opportunity to share my life with someone, but now I have you," she told him with tears in her eyes.

Ed assured her he would not be in the way this time. "I promise I am not going to be on the front line this time. Rick and I planned this one perfect, a great diversion to lead him into a trap that we will spring with many cops and our top SWAT teams. We will have him. I promise you. And we will get married soon enough," he said.

Stephanie told him she couldn't wait to start making wedding plans and looking at different wedding gowns and elegant halls in which to hold the wedding reception. Ed smiled and tried to act like he was happy, but he knew how expensive weddings were, and the thought of a lot of money leaving his bank account crossed his mind.

Rick told everyone it was getting late and that he wanted Cate and Stephanie taken back to Central Division for their safety until the mission was complete. Cate remembered that she had left her

DNA report on the victims at Dr. Farrell's office. She asked Rick if she could pass by and get it first. Rick sighed as he looked at his wrist watch. It was 5:30 p.m. He wanted to get his team and all the vehicles into position within two hours tops.

Ken spoke up and made a suggestion. "Rick, it's all right. I will take Stephanie and Dr. Adams to Central Division as soon as we stop by Dr. Farrell's office and get the DNA report. Jack can go with you guys to the safe house, and I will meet up with you there soon enough."

Ken's partner, Jack Kerns, rolled his eyes at Ken, but Rick told him all right but to get back to the safe house in North Park by 7:00 p.m. Ken told him he would be there by then to get ready and then left with the two women. Rick and Ed headed down with Jack to get into his Envoy. Rob had driven Ed's motorcycle to the safe house and was waiting for them to arrive.

Forty-five minutes later, Ken pulled into the parking lot of the medical facility where Diana worked. On the freeway on their way there, Ken had felt like they were being followed by a sedan, but the vehicle had stayed with the traffic on the freeway when Ken took the exit ramp. Cate was about to open her door and exit the vehicle when Ken told her he would go get the report from Dr. Farrell. He told the women to stay in the vehicle and lock the doors, and he would be right back. Cate and Stephanie followed his instructions, and Ken walked through the back door and was let in by a security guard.

Dr. Farrell had just finished putting away some of her files in her office and was about to shut off the lights in her lab and head home for the night when there was a knock on the door. She went over and looked through the glass window. She smiled at Ken and waved to him to come inside; the door was open. Ken walked up to her and asked if she was alone. Diana told him her staff had left for the evening and asked what he was doing there at this hour of the night.

"I was about to take Stephanie and Dr. Adams back to Central Division, but Cate forgot her DNA findings. Do you have them?" Ken asked.

Diana told him she did and went to her desk to get it. She asked about the task force's next plan to catch the killer. As she handed Ken the folder, Ken smiled. They embraced and kissed deeply. Diana broke off the kiss, smiled at him, and shook her head.

"Ken, we have to be careful about this. You're still a married man, and a colleague I have worked with for a long time is in your car. Please, not now. But tell me what's going on," she said, emphasizing to Ken that they needed to keep their sexual relationship quiet from their friends and coworkers.

"Ed and Rick came up with the idea that since the killer is always following our team members around, why not use decoys of Ed and Stephanie to lure him out and get him out in the open. They are planning this tonight at the site of the new safe house in North Park," Ken revealed to her.

Diana was surprised to learn this. "Well, you had better get going, Ken. You've got to get Stephanie and Cate to safety first," she told him. Then she cursed and told Ken she just remembered that she had found evidence to link one of the recent victims to Nathan Malcolm's victims—a matching strand of female hair.

Ken told her that was great. She said she needed Cate to come up and look at it in the lab's microscope right away. Ken called Cate on his cell phone and told her to come up to the lab. Diana turned the lab lights back and donned her lab coat.

Stephanie and Cate were seated in the backseat of Ken's car, patiently waiting for him. Stephanie looked up and noticed the lights come back on in the lab on the top floor of the building. Cate wondered aloud what was taking Ken so long, and then her cell phone rang. She answered it. Ken was calling to tell her about Diana's new find. Cate became ecstatic at the news and said she would be right up. As she got off her cell phone, Stephanie asked her what was going on.

"Diana just called; she found a link between victim Ashley Cook and the first victim of Nathan Malcolm. I want to go up to her lab and look at it really fast. Ken is coming back down to stay with you."

As Cate exited the car, Stephanie told her not to be too long because they needed to hurry. She watched Cate enter the back door as the guard opened it for her.

She then looked around the deserted parking lot. The daylight was now gone, and the darkness of night had fallen over the city of San Diego. The full moon cast its rays down onto a reflecting mirror of a parked vehicle. The light's reflection hit Stephanie in the face. When she looked in the direction of the light, she saw two white vans parked side by side in the rear parking spaces. Stephanie knew they belonged to the facility for medical use, and she remembered one of the witnesses describing a white cargo van. Stephanie unlocked her side door and walked over to the vans, still wondering what was taking Cate and Ken so long to come back down.

As Stephanie approached the vans, she looked at the one on the left; it had large black lettering identifying it as a county examiner vehicle. She then turned her attention to the vehicle on the right and noticed the lettering was covered by a magnetic sign on both sides. The sign read, *Fresh Flowers*. Stephanie removed one of the false signs, knowing someone was deliberately trying to hide the van as a flower delivery vehicle. She quickly tried the side cargo door, but it was locked. She hurried to the back double doors and tried the door handle. It was open. She opened both doors and looked to the upper right of the interior. She found what she was searching for—a torn piece of carpeting that was the same kind of material and color found beneath a victim's fingernail. Stephanie thought quickly, *I saw the ring on a chain around her neck.* She quickly took out her cell phone to call Ed right away.

A few stories above her, Cate walked very slowly across the floor. All the lights she had seen turned on from the parking lot had been turned off again. As she made her way to Diana's lab, she noticed the door was still open. She called out for Diana and Ken but got no reply. She found the light switch on the wall and flipped it. She again called out for Diana as she walked around the large center table. She looked down and screamed in horror. On the floor was Ken Rogers lying in a pool of his own blood. Cate screamed again. The security guard heard her screams, left his desk, and ran to see what was wrong.

Stephanie tried to call Ed and got his voice mail. She heard Cate's screams and looked up. She then looked inside the van at the damaged material. At the beep, she left him a message: "Ed, please listen to this and hurry. I found the cargo van used in the abduction of that young girl! It's one of the medical vans from Diana's office—" but before Stephanie could finish her sentence, a gloved hand clamped over her mouth fast and tight.

She felt a tremendous shock to her right side, stunning her; her attacker had shocked her with a stun gun. The low-current electric charge immobilized her muscles, and she dropped her cell phone to the ground. The attacker then forced Stephanie into the van and closed the doors behind them. Stephanie was still conscious but had no muscle functions from the shock. But her gaze fixed upon her attacker—Dr. Farrell.

"My dear Stephanie, you're a very smart, clever girl. You figured it out all by yourself, along with your dear Ed. I wish I could kill you like the others, but someone very special wants you alive," Diana told her in a soft voice.

Stephanie lay on the floor of the van as she watched Diana reach into a plastic bag and take out a black cloth, which she used to cover Stephanie's nose and mouth.

"Just breathe in the sweet chloroform, Stephanie. We are going home now, and you're going to a have a new life."

As the sweet, potent fumes of the chloroform took effect, Stephanie slowly closed her eyes and fell unconscious. Diana held the cloth in place a few seconds longer to be certain she was out.

Then she quickly placed the cloth back in the clear plastic bag and into her jacket pocket. She hurried into the driver's seat, started the van, and took off to her secret destination.

Upon discovering the body of Ken Rogers, the security guard used the phone in the lab to call the police. Cate called Rick on his cell phone to inform him of what had happened. She screamed it at him as he answered. Ed and Rob, who were in one of the communication rooms with other policemen, heard Cate yelling at Rick, and they knew something bad had happened.

Rick got off the phone. "Ed and Rob, come on. We have to go to Dr. Farrell's medical office. Ken Rogers is dead!" Rick screamed at them.

Rick and Rob ran to get into Jack's car, and Ed ran to his motorcycle, knowing he could maneuver through traffic faster and get there sooner.

As Diana drove along the Mission Valley Freeway, she kept a steady speed to keep from alerting any police cruisers she might pass along the way. She looked at Stephanie in the rear view mirror and saw that she was still unconscious. She placed a call on her cell phone, and a man's voice answered her.

"I have her; she is safe. I will be at the house in a few minutes. We have to move fast because Ed and the rest of the police will be looking for her. I had to kill my boyfriend because he was about to find out it was me all along," Diana told her friend, and he asked her if she had harmed Stephanie in any way.

"No, I only chloroformed her. She is safe, I promise you. But we have to move her out as soon as I get there!" Diana ordered.

"Don't worry about that. Just get here as fast as you can get here unseen. I still have plans to make for my dear opponent," he told Diana and then hung up. The Entity felt satisfied that the first part of his plan was complete. He had Stephanie all to himself, and he could now kill Ed Brooks and get out of San Diego with her.

Ed arrived at the facility before Rick and the others. He ran up to the lab on the third floor and was met by Cate and a whole slew of uniformed policemen methodically looking through Dr. Farrell's lab and office. Cate explained to Ed what had happened, and he asked her where Stephanie was. She told him she had left Stephanie in Ken's car to come up and view the new evidence Dr. Farrell had found, but she had found only the body of Ken Rogers on the floor of the lab, and both Stephanie and Dr. Farrell were now missing. Ed started to look around the lab for clues. He then took out his cell phone and called Stephanie, but there was no answer. Ed knew right away she had been abducted by the Entity. He became enraged but also knew that he was helpless. He couldn't help her if he didn't know where she had been taken.

When Rick and the others entered the lab, Cate ran to Rick, and they embraced. Rob went over to Ed, handed him a cell phone, and told him he had found it ringing on the ground in the parking lot.

"This is Stephanie's cell phone. She's missing now," Ed told them as he listened to the new voice mail on his phone. It was Stephanie alerting him of the white cargo van she had found at the facility. The panel carpet inside had been damaged. Her voice then stopped, and there was static before the call ended.

"She found the van that was used by the killer. It was one of this medical forensic team's vans!' Ed told Rob.

One of the policemen called to Rick to tell him he had found something. He handed Rick a small bottle he had found on the countertop. Rick smelled it and made a face. He let Cate whiff its contents to see if she could identify what it was.

"Chloroform. It's used as an anesthetic to render someone unconscious," Cate told him.

Jack Kerns made a face. He knew all the pieces were coming together. Another policeman called to Rick and his team, and they ran into Diana's office. They had found interesting items in her locker.

Ed made his way over to the locker first, and he saw two black sets of scrubs stitched together to form a black hood and sleeves. *The Entity's style of outfit*, Ed said to himself as he looked on the floor of the locker. There was a nylon black bag. Ed pulled it out, opened it, and found black latex gloves and a lock pick gun, along with a plastic case that held many sharp steel postmortem knives. He and Rick looked at one another and now knew that Diana Farrell was the Entity, and she had abducted Stephanie.

"Right under all of our noses. No wonder there was never any DNA evidence. And she knew everything about us: where we lived, the safe houses. She had deep insight into everything we were doing, and now she has Stephanie. Call dispatch and get them to tell us her address!" Ed shouted to Rob.

Rob took out his cell phone and made the call. Rick saw the sad look on Jack's face and asked him what was wrong.

"Dr. Farrell knew everything about us and the investigation from Ken. He told me she had come on to him, and they started having an affair. So I'm certain Ken told her everything we were doing on the case and the locations of the safe houses. I told him he was going to get into trouble and that he should end the relationship, but he kept telling me he could trust her and no harm was going to come out of it," Jack admitted to them.

Rick cursed and called Ken a stupid idiot.

Rob quickly wrote down the addresses he got from dispatch and then told Ed and the others, "Dr. Farrell has two homes. One is all the way west of here in Village Center. The other home is 8542 Hill Street. The house right next to Nathan Malcolm's old address in Sunset Cliff Estates!"

Ed shook his head in disbelief. "She's his daughter. It all makes sense now. She got him out of the house the night of the fire. He's still alive. He has to be!" he screamed as he ran to the parking lot.

Rick called for him to wait. "Jack, call Central Command and the FBI. Tell them to get units to both locations, seal off every freeway and the airports, and have checkpoints set up at the marinas. Get an APB but out on all of Diana Farrell's vehicles, along with the make and model of the cargo van!" Rick ordered and then told Rob to come on. They raced behind Ed to get to their car.

Ed didn't even put on his helmet. He started up his bike and roared out of the parking lot toward Sunset Cliff Estates. He peeled through the intersection even though the light was red. He didn't care. The heavy force of wind and air hit his face as he sped up to sixty miles per hour on Van Horn Road and made his way onto the freeway. He cursed at Nathan Malcolm and his daughter. They were going to harm Stephanie.

"You sick bastards, I'm going to kill you both!" he swore as he quickly turned onto the on-ramp of the San Diego Freeway. He passed one hundred miles per hour as he raced to save Stephanie's life.

Chapter 11

Diana drove backward up the long driveway of her home. The double-sided garage door was already open for her arrival. She parked the van next to her other vehicle, a dark metallic gray Ford Expedition. The garage door closed once she was inside, and she met her ally, who had been waiting for them to come. He was dressed completely in black; he even wore a black face mask, as if it was a Halloween costume.

He opened the back doors to the van and saw that his prize was still unconscious. He was overwhelmed with emotion; he had only ever viewed Stephanie from a distance, and now she was here for him to have. He studied her; she was motionless except her chest rising and falling as she breathed. He clenched and ground his teeth together as he reached out with his gloved hand and gently touched her legs and buttocks through her tight blue jeans. He knew her skin and figure was smooth and would be firm to his touch. He reached inside the van with both hands and pulled her wrists toward him. He took her limp body in his arms. Diana came around to meet him. She looked at Stephanie's face and then felt her wrist for a pulse and was satisfied. Diana knew she would be waking soon.

"We better get her inside the other truck. She will be waking up soon, and we don't have much time. I will sedate her with an injection to keep her out for as long as it takes us to transport her to our new home," Diana instructed the man in black.

He became enraged at her words. He had other plans first, and he answered Diana with his deep raspy voice, which trembled with anger. "I told you I want to confront Ed Brooks first. Then, after I kill him, we move her out. I know he is coming now, so help me prepare," he instructed Diana as he carried Stephanie into the house and up the first flight of stairs.

They entered the large living room, which was open to the kitchen. He placed Stephanie in a wooden chair, and Diana quickly tied her hands behind her with thick rope; she also bound her feet and fastened the rope to the bottom support of the wooden chair to make certain Stephanie wouldn't be able to kick her legs free.

As Diana worked to quickly secure Stephanie, the Entity took off his glove so he could feel the very soft skin of Stephanie's face. He bent down and pressed his hooded mask against her soft hair. He could smell her sweet perfume. He couldn't wait to have her all to himself, alone.

Diana saw him getting aroused by Stephanie, and she became very angry. "You better contain your pleasure. We are not safe yet. Just as most men fall to the weakness of a woman, you're about to jeopardize everything we have planned and prepared for, just for this woman." Diana stood up to face him after she finished tying Stephanie's feet.

She couldn't see the anger she had caused as he stared at her through his mask. He stiffened his right hand and slapped her hard across the face, cutting her lower lip.

"I started this whole ordeal in preparation for revenge, and I needed your help to regain my strength and plan the deaths of my enemies. I made you what you are. I know you wanted me to kill her from the start, along with him. But my feelings for her changed. She is very different from all the others I have killed. She is a pure, soft soul, something that has been missing from you females for a long time. Now you can either help me, or I will slay you like the others here and now," he told Diana as she licked the blood from her lip with her tongue.

She smiled at him and told him she was still loyal and willing to help him.

"Good. Now hurry and start the Bunsen burner and heat up my blades. He is coming."

Diana turned to the kitchen countertop, turned on the gas, and used a match to ignite the very deep blue flame of the burner—the hottest flame possible. Holding the handle of a very sharp steel dagger, Diana passed the blade through the flame to make it hot enough burn human skin. As he watched Diana prepare his weapons for him, the Entity heard Stephanie moan softly. He touched her face. She started to wake, and her head tilted to the right as she tried to clear her thoughts and focus on where she was.

"That's it. Awaken, Stephanie. The end is almost here for my enemy. A new beginning awaits us both far away from this place," the Entity spoke to her.

Stephanie blinked a few times, squinting. When she finally managed to open her eyes fully, her surroundings looked very blurry. But she knew she had been drugged with chloroform. She shook her head hard to clear her vision, and she now saw the very large black figure standing in front of her. She turned her head to look behind her and saw Dr. Farrell heating up daggers and two large swords with an open flame. When Stephanie tried to move, the Entity told her to be calm and no harm would come to her. She tried to free her hands but couldn't.

"What the hell do you want? Where am I? Who are you?" Stephanie yelled at the Entity as she looked back at Diana, who just smiled at her; she would let her counterpart explain everything to Stephanie now.

Before he started to speak through his dark face mask, he cleared his throat as much as he could so she could understand his deep raspy voice.

"Congratulations, Stephanie. You and Ed put all the pieces of the puzzle into place and concluded who Jack the Ripper was. But you didn't know who I was and what my relationship to Francis Tumblety was and why my dear Diana is involved," he told her, but Stephanie was about to surprise him. She already knew all the answers to his riddles.

"You're wrong! Ed and I know everything now. You are related to that sick son of bitch, Francis Tumblety, along with this crazy bitch who has been helping you. So who the hell are you now? Show me your face!" Stephanie screamed at him.

He slowly removed his hooded face mask and revealed his identity to her. He face was scarred, having been burned badly. The inferno had even permanently singed away his eyebrows. Stephanie knew who he was—Dr. Nathan Malcolm. But she was indeed surprised that he was alive. She could still make out some of his facial features. His eyes were still intact. But Stephanie whispered that he couldn't be alive. He smiled at her; it was time to tell her what happened that night four years ago.

"Yes, I am still alive; I wouldn't be here now if it wasn't for the love and great support I received from my daughter, Diana. She helped saved my life that night, but we had planned our route of evasion a year before that. I discovered through my father's personal items who my great uncle was and the greatness he had achieved in life. I showed Diana the journal of our great uncle, Francis Tumblety. He wrote in detail of the whores he killed in England in that foul dump known as Whitechapel. He was a true man who destroyed whores who deserved to die. I met them here in my own present life, starting with my own wife, Jane, who had abandoned me and left me all alone. But in time she got her retribution as she died a slow, agonizing death. Diana grew older and stronger, and I let her read the journal. She knew what our family bloodline entailed and that we were to cleanse the new world again in the present."

"So Diana is your daughter. She changed her last name from Malcolm to Farrell upon the death of your ex-wife. But how did you survive the fire at your house, and who was the person who even

Dr. Cate Adams confirmed was your badly burned corpse after the autopsy?" Stephanie wanted to know.

"I indeed fought with your daring Ed Brooks in the house. I was about to set the fire to a dead man's corpse when he took me by surprise. One dark night Diana had found a poor dear lost soul who matched my height and weight. We knew his face and fingerprints would be destroyed in the intense fire I was going to set, so Diana knew the only way to confirm the dead man's remains as my own was through dental records. She took a mold of my teeth with plaster and made a composite mold with the clear plastic Invisalign braces and fitted them into his mouth perfectly so any autopsy expert would find my dental remains and confirm the corpse as my own. But I almost did die at the hands of your dear fiancée. I was burned beyond hell itself as the fire raged in the house. Diana was waiting behind the stairwell door, and she covered me with a large fire blanket. She guided me downstairs, out the back door, and into this home, which she had purchased months before. The plan was well formed. But I was unable to kill Ed Brooks that night. With Diana's help again in treating my wounds, I grew stronger, and I taught her how to use knives and kill our enemies. Together we were ready to exact revenge on everyone."

Stephanie now knew how the whole ordeal had started and built to this point. She knew it had been Diana dressed as the Entity the night she killed so many of their friends at the safe house. It had been her driving the sports motorcycle through the mall, able to quickly avoid being captured by her sheer strength and quickness. The attack by the Entity at the lab when Diana was injured the night Rick and Cate were there had all been a set-up to take any suspicion away from Diana. Stephanie remembered seeing Diana wearing an old ring on a chain around her neck one day; she knew it was one of the rings Francis Tumblety had taken from his fourth victim and placed along with his journal in the old wooden box.

Nathan took out the other ring, which was suspended on a gold chain around his neck. He smiled and told her it was a true family treasure handed down by their great uncle to mark their victory in their will to rid the world of whores and their enemies. Diana told Stephanie that she felt very sorry for what her father had gone through and the pain her mother had caused him. She knew her place was to help him with all his needs and his revenge.

"So what do you want with me? Why not just kill me at the lab earlier?" Stephanie asked Diana, who said she would let her father answer that question.

"Because, Stephanie, I had a change of mind and heart about you. I did order Diana to take your life when she had the chance, but I saw you making love to Ed one clear night in his bedroom. I studied you so deeply. You're a very beautiful woman, and I want for myself. We are going to take you with us to a far-off place where no one will be able to find you. We will leave once Ed gets here and I kill him. You will be my future bride, Stephanie," Nathan told her.

He glided his fingers over her face and lips and lowered his face toward hers. He wanted to kiss Stephanie's lips, but she broke free of his grip and turned her head away.

"I'm sorry to tell you this, but I have a thing against marrying a serial killer who is a crazed, sick fuck! I am going to marry the man who is going to save me and kick your ass!" Stephanie yelled him.

He and Diana stared at one another and then started to laugh at the thought that she believed Ed would be able to save her. Just then, they heard the sound of a loud engine getting closer. Stephanie knew it was the sound of Ed's motorcycle. She screamed his name as Nathan yelled at Diana to pass him the heated swords. Ed didn't stop as he jumped the curb in front of the house and drove straight toward the large double windows. He leaped off the bike just in time, and Diana and her father jumped out of the way as the motorcycle crashed into the living room and came to a halt when it hit the large stove in the kitchen. The tremendous impact caused Stephanie to rock to her right side in the chair and fall to the floor.

Ed landed on front lawn. As he looked up, he found his handgun. Then he jumped to his feet and leaped into the massive opening he had created. He saw Diana and didn't hesitate. He took aim and fired at her. Diana leaped behind countertop, just avoiding the bullets. The Bunsen burner fell to the floor when Diana accidently kicked it. Stephanie saw it right in front of her; the flame was still lit. She fought with all her might to stretch her bound hands toward the hot flame to burn away the rope.

Ed quickly dropped the empty magazine and was about to insert a full clip into the gun when Nathan hit him hard from behind with a shoulder tackle. Ed looked up from the floor as Nathan stood over him with both flaming-hot swords in his hands. Nathan screamed and swung them hard at Ed, but Ed quickly rolled to his right and swept Nathan's feet out from under him. Nathan fell to the floor, and Ed kicked him hard. The swords flew from his grip and ignited the carpet in the living room.

Stephanie leaned forward and then crashed the chair backward against the hard marble floor and was able to break the wooden back in two. Now she was able to reach her hands up to the flame. It started to burn the rope, but Stephanie screamed in pain as it also burned her hands. Diana saw that she was trying to free herself. She picked up one of the daggers and charged at Stephanie to strike her, but Ed caught her arm, spun her around, and hit her square in the face. She flew backward to the floor. Nathan made it to his feet and tackled Ed from behind. The two men hit the floor hard and exchanged furious blows.

Stephanie pulled her hands free from the singed rope. She reached for one of the daggers and cut the rope to free her feet. Diana charged at her again, kicking the dagger out of her hand, but Stephanie kicked her hard in her thigh, stopping her in place. As Stephanie leaped to her feet, she reached around Diana's head, grabbed her long hair with one hand, and then punched her in the face with her other hand repeatedly, cursing at her the whole time. Diana bent her head and drove Stephanie into the wall. Both women fell to the floor. The fire from the carpeting now engulfed the large curtains and kindled the walls of the home.

Ed realized this was a repeat of his first encounter with Malcolm. He pulled him up from the floor and with a thunderous blow smashed the killer in the face and then the chest. Nathan reached behind his back, where he had a sharp dagger strapped in a sheath. He quickly grabbed it, and as he bent down to avoid Ed's incoming punch, he stabbed Ed deep in his right thigh and left the dagger embedded in his muscle. Ed fell to the floor, crying out in pain. Nathan screamed as he kicked Ed in the face and then bent down and pushed the handle of the dagger, driving it deeper into Ed's thigh. Ed screamed in desperation and tried to get away from Nathan, who reached out and picked up a heated sword.

Stephanie knew he was about to kill Ed with it. She looked around for Ed's gun but didn't find it. Diana leaped to tackle her, and Stephanie ducked. Diana missed her and hit the refrigerator hard. Stephanie kicked her where she lay on the floor and found a can of aerosol oven cleaner on the counter. She picked up the Bunsen burner with her left hand, sprayed the highly flammable substance into the path of the flame, shooting a stream of fire directly into Nathan's face and eyes. He screamed in pain as the fire blinded him and swung the sword furiously in her direction. Stephanie dropped both the can and burner.

Ed reached down and pulled the dagger out of his thigh. As he was about to get up, Diana kicked him hard in the gut, and Ed dropped the dagger. Diana grasped it with her right hand and swung it over her head to strike Ed. He caught her hand and fended her off as he tried desperately to free the weapon from her tight grasp.

He then remembered the karate move Stephanie had used on him. He bent her hand low and then back up and held the dagger against her own chest as he threw Diana in the direction of her father, who was still swinging the sword violently. The flaming blade cut Diana's neck like butter, decapitating her. As her head fell to the right side and her body fell to the left, Nathan was able to get a glimpse of it from his right eye. He screamed in agony that he had killed his own daughter. He turned and saw Ed and Stephanie holding each other on the floor.

"You!" Nathan screamed.

As he was about to swing the sword at them, Rick and Rob opened fire; round after round of bullets struck him in the chest and neck. Nathan flew off his feet backward, dead, and the flaming sword fell onto the fallen motorcycle, which was leaking gas from its tank. Rick quickly helped Stephanie to her feet, and Rob used all his strength to pick Ed up. The four of them ran and then leaped out of the shattered window just as a tremendous explosion rippled behind them, propelling them through the air as the flames shot high over them. They came crashing down to the grass face-first. They kept their heads low. When the flash of the fire ceased, Rick looked up and then behind him. He yelled, "Clear!" to the others.

Stephanie got up and ran over to Ed. She hugged him where he lay on the ground and started to cry from both pain and thankfulness that he had saved her life. Rob and Rick got to their feet and stared at them. Jack rushed over to Ed and Stephanie with a first aid kit from his vehicle, and several patrol vehicles came to a screeching halt in front of the house, their sirens and flashers blaring. As the policemen exited with their guns drawn, Rick and Rob showed their badges, and Rick ordered the head sergeant to get ambulances and the fire department to the location right away.

Jack put pressure on Ed's deep knife wound to stop the bleeding. Stephanie just held him in her arms and they kissed.

Ed had tears of joy in his eyes and knew it was all over now. "It's over, Stephanie. He's gone, and Diana. I told you I wasn't going to let anything happen to you."

"I know, Ed. Now just shut up and let Jack heal you up, because you need to walk straight when we walk down the aisle as husband and wife," Stephanie told him.

They kissed again deeply. Rob and Rick shook hands, knowing it was finally over. Chief John Chase arrived with his staff and escorts, and Cate got out of one of the squad cars, along with Rob's wife. They ran to their husbands and embraced them. Chief Chase was puzzled as he watched the three happy couples together. He was then filled in by the head lieutenant on the scene about how Detective

Ed Brooks had saved the life of Stephanie Morgan, resulting in the deaths of serial killing suspects Nathan Malcolm and his daughter, Diana Farrell.

Chase screamed to the arriving forensic team that he wanted immediate confirmation of the deaths of Malcolm and Farrell, and he wanted their remains secured right away so no arriving media would be able to get photographs of the bodies. The forensic team moved in behind the firefighters, who were containing the fire, and the chief walked over the ambulance where Ed and Stephanie were now being treated. He shook Rick's hand and then Rob's hand and congratulated them and Rick's whole task force. Next he turned to Ed and Stephanie and told them he was very happy that they'd made it, and they would receive high commendations from the city for their excellent work on this case. Chief Chase then asked Rick to brief him and his staff on everything that happened and who was involved. As Rick walked with the chief to get ready to brief the media, the EMTs finished bandaging Stephanie's burns and Ed's knife wound. They told him he needed to receive staples at the hospital to close the wound.

Ed smiled and told Stephanie, "At least this time my wounds are not life threatening."

Two hours had passed since the deaths of Nathan Malcolm and his daughter. Ed and Stephanie watched together as their remains were placed into two black body bags and loaded into a large coroner's van, which was escorted to the medical facility by four patrol vehicles. The vehicles had to pass through the growing swarm of media and gathering crowds of the neighborhood that were getting ready to listen to the late media briefing by Chief of Police John Chase and other high-ranking staff members to announce the death of the Entity serial killer and his daughter. They would also answer rumors that he was related to Dr. Francis Tumblety, who was indeed Jack the Ripper.

Ed and Stephanie watched the brightness of the lights and the flashes of cameras going off around the podium, which was set up right in front of the charred house. Then the ambulance doors closed, and they were en route to the hospital to receive further treatment.

Stephanie turned to Ed, who was sitting next to her on the soft bench, and saw he was very upset. "Ed, what's wrong? You look mad now," she said as she held his hands.

"I lost my beloved Harley Davidson Fat Boy. I'm getting myself another as soon as we get back from the honeymoon," he told her.

Stephanie just looked at him with tears in her eyes, and Ed took her into his arms.

Chapter 12

One Year Later

E d married Stephanie just two months after the most brutal serial slayings in the world came to an end. But the couple hadn't prepared for or expected the rush of the media and the strong surge to get them in front of every news correspondent and major news station for repeated interviews about of how a team of a hardnosed detectives and a vibrant and very intelligent FBI profiler had worked together to solve the most infamous serial cases ever known.

Ed told every reporter and news host that he just followed up on the work of investigators and authors who had named Dr. Francis Tumblety as the lead suspect in the Jack the Ripper case. With Stephanie's help, they were able to prove that his distant nephew, Dr. Nathan Malcolm, and Dr. Malcolm's daughter, Dr. Diana Farrell, had carried on Tumblety's tradition of serial slayings. Ed and Stephanie Brooks told the whole world that they didn't intend to write any books or make any deals for movie rights. The couple had no plans to financially profit from their experience with this case. They just repeated over and over that finding their love was their true reward. They would now be able to go on their long overdue honeymoon and had agreed to take a long tour of the many beautiful countries and famous cities in Europe.

When they were finished with all of their interviews, they visited Paris and Rome and stopped in Zurich and Madrid. They were now in England. They came upon the city of Leytonstone. After visiting St. Patrick's Roman Catholic Cemetery on Langthorne Road, Ed decided he wanted closure on the whole Ripper ordeal. He wanted to visit the place where the nightmare had started way back in 1888. Stephanie didn't argue with him; she also felt a need to pay their respects to the resting place of Mary Kelly, the last known victim of Jack the Ripper.

Stephanie laid a nice arrangement of fresh flowers by the tomb marker. Ed and his wife felt a deep sadness for her because even though Mary Kelly had lived a short life many years before they were born, Ed felt a touch in his heart for her when he looked at photographs of her before her death. He and Stephanie knew that she had been a beautiful young woman who was full of life; she hadn't deserved to have her life end at only twenty-five years of age. Ed had found some recognition, peace, and closure for Mary Kelly by proving to the world who this beautiful young woman's killer was. That touched him in a way, even though they were many years and miles apart.

Stephanie reached over to hold Ed's hand and rested her head on his right shoulder.

"You did what you set out to do. I remember you told me you wanted to prove to the world who committed these unspeakable acts and to keep all the innocent and good people safe from harm. You are more than a hero, Ed; you're a brave man who fights for the good and just in this world. It's one of the qualities I fell in love with about you. And I know you retired from the force just a few months ago, but you are about to get a new job very soon, tough guy," she told him.

Ed looked into her eyes and asked his wife what she meant.

"You're going to become a father. I'm three weeks pregnant," Stephanie told him with joyful tears in her eyes.

Ed picked her up off her feet and kissed her at this happy news. As they started to walk down the path and exited the cemetery on the clear autumn day, they held hands, and Stephanie started telling him about all the plans they needed to make for the baby.

"Now, Ed, I know we are still living in the condo, but we have to buy a three-bedroom home in a good part of San Diego, and we have to search for a very good school system for all our kids to come. My parents and I talked about having them move to the city so they can help babysit when we are busy with work and other things."

As Stephanie continued, talking about painting the nursery once they knew the sex of the baby, Ed just smiled back at her. He was very happy for them but couldn't help thinking his retirement had been short-lived.

About the Author

Mark Barresi spent four years in the army infantry, training at Fort Benning and then Fort Campbell, where he expanded his military knowledge and skills while going to college and taking creative writing courses. He has followed the paths of his favorite established authors, James Byron Huggins and Clive Cussler, and has authored four books and established himself as one of the great new talents of the action and horror genre. In his spare time, apart from writing, he is a strong supporter of conservative issues affecting US policies and the country's direction, following the same paths and beliefs as iconic actors John Wayne and Charlton Heston. He is a lifelong member and outspoken supporter of the NRA and gun rights for private citizens. He enjoys traveling, collecting antiques, and being an animal rights activist, caring for abused and neglected animals. He plans to write two more novels in the near future: *Daughter of Affliction* and *Forbidden Passageways*. He currently lives in New York City.

Other Titles by Mark Barresi

The Dark Mist of Autumn

Evil's Redemption

The Encounter Over Alaska

References

Jack the Ripper: First American Serial Killer by: Stewart Evans and
Paul Gainey